Cool Waters

Michael Knell

ISBN: 9781796723328

Suitable for teens to ton-ups,
although snowflakes might
need to be near a fridge.

Other works include:

The Forces of Grey
The Elephant's Nest
Brotherly Matters
Damon – The Providence of Pan
Tales from Fat Sheila's
The Boy Who Could Do Magic
Once More Around The Block – Old Men
The Life and Times of JOHNNY MO Private Eye
The Choirboy and other Ghostly Stories
The Queen's Chambers (Stage Play)
The Legend of Itchen Castle
A Boy for Christmas
Strange Short Stories
The Boys of the Trinity
The Master of Moreditch Manor
APPOINTED
Haggerty's Cottage

For details on these and more information
visit: **www.michaelknell.com**

The characters and events depicted
in this novel exist only within
its pages and in the
imagination of
the author.

Chapter One

How Kelvin Waters came to be in Chestnut Dale is a story he wouldn't tell you. Not yet eighteen years of age, he'd been abandoned as a toddler and raised in council care that had seen him pushed between pillar and post; used and abused in more foster homes than he cared to remember. He had many stories he wouldn't tell you. However, finding himself in this small outskirts town, he'd taken quite a liking to the place. A suburb to the southeast, not anywhere near so threatening as several other areas he'd known, by far its biggest attraction for him was Nellie's Inn. A Victorian pub time had forgotten on the corner of High Street and Market Street, its patrons were mainly gay men above the age of sixty. With the place too quiet to ever warrant a police raid, the retired drag queen running it never bothered to ask him for proof of age. It was somewhere he could earn a few quid in safety.

Kelvin didn't consider himself as gay. It was simply that in this pub he'd found a generosity in guys who were of an age where that didn't matter. All they wanted of him was a little company. For an evening of vibrant conversation, a chummy hug and the touch of a hand, with the occasional peck on the cheek thrown in at chucking out time, they would reward him handsomely. Although in a way he was charging these people for his company in order to survive, he considered them his friends. He'd suffered from trying a similar venture in the Soho area. It was a risky business up there, one where all too often more had been demanded of him, and many times he'd had to do a runner and go hungry the next day.

That hot Friday evening in August, sitting on his own at a table in the pub, Kelvin was sipping a complimentary vodka and orange juice while waiting for the clientele to arrive. The regulars usually started drifting in around eight o'clock, and Nellie always provided him with a free drink for his wait. He was an athletically built young lad with silky jet-black hair, the darkest blue eyes imaginable, and a slightly olive glow to his complexion. With a good disposition and the cheekiest of faces, Kelvin made excellent wallpaper, and Nellie knew just how important that was for putting money in the till.

Only looking a couple or so years older, the guy wandering into the pub at seven-fifty was a good-looking specimen too, although one where you would definitely think twice before picking an argument with him. His fresh face, spikily-short blonde hair and friendly blue eyes did little to conceal the fact. He looked around to see, apart from the lad at a table on his own, the place was devoid of customers. Photographs and posters around the walls told him the aging man behind the counter had once been a drag queen of renown. He sauntered across and ordered a pint of the best lager off him, paid for it, and then ignoring the range of vacant tables, he made his way over to the one where Kelvin was sitting.

"Hello, Cool. Don't mind if I join you, do you?" he asked, gulping heavily from his glass as he sat down.

Kelvin looked across at the guy, and frowning puzzlement, he asked, "How did you know that was my nickname? Nellie doesn't know it, no one here does. I don't know you, do I?"

"No, you won't know me, the name's Hunter Jackson, but I know an awful lot about you, Kelvin Waters. Cool is a pretty cool label for someone named after the temperature scale for absolute zero. Your carers certainly liked it. Whenever you bunked off, they only had to phone up and say the name of that film, Cool Running, and that said it all."

"Oh, no, you're some lowlife from Social Services, aren't you? How did you find me?"

Hunter chuckled. "No, relax, I'm not here to lecture you on any rules you've broken." Still feeling parched, he swallowed down another huge mouthful of his pint.

"What do you want, then?"

"You, of course."

"Sorry, I'm not for rent."

"Lying is your only real fault, isn't it? Still, I guess with the life you've had, it has to be excusable."

"Huh?"

"You're here tonight because you *are* for rent. You can be found sipping a screwdriver at this table about the same time every Friday and Saturday evening. It's okay, I know, it isn't anything bad, you only offer your company, talking to guys for a few hours. With a bit of luck, you'll get several drinks bought and make about twenty quid tonight, won't you? But if you wanted to, you could come with me and earn a great deal more. I'd really like you to come with me."

"I don't normally . . ." Kelvin surveyed the guy closely. He could see he dressed well, smart casual, so obviously he had money, and being there wasn't much difference in their ages, he'd probably be better company than most of the old boys who'd be in later, they'd have more in common. Searching his brain, concluding they hadn't met before, did nothing to stop a nagging feeling he might just have forgotten. "How much more are we talking about?"

"As much as you need. And that is need, not want."

"What do you mean?"

"If you come with me, you'll always have what you need, and that's not necessarily what you might want. Maybe you'd like to have a million pounds, but you don't *need* a million pounds right now, do you? Squatting in that empty shop in Bessemer Road, you only need to find enough money to buy your food for next week. Although, I can see a new pair of trainers wouldn't go amiss."

Ignoring for now how the guy could know where he was squatting, Kelvin forced down a difficult swallow. "You're well-loaded, aren't you? What would you expect me to do for enough to buy a new pair of trainers?"

"Not a lot. Just come with me and promise you'll never lie again unless you really have to."

"Oh, no, don't tell me! You're some mad Holy Joe here to save me, aren't you?"

"Isn't it worth a new pair of trainers to find out who I am?"

"I'm not really gay. I don't do anything. And I don't need to be a born again Christian."

"After a while, it gets difficult to stop lying, doesn't it? And especially to yourself. I told you I knew a lot about you, and as I know you've been forced into doing more than you've wanted to on a few occasions, if it helps you to make that decision, I swear I wouldn't force you into anything. I've got to admit, though, I can't think of anything that'd beat the two of us banging each other for the rest of our lives."

"Bloody hell! What do you *really* want with me?"

In a couple more gulps, Hunter finished his pint. "A refill would come in handy. It must be the heat today, I seem to have downed that one a bit quick."

"You want me to go to the bar for you? I'm not a skivvy."

"Only when you're ready to get yourself another one. You don't have to go up especially for me."

Kelvin laughed. "You've got a long wait, then. I'm skint."

"If that's true, I'll buy the drinks, but with your past record for lying, I'd need you to prove it to me, wouldn't I? Show me your wallet."

Smirking, and not without considerable difficulty while he was sitting, Kelvin wrestled his wallet out of the tight right-hand pocket of his jeans, holding it out and flipping it open.

"Fuck!" exploded out of the lad's mouth, as he stared down wide-eyed at all the notes inside it.

"I guess you must need more than food and a new pair of trainers, then? Okay, you're paying and mine's a lager."

"But how?"

Hunter reached over and snatched a twenty pound note out of the wallet. "I'll go up and get them."

"No, you mustn't!" Kelvin protested. "It's not my money, honestly. I don't know how it got there, but it isn't mine."

"Yes it is. Didn't I say you'd always have enough for what you needed? I reckon you've decided to come with me."

"Are you a dip? Did you just plant this money on me?"

Standing up, grinning, Hunter said, "No, I didn't just plant it on you. Same again, is it?"

"Um, I don't know if I should. This money definitely isn't mine. I've never had that much before in my life."

"You'd better get used to things being a bit different from now on, then, hadn't you? Don't run off, I won't be long."

Kelvin hadn't finished his drink, so Hunter only took his own empty glass as he moseyed over to the bar.

Staring after him in a state of confusion, the lad couldn't have legged it out of there if he'd wanted to, he was unable to tear his eyes away. He was still staring when the guy returned and placed a vodka and orange juice in front of him.

"I didn't do one," said Kelvin, rather pointlessly.

"Proves how sensible you are, doesn't it? Here, look, even with the high prices they charge, you've got change." Hunter handed over a tenner and some coins.

Putting the money away, Kelvin explained, "Nellie does the best she can with the prices. It's not a busy pub, as you can see. She may not be able to keep it going much longer. It's a shame, really. She's a good sort and her regulars don't have anywhere else like this to go for miles."

Hunter winked. "If she's a good sort and the pub would be missed, don't you think we should do something about it?"

"Huh?"

"It'll be bad enough them losing you. We can't have the old queens losing their pub as well."

"You can help?"

"I don't know Nellie, it'll have to come from you." Hunter took a sealed envelope out of his inside pocket and handed it to Kelvin. "Give that to Nellie just before we leave and tell her she's not to open it until after we've gone. There's a bit of money in there that might help. You can say it's like a parting gift because you won't be back."

"Thanks, Nellie needs every penny she can get, but what do you mean, I won't be back?"

"You'll like it where you're going."

"You reckon?"

Taking a gulp of his drink, Hunter nodded the confirmation, and Kelvin screwed up his face, not understanding.

"But how do you know what I like?"

"Trust me, I know. Now, drink up, we've got a long drive ahead of us before we eat and I'm starving. I haven't eaten all day. I don't like the look of the places around here."

"There's only a few fast-food joints, and they're all pretty iffy, but you don't intend to drive on an empty stomach after gulping down two pints, do you? You'll get us killed."

"No, I won't. I popped something special earlier."

"Something special?"

"It's hardly known about, but there's a pill that pretty much kills alcohol. Next to nothing gets into your bloodstream."

"Crikey, that must be awful handy when you're driving."

"Yes, it is, and there are a lot of other handy things like that you'll learn about with me. We'll get to them all in time."

"When do we start?"

"We can start soon after I get you home."

"And where's that?"

"Puffney Bigshot. If we're lucky, it'll take roughly an hour to drive there at this time of the evening. You aren't going to change your mind, are you?"

"No, I guess not, but you're a pretty meaty guy, I wouldn't be able to fight you off. No funny business, you promise?"

"I promise. I can wait until you stop lying to yourself."

"You really think you know me, don't you?"

"I do know you. Come on, drink up, I don't like the look of those two shady characters hovering around outside. Perhaps we ought to make a move soon."

Kelvin looked round, thinking he might recognise a couple of the old boys. Unable to see anybody, he stood up to get a better view over the frosted part of the glass. After bobbing about, he said, "I can't see anyone out there."

"Exactly!"

"Huh?" Kelvin sat down again, befuddled.

Nellie wasn't best pleased to learn Kelvin was leaving. He was good for trade, like a breath of fresh air in her punters' stale lives, and they would miss him. She took the envelope and thanked him, pinning it on the notice board behind the bar. There were a few hugs and warnings to be careful and to look after himself from Nellie, and wiped damp eyes on both their parts, before he left with Hunter.

In the car park behind the pub, Kelvin wasn't surprised to learn his new friend drove a black Jaguar saloon. He looked the type; rich and towards the conservative. Buckling up in the shotgun seat, although not exactly worried, he did feel a little vulnerable when the central locking engaged.

"Do you need to pick up anything from the squat?"

"No, I don't leave anything important there, I might not see it again, but how did you know where I was living?"

"It's in the folder on the back seat," said Hunter, nodding to it as he started the car. "You can read it, if you want; make sure there's nothing wrong."

"You *are* from Social Services!" Kelvin cried. "Because I can't find employment, you want me to be your meal ticket until I'm eighteen." Stupidly, he unbuckled the seatbelt and tried to get out of the door, fully knowing he'd heard it lock.

"I told you I wasn't and I don't lie. Read the folder and it'll prove it. Oh, and buckle-up again. I like my speed."

Realising it was too late, there was no hope of escaping, Kelvin leaned over and grabbed the folder before reluctantly refitting the seatbelt. It was a thick folder, he discovered, as the car shot off up Market Street. Then, turning to the first page, he couldn't believe what he was reading.

"You think my parents were druggies and they're dead? I was told the police found me as barely a toddler on the steps of the town hall and nobody knew the first thing about me. I was unconscious, freezing cold and soaked through. Because they didn't think I was going to make it, they sent for a vicar and it was him who christened me Kelvin Waters." The lad turned to stare at Hunter, open-mouthed.

"Keep reading, you'll work it out."

There were so many pages that Kelvin scanned them more than read every word, soon realising there were things there that nobody should know. There were others he didn't know himself, like how Arthur and Rita Higgins, one set of foster parents who'd regularly abused him, had perished in a house fire. He was shocked, reading how they had done the same things to their son, Tom. One night, a few years after Kelvin had left them, Tom had taken his sister and his two foster brothers of the time outside to safety, and then he'd gone back and set fire to the house. His wicked parents had died in their bed from smoke inhalation, sometime before the flames charred them to beyond recognition.

As he turned them over, page after page held surprise after surprise for Kelvin. There was so much in detail, some of it he'd have sworn it was impossible for anyone to know. How could anyone be aware of all of the places he had gone and where he'd slept when he'd run away? Embarrassingly, there was even a list of the nights he'd cried himself to sleep when, at eight years old, he'd bunked off for the first time and not been found for two weeks. He knew he hadn't told anybody those things, so if someone had been aware of them, why hadn't he been picked up earlier? Far more embarrassingly, later on he found a list of all the foster homes where he'd been abused since that time. They were all printed there, recorded in black and white. The more he read, the more he found the account accurate to beyond belief, and that didn't make any sense to him. Coming to the end of it, where he was reminded he'd given one of the old boys a freebie hour of his time, chatting to him in the pub last week because the bloke's money hadn't come through, he turned and stared at Hunter, speechless.

"You mustn't be embarrassed. I was in care too. I suffered everything you did," said Hunter, only momentarily taking his eyes off the road to glance at him as a bend was coming up and they'd passed doing a ton a good few miles back.

Kelvin forced a swallow down. "You were . . ? At four?"

"I was six. and like you, I expect, I didn't know what it was about then. And also like for you, it happened to me many more times. I was farmed out to perverts at six, eight, ten, eleven and twelve. After that, I'd grown to be too much of a handful. I hit out. If you want to keep score, I had one more home than you where I had to do bad things, and you had two more than me where you were beaten and made to work like a slave. And if you don't count the return stays, we both only knew five good ones. Those police checks they brought in a few years back did nothing to help us, did they?"

"What, that Perverts' Charter?"

Hunter laughed. "Yeah, I've heard it called that. It's a good description. The overwhelming majority of perverts don't have a criminal record, so once one's been checked out, it's like they've been given a free pass to abuse kids. It's why so many perverts foster these days. They know any complaints about them aren't going to be believed. It's also why there's fewer good homes now. Believing it'd all explode one day, many of the ones providing good homes gave up fostering in case they should be tarred with the same brush."

"Why do you know everything about me? And how?"

"Any boy who has the guts to run away at the age of eight has one hell of a lot of resilience, making him interesting to the people who now employ me. They went out of their way to find you, and they've been watching you ever since."

"What people?"

"A secret organisation. Called CoT, it started up in Britain not long after World War II, a conglomerate of important people with a bit of clout, some people blessed with top-class brains, and a few like us, those with a first-hand knowledge of how bad the world can be, but since then it's spread to have chapters in countries all around the world."

"CoT? Is that an acronym? What's it do?"

"CoT stands for Cup of Tea. It needed an innocuous name, and in the days when it got off the ground, no matter how bad things should get for anyone, a cup of tea always made them feel better. It's what CoT does, it makes things better."

"What things?"

"Miscarriages of justice, for one. Sorting out people who take advantage of the vulnerable or those not so fortunate for another, and there's plenty more. CoT can't solve everything that's wrong, but it does manage to make quite a lot of things better. It's sorted out many nasty people in its time, and even toppled the odd government here and there. You know now that Arthur and Rita Higgins' son made them pay for their ways, but they aren't the only carers who abused you to have suffered. CoT dealt with the worst of the others."

"Bloody hell! You killed them?"

"No, but they paid a high price for what they did. So, now it's crunch time. How do you feel about being my partner?"

"Your partner?"

"I need a partner. For CoT work only if you want, but I'd really like it to be more; a hell of a lot more."

"But why would you want me?"

I told you they'd been watching you. Knowing how I was looking for a partner, they sent me your profile, and then I started watching you too. James Bond can have all the pretty girls he wants, I just want one gorgeous guy who pretends to be straight, when in fact he's so straight, he can knock three off over a gay mag before getting up in the morning."

"Jesus fuck! You really have been watching me!"

"Yes, and I liked what I saw."

"But I don't. I never have. That's why I pretend."

"Discovering you're gay isn't easy for anybody to accept, but there comes a time when you realise nothing will change it, you *have* to accept it, and when you do, you find it's not so bad. You just haven't got around to accepting it yet, but you will one day. Actually, I think being gay is better."

"Better?"

"For straight guys, it's all over when the fat lady sings, but if you're gay, that's often only the time when you'll reach out for a starting handle, while giving thanks to on high for being blessed with a second motor."

"Bloody hell, Hunter!"

"So, what's the answer? Will you be my partner?"

"Yes, okay, I accept it, I'm gay, and now I have accepted it, who *wouldn't* want to know you better? You sure beat what was in that mag. Oh, and who wouldn't want to help CoT?"

"That's a relief! Well, from now on we need to trust each other implicitly, and that means there must be no secrets between us. None at all. And you are going to have to learn how not to lie anymore, not unless it's totally unavoidable, and it's very important you never lie to me."

"That won't be easy. The lying bit, I mean. I've had to lie all my life to get by. It almost happens automatically now."

"You'll manage it. I have. I only lie now when I'm forced into lying, and the lying you're forced into comes easy for us, doesn't it?"

"How do you mean?"

"Don't tell me you didn't say everything was hunky-dory when the children's welfare officer came round to check up on things, knowing full well if you didn't and spilt the beans, the dog, cat or rabbit would be dead before morning?"

"Oh, yeah. That happened all the time. We really are alike, aren't we? Except, of course, I can't do what you do."

"Like what?" Hunter turned to frown at him.

"Only you could've put that money in my wallet, and yet no matter how good a pickpocket you are, with the tightness of my jeans, you couldn't have got it out of my pocket. I had a job pulling it out myself. How did you do it?"

"I didn't lie. I hadn't *just* planted it. You take your jeans off at night and I put it in your wallet while you were asleep last night. Thinking you had no money, you were hardly likely to take it out and open it before we met in the pub, were you?"

"You crept in and I didn't hear you?"

"There's a knack to not making a noise. Don't worry, I can teach you how to do it."

"Um, that's strange. You've just overtaken a stealth car, I saw the sign lying down on the back shelf, and we're doing over a ton. Why haven't they started to chase us?"

"There are no flies on you, are there?"

"No, a zip's faster. Sorry, forget that, it's become a habit, I was doing the wordplay thing I'd do at the pub. The old boys liked it. So, why isn't the police car chasing us, Hunter?"

"Maybe the coppers didn't see us."

"They're orifices of the lowest order, got eyes like hawks, they wouldn't have missed seeing us."

Hunter laughed. "Orifices of the lowest order? Really? You can say arseholes, you know? I won't mind."

"Sorry, I was trying to limit my swearing. I had an idea you didn't swear. You seem so clean-cut."

"Oh, I swear, but usually only when it's deserving."

"Well, they're deserving. Why aren't they chasing us?"

"Let's just say CoT has a lot of tricks up its sleeve. Police searches and ANPR checks flag our cars as DNH."

"What's DNH?"

"Do not hinder. They think we're special cops, or MI5."

"Bloody hell! Um, if you were in care until only a couple or so years ago, how do you afford to drive a car like this? Did you win the lottery or something?"

"No, CoT merely thought a greedy bastard who got rich by conning people should put his money to better use. I helped to clear out his bank account, and in such a way that the bank thought he was trying to pull a fast one and refused to cover his loss. He doesn't know it, but he also bought our house."

"Oh, wicked!"

"We do many things like that. Yes, we benefit, but because we do, we are able to help others."

Half a mile before Puffney Bigshot, Hunter eased his foot off the accelerator and swung the car left, into a country lane.

"We nearly there, are we?"

"Yes," Hunter replied, grinning, as the car turned right, on to a tarmac driveway. "What do you think?"

"That's it? That's not a house, it's a mansion!"

"Well, it was a very big bank account. That bloke hurt a lot of people," said Hunter, sweeping the Jaguar around the car park in a semicircle to park tidily outside the front door.

"You don't walk on water, do you?"

"No, but if you want to give it a try, it does come with an indoor and an outdoor pool."

"I think I've died and gone to heaven."

"No, you haven't, but we can get close to heaven later on, if you want. I've told you how much I'd like to. I'd need to eat something first, though. How does a big fat juicy steak with all the trimmings grab you?"

Kelvin giggled, "What's steak?"

Laughing, Hunter punched Kelvin's arm, playfully. "Yeah, I know. I was seventeen before I had my first one. Come on, let's get you indoors, you've got to meet our fairy Mary and her husband Andy. They've been waiting to see you."

"Fairy Mary and Andy?" Kelvin questioned, frowning as he scrambled out of the car. "Who are they?"

"Mary and Andrew Parks, a magic middle-age couple who live in a cottage just up the lane."

"Magic?"

"They're magic to me. I couldn't keep the house clean and tidy, and as for cooking, I know when I'm beaten. Even when it comes to the grounds, I wouldn't have a hope there either. I barely know a daisy from a dandelion."

"They're servants? You've got servants?"

"No, just good neighbours. Friends who look after me. I guess they feel a bit like my family would, if I had one."

"Crikey!"

***

They'd had a tiringly long day, tying up the loose ends on a particularly challenging case, and D.I. Crabbe was about to be dropped off outside his house by D.S. Weathers when they noticed a lot of blue light activity a couple of hundred yards further along Dullbury Road.

"We ought to go and check that out, Stormy," the inspector said. "If someone's playing silly buggers on my doorstep, I'd like to know about it."

"Righto, guv," said Stormy, driving on past his inspector's house to join the four police cars and an ambulance putting on a lighting display worthy of a nightclub's dance floor.

Everyone at Dullbury Central nick knew Colin Weathers as Stormy, and he didn't much mind the nickname. It seemed befitting of a man with a short fuse. The slightest provocation and the thirty-year-old single guy would turn into a category five, and that's a mighty bad hurricane. Brass and criminals alike trod carefully when Stormy was around. Probably, the only reason he was still on the force was because he could be relied on. If anything got hairy, they sent for Stormy, and he soon sorted it out.

A well-seasoned copper, one of the old brigade a few years off retiring and now turning a little rotund, Jeffrey Crabbe also had a nickname, though not one used in front of him or his sergeant. Should Stormy hear anyone calling his guvnor Old Crabby Claws, they'd be wondering what day of next week they'd landed in. The two worked well together, almost like they were father and son. It was not something he could remember himself, but like his boss, Stormy preferred the old ways. Back in the days when coppers could bounce prisoners off a cell's walls, most of the crimes were solved. Now, even with modern technology and only half of reported offences getting to be recorded as a crime, they'd have to be extremely lucky to hit a success rate of ten percent.

Realising who'd turned up, the six coppers hanging around, seemingly doing nothing but talking and cracking jokes, two casually leaning up against one of the police cars and another sitting on its bonnet, suddenly found they had things to do. It was a comical sight, but the inspector wasn't amused.

"What's going on here, then? Having a party, are we?"

"No, sir," a red-faced constable replied. "It's two old-timers not coping very well; a man and woman both getting on for eighty, I'd say. PCs Jones and Watson are dealing with them now. We thought the women would handle them better."

"So, it's this house?" D.I. Crabbe asked, pointing. "Not the one where we've got a car stuck on the drive?"

"No, that's Burton's car, first to attend. It was the woman in there who did the nines."

"There's a bloody body cart waiting there, why haven't the scoopers taken over?"

"They tried, but the old man in there took one look at them, and in no uncertain terms, he started screaming and shouting, effing them off out of his house."

"That doesn't sound like old Fred, not unless he had a good reason to want them out."

"You know him, guv?" asked Stormy.

"Yes, Frederick Wilkinson, lost his wife about five years back. He took in Mavis Wilson a year or so ago after she lost her husband, only for the company, mind you, nothing else. I think we ought to have a word with old Fred, Stormy. I want to know what's going on."

A look and a nod towards the door from the inspector and, counting their blessings, the two women police officers beat a hasty retreat. They'd been getting nowhere with the teary-eyed couple sitting in rickety old cottage chairs.

"Now then, now then, what's going on here, Fred? It's not like you to need our services."

"Jeff! I don't need them, it was Mrs Troughton who called you out, not me, but what are you doing here?"

"Saw the lights and thought I'd make a social call, Fred."

"A social call?"

"Yes, but now I'm here, you can tell me where nearly all your furniture's gone. Why are you sitting in those rough old wooden chairs? The last time I was here, you had a leather three-piece-suite in good nick. And what's happened to your father's medals? The display case over there's empty."

"We had a bit of a clear out. About a week ago, it was. Silly keeping all that stuff, it was only collecting dust."

"I'm a copper, Fred, I know a porky when I hear it. Are you up against it? I know for definite you wouldn't have got rid of your father's medals unless you hadn't a choice. You were proud of them, and rightly so. Christ, Fred, the whole bloody country had a debt it couldn't pay your old man for what he did to get them. What's going on here?"

"It's a personal matter, Jeff, and we really don't want to talk about it."

"Well, I do, I want to talk about it. Stormy, go and get me the names of the two scoopers outside, I've a feeling they've got something to do with this."

"Righto, guv," said the sergeant, hurrying out of the room.

"Please don't interfere, Jeff. If your lot get involved, it will only make matters worse."

"Worse? They couldn't be much worse, could they? What if I were to make it unofficial? No police involved. Would you tell me then?"

"I think you should, Fred," Mavis said, sniffing, and wiping her eyes with a scrunched-up laced handkerchief. "We've not much left now we can lose."

"It would definitely be off the books?"

"Scout's honour, Fred. And that's worth a hell of a lot more than police honour these days. I know, I was a boy scout. So, it wouldn't have been because of their choice of aftershave or lipstick, why did you throw those two paramedics out?"

"It was only Jenny Cole we didn't want in here, we don't know the male one. It was Jenny who got us into this mess."

"What did she do, Fred?"

"We think now she only works on an ambulance so she can find vulnerable mugs for her husband. She turned up after Mavis had a fall last year, badly twisting her ankle. Unable to get about for a while, she needed more care than I could give her. As you're aware, we're not a couple in the marital sense, so a nurse was required for some things, and a nurse who does house calls on the National Health is rarer than rocking horse do-do these days. I'm not usually so gullible, but you believe a paramedic, don't you? That Jenny convinced me we would have no problem paying for a private nurse, all we needed was a short-term loan, and she said she could get a good deal on a loan for us with her husband who happened to be in the business. We trusted her, Jeff, we didn't read any of the small print. You can probably work out the rest."

"How much so far, Fred?"

"Almost everything we had. We just live off our pensions now, and as that's not enough to cover what the balance goes up by every month with all the added interest, the house will have to go next."

"Don't you go doing anything silly, now, Fred. The house stays. I'll sort it out for you."

"No, you mustn't! You promised you wouldn't involve the police. Scout's honour, Jeff, remember?"

"Yes, and I'll keep that promise. But I didn't promise you I wouldn't ask other people to get involved."

"What other people?"

"People who handle this kind of thing better than us. When they close a shyster down, they don't open up with a different name a week later. They lose everything."

"Really?"

"Jenny Cole and Tony Reagan are the names you wanted, guv," said Stormy, reappearing. "Tony's probably okay, an ex-copper with a commendation and twenty years under his belt, but if you ask me, Jenny seems a bit shifty."

"She is, she's a rotten fish, Stormy. You can get off home now, I'll walk back to mine from here. Oh, and get rid of that bloody circus out the front."

"Righto, will do, guv. See you in the morning."

Stormy left, and Jeff took out his phone. Not exactly au fait with modern technology, it took him a little while to find the number stored on it for Gregory and touch the screen in the right place to have it dialled.

"Yes," said a voice.

"Greg? Is that you?"

"Of course it's me, Jeff. Who else would it be?"

"How did you know it was me? They told me the number doesn't come up if I use this phone."

"Oh, it comes up on mine, Jeff. And I knew it was you and not someone using your phone because mine has a few bells and whistles. It's got voice recognition."

"Good Lord!"

"It comes in handy when it's one of those cold callers who hack a number stored in your contacts. If it doesn't recognise the voice, I say, 'Fire Service, what's the emergency?' and I never hear from them again. What can I do for you, Jeff?"

Chapter Two

It was ten o'clock when Hunter's phone rang. He sat up in the bed only for as long as it took him to accept the call and put his phone into speaker mode. It had been a heavy night.

"Urgh?" Hunter grunted, questioningly, before collapsing back onto his pillow.

Dreamy-eyed, Kelvin giggled from the next pillow. Last night had been like an epiphany for both of them. Apart from following Hunter into his bedroom when they'd turned in, despite being given a bedroom of his own, and feeling more nervous than he'd ever felt in his life, he couldn't remember how anything had started. Not that it mattered now anyway, but he recalled he'd been mumbling, 'I love you, Hunter, you could never know how much I love you, and I know I'll love you forever.' He hadn't cried since he was eight, not once, but when Hunter had told him he'd love him for longer than that, he'd broken down and bawled.

Kelvin was sure it hadn't been because of the drink. He'd only sipped a small glass of red wine out of a freshly opened bottle with the dinner. The two screwdrivers he'd had earlier at Nellie's Inn would have been lost in history. But start it had, it must have done, and no one was more grateful it had than him. Without any shadow of doubt, it had been the best time he had ever known in his life. They hadn't just spent the night enjoying each other, they'd both found feelings they'd never known existed, exploring them to the limits of ecstatic endurance. While confessing at every opportunity how much they meant to each other, the night had been spent enjoying a wonderful voyage, where they had laughed and played and swum in an ocean of love that went on and on without end, and with each new experience they'd wanted to soar through the sky, shouting it to the world. Finally, they felt complete, and life made a lot more sense.

"It sounds to me as if all your wishes came true, Hunter. I thought they might, it's why I left it until now before calling you. There's a job in Dullbury, if you can manage it."

Hunter rubbed his eyes. "What time is it?"

"Gone ten."

"Really? I don't think we got much sleep last night."

"You may not be alone. Nellie looked like she hadn't had any this morning. It was only because she'd seen you give Kelvin the envelope she didn't tear up the cheque. She was waiting outside the bank before it opened, and I swear it, she skipped all the way back to the pub."

Kelvin sat up, shaking his head, a puzzled look growing.

"Who are we hitting and why?" Hunter asked.

"A loan shark, we used to call them, but some of them are a lot worse than that now they can be found doing business legally on every high street. There's one in Dullbury owes an old couple big style. I'll email you all the details."

"Okay, Greg, we'll make a start on it this morning."

Ending the call, Greg laughed, "Yes, I suppose that'll be providing nothing else comes up, eh?"

"You've got a job?" Kelvin asked, staring wide-eyed

"We have. We're partners, remember?"

"Yeah, I know, but who's Greg? I thought I recognised his voice, and what was that about a cheque? It didn't feel like a lot, I thought it might've been a tenner or a twenty, but was there a cheque in the envelope you got me to give to Nellie?"

"You do know his voice. When he's not Greg, he's known as Bob, the bloke you gave a freebie hour to in the pub, and I didn't lie by saying there was a bit of money in the envelope that might help, I just didn't tell you it wasn't cash."

"How much was the cheque for?"

"It was enough for Nellie to buy the freehold and get out of her tie to the brewery, do a few updates, shop for her beer at sensible prices, and make a profit. Two hundred grand."

"Fuck me!"

Hunter laughed, "Again? Don't you ever have enough?"

Kelvin laughed too. "No, not like that, angel features. I'm feeling just as knackered as you. It was a really good night, though, wasn't it? Do you think we broke any records?"

"You nearly broke something, I know that much. You were insatiable. I lost count."

"Sorry, I think it might've been that steak, I've heard it can do things to you."

"Remind me to say my prayers tonight."

"Why?"

"In case God does exist, I ought to say thank-you."

"Well, if you do, pass on a thanks from me too. I can hardly believe what's happened to me since yesterday. Not only are you beyond belief, you weren't joking about Mary and Andy, they really are magic."

"They certainly like you. Did you notice Mary gave you the largest steak?"

"Yeah, and did I ever need it? How do you know Bob? And why would you have been carrying two hundred grand about with you yesterday? I thought you said you hadn't been to Chestnut Dale before."

"I hadn't, not until I arrived in the night to fill your wallet. I know Bob because as well as being Greg, he's also known as Commander Raines, one of CoT's top brass, and he happens to live in Chestnut Dale. You could say we were killing two birds with one stone. It wasn't only me trying to convince you to become my partner, Nellie's Inn is Greg's local, and he couldn't give Nellie a cheque to save the pub, it would've blown his cover."

"Crikey! You seem to splash an awful lot of money about, how much are you worth?"

"Oh, I'm priceless, but if you mean how much have I got in the bank, the real answer's zilch."

"Zilch? Nothing?"

"I don't check it often, but I believe there's something over four million in different accounts. The thing is, though, none of it really belongs to me, does it? I only get to use it."

"Bloody hell!"

"You'll get used to it, I have. Come on, we ought to make a move, we've work to do. We can share a shower, if you like, all the bedrooms have an en suite with a double shower, but you'll have to promise to behave."

Kelvin giggled, "Okay, then, I promise I'll be good."

Hunter laughed. So, what if they were a bit late?

***

Royston Cole was a cocky kind of bloke. When his wife had told him of the previous evening's events, worried by them because the police had been there and she'd had her name taken, he'd laughed them off. He reckoned, although what he did was a bit underhand, it was legal. In compliance with the law, he was registered as a money-lender, and the punitive loan contracts some of the idiots chose to sign were perfectly legal too.

He wasn't even worried when he recognised D.I. Crabbe and D.S. Weathers come into his shop to wander around it at lunchtime that day, with the sergeant taking photos of a few things with his phone. The police often paid the shop a visit, looking for stolen items, but even when they found some he knew they couldn't touch him. He always had the necessary paperwork to prove who he'd bought the stuff from in good faith.

It was a large shop, spread over two floors on the corner of High Street and Tapperton Road. At the back of the ground floor there was a counter with a grill, similar to a post office, where customers paid for the valuable items, or got paid for them, with an office beside it where Royston liked the loan contracts and easy payment deals to be signed. Signed there, on his premises, there was no cooling-off period in which a mug could change their mind. Most of the rest of that floor was mainly given over to electric and electronic goods, with one whole wall a secure glass cabinet full of mobile phones, laptops, pads and games machines. On the other side to the office, through a door that led to the outside, surrounding a yard that was also accessible by double gates onto the side road, were lock-up buildings where the furniture for sale was on display, while on the first floor, up stairs near the front of the shop, was the jewellery and ornaments department.

Kelvin and Hunter wandered into the shop at three-thirty. It had been a thirty mile journey to Dullbury, and on a Saturday afternoon, especially during the summer months, traffic was heavy out that way, the fast car being of no help. Hunter was dressed down a little, not exactly shabby but far from looking the well-dressed guy he had yesterday, and he'd stressed to Kelvin, no matter what might happen when they got there, on no account must he laugh.

"Need any help?" asked a young lad, plainly staff.

"Yeah, I wants to see the fucking bloke in charge," Hunter said, with all the finesse of a yob.

"Are you free, Mr Cole?" the lad cooeed, up the shop.

Kelvin bit his tongue. That had nearly done it for him, and he knew it still might if the bloke cooeed back, 'I'm freeee!' He'd seen reruns of a camp television show in Nellie's where it had been followed by a mince. Thankfully, the bloke only walked towards them.

"Can I help you?" Royston asked.

"How the fuck would I know?" asked Hunter.

"Pardon?"

"If you don't know if you can help me, what the fuck are you doing here? If you *can* help me, you're supposed to ask me if you *may* help me, you tosser!"

"I'm sorry, we'll do it your way, then. May I help you?"

"You may. I want to buy back all the stuff my grandpa had to sell you, and I want it delivered and put back where it was within the hour. It's Mr Wilkinson, 108 Dullbury Road."

"He's your grandpa?"

"Are you thick, mate? I just fucking said so, didn't I?"

"Um, it won't be cheap. How do you intend to pay?"

"Do I look poor? With my fucking plastic, of course!" said Hunter, flashing a gold debit card.

"Just give me a minute and I'll see how much we still have of it, and what it'll cost you."

"Don't be long, then. I'm on a bloody promise, I am."

Kelvin was biting his tongue awfully hard, by now.

It wasn't a minute, it was at least five minutes before the man came back. After adding up the jottings on his notepad, he said, "You're lucky, we still have everything, but to buy it back, I'm afraid it will cost you four thousand, seven hundred and fifty pounds. We have to make something out of it."

"Cheap at half the fucking price! Well, don't hang about, get it loaded."

"We'll just put your card through first, sir."

The card was accepted without a problem, and then as if somebody had fired a starting pistol, the staff members began running around, stacking Fred's stuff into a large van. Thirty minutes later, Hunter and Kelvin were watching along with D.I. Crabbe and D.S. Weathers as, in a state of bewilderment, old Fred hobbled around his house, showing the deliverymen where each piece of their returned belongings needed to be put. Mavis was back on her handkerchief again, but this time they were tears of joy.

"Do we get to know how and what you've done?" asked the inspector, once the deliverymen had gone.

"Well, we didn't do a lot, really," Hunter said. "We simply bought Fred's stuff back with a debit card we made, one that is drawn on Royston's personal bank account, so *he* kindly bought the stuff back for us. But the best bit is still to come."

"And what's the best bit?"

"We've something a bit naughty scanning Royston's bank account and business accounts now, collecting information on every input they've seen for as far back as the bank has kept records, and once it's completed its task, starting with the most recent, it'll return as many of those payments it can, close the accounts, and then remove every trace of them."

"You can do that?" gasped the inspector.

"No, but that something is awful good at it. The only reason you won't have heard of it is because no one has managed to catch the blighter yet. Good, internet banking, isn't it?"

"So, are you saying Royston Cole will go bust?"

"Probably, unless he has offshore investments. He won't be able to pay his bills, his credit rating will plummet, meaning he'll lose his licence to lend money, and he won't be able to receive any payments servicing outstanding loans as his bank accounts won't exist. And in such a poor financial state, it's very unlikely a bank will let him open up another one. If the second-hand sales at his shop and his wife's job don't keep his head above water, you could see him queuing up at the only bank that'll have him, the food bank. Convincing any other kind of bank they'd lost his accounts would take him years, if he could manage it."

"If you asks me, it couldn't happen to a nicer bloke," Fred chortled, from the comfort of his favourite armchair, where he was proudly positioning the medals in their display case.

On the drive back home, Kelvin said, "I know I hardly did anything, but I don't half feel good about what we did. It's like I'm glowing inside."

"When everything goes right, the job satisfaction you get is a really big perk."

"Do jobs ever go wrong, then?"

"Only rarely, but it does happen. It's not easy to plan for the unforeseen. We don't give up, though. It just makes us even more determined to get it right the next time."

"Something's puzzling me about that job, though. I know Fred and Mavis have got their stuff back, and soon the direct debit to service their loan won't have a bank account to pay into, but won't that just make the amount they owe Royston shoot up more? And anyway, what's to stop him banging on their door and asking for cash?"

"The first bit in Greg's email, where he said he was happy he could cook now that he'd cracked an egg and successfully separated the yolk from the white, had nothing at all to do with a chucky egg. It was telling us we weren't the only ones involved. Another CoT team had been successful overnight in going in and removing, or separating, the contracts from Royston's safe, leaving it okay for us to do our bit. An egg to us is a safe, or a secure unit. CoT has the contracts now, and if they haven't already, they'll be destroyed. And that means if Royston should turn up on anyone's doorstep and ask with even the slightest bit of pressure for a payment, when in the eyes of the law he doesn't hold a signed contract as proof of a debt, he would be committing a nickable offence known as demanding money with menaces. Don't worry, he won't give them any more grief. Royston is what's known as a sharpster and nothing more. He makes his money out of knowing the law backwards and keeping just within it. He's not a heavy, and neither is he surrounded by them. Look at the way he just stood there and took how I was speaking to him."

"Is that why you did that?"

"Of course."

"Jesus! CoT is really good at what it does, isn't it?"

"The best," Hunter replied, winking.

"What would you have done if Royston had got heavy?"

"If he had, I'm afraid he would have regretted it. He would have had to meet my dragon."

"Dragon? You wouldn't by any chance mean the Terror of the Dragon, would you? Don't tell me you know it!"

"All CoT members working in the field are trained in the Terror of the Dragon, and I'll have to teach it to you, but how do you know about it? Not a lot of people do."

"I've spent many a winter's day reading books in a library to keep warm. I read one about Johnny Mo last year, thinking the Terror of the Dragon had to be something the author had made up because it seemed so far-fetched, but when I did a search for it on the library's computer, I found out it really existed. It said it was a highly secret martial art most notably associated in the UK with Johnny Mo and his team of private investigators in the sixties, and it was kept a closely guarded secret because its prime purpose was to kill an opponent. It as good as said the book was true."

"Oh, it's true, alright. It's because it's true it could only be classified as fiction, and if you're taught it properly, you can adapt most Terror of the Dragon moves to only incapacitate."

"It is true? They really did save the world?"

"The world might've survived, but if they hadn't solved the case in time to stop that rogue agent pressing the button, it's possible the nuclear winter we'd have suffered would've seen the end of human life. Actually, it was Johnny's adopted son, Kamal, who first taught the Terror of the Dragon to our CoT members in the seventies."

Kelvin gulped, "Kamal?"

Hunter laughed. "Yes, don't you remember the mixed-race street urchin they hired as their guide in Marrakesh? First you pity the boy, then you want to cuddle him and take away his troubles, and then when he gets older you're in awe of him. I doubt there can be a gay guy who's bought that book and not found it hard reading, and I don't mean difficult."

Kelvin failed to hide a giggle. "Of course I remember. How could anyone forget Kamal? When he found out who it was, jumping up and down, saying, 'You Johnny Mo, mister? I work Johnny Mo? Oh, Kamal friends they no believe!' it had me choking up. And further on, after MISIC had wangled the adoption and Johnny and Karl taken him home, it got to be very hard reading about him in that library. I wished I could have taken the book out, but with no address, I couldn't. Do you think they're all still alive?"

"The last I heard, they were enjoying their retirement on an island they bought in the sun. But before you get all dreamy over that book again, I've got something to bring you down to earth with a bang. It could be your worst nightmare."

"What?"

"We've an undercover job starting soon, in September, and it's as security guards at an all-girls' boarding school."

"Hell, that is my worst nightmare!"

"I know, I nearly wet myself when I read about you trying to do what you did in Nellie's Inn at that old gal's pub."

"Don't remind me about it. That was a big mistake. I'm not kidding you, those women were like wild animals, pawing me everywhere and trying to get my clothes off. I barely got out of there alive."

"Yes, well, from what I've heard about all-girls' schools, I think we could be in trouble there. If it's not to go the same way, we might need to camp it up a bit."

"I'm freeee!" Kelvin giggled.

Hunter playfully thumped him.

***

Over the following three weeks, there was little to convince Kelvin he hadn't died and gone to heaven. Hunter opened a bank account for him, transferring a sum of money into it that made his eyes water just trying to read all the figures. For the first time in his life he went out and bought clothes from a proper clothing store, not a second-hand shop, and he filled the large wardrobe and chest of drawers in his bedroom with them, although technically it wasn't really his bedroom. Off a corridor, it was directly opposite the bedroom he shared with Hunter, and only the room where he kept his clothes.

In a whirlwind experience, on several non-racing days, he'd also driven Hunter's Jaguar around the car park of a not too distant greyhound stadium, being given driving lessons by him, sent off for a provisional driving licence, bought himself a car, a phone and a laptop, and applied for a passport. And as if that wasn't enough to keep his head reeling, for two hours every day, Hunter was teaching him the Terror of the Dragon, and he was proving to be a fast learner. The lessons were tiring, but with all the bodily contact involved, not so tiring that they didn't often end with them enjoying each other in either their bedroom or the indoor pool.

Kelvin still found it difficult to believe how much his life had changed for the better. By refusing to accept what he was, while knowing he'd never be able to be what he wasn't, he'd thought it was inevitable. One day youthfulness would leave him, he'd no longer be able to earn money from being good company, and he would become a sad and lonely old man. And then, out of the blue, Hunter had turned up. No one he'd known had ever been that good. He was undeniable, everything he knew he wanted but was too afraid to admit, and unbelievably, Hunter had said he felt the same way about him. Thankfully, he'd had enough sense to recognise it was likely a once in a lifetime moment, and somehow he'd found the courage to finally accept the truth.

By accepting the truth, Kelvin had exposed something that neither of them had met before. It was more than a look of relief he'd seen on Hunter's face, more than relief he'd felt himself, and for a few moments it had passed unknown. But too strong to stay unknown, slowly it had dawned on them, it was more than just a like and a want they had for each other, they were the two halves that made a whole. It had always been a stranger, even something alien, but no longer, it was that four-letter word called love, and now they knew it, they also knew the world and its partner could never break that whole. They had both done something that night they'd never dared to do before; they'd made a commitment. Kids in care, not knowing whether they'll be somewhere for only a day or a few weeks, don't make commitments or do anything that might hurt them, not even make real friends.

Should another heaven exist, Kelvin realised it would really need to go some if it was to beat the one he now shared with Hunter. He lived in a heaven. It was the first place he'd been able to call home. And something that would produce a grin whenever he thought of it, Hunter had to be right about gay being better. Being they were both what was called versatile, there couldn't many straight couples around who'd be able to confirm their love as often as they could in a night.

On the Monday following those first three weeks, came the day they started the undercover job. As they left home that morning with Kelvin driving his Volvo V90 estate car with L plates on, the one Hunter had almost insisted he buy because estate cars were always handy to have and in that model he couldn't go *too* mad, they were both hoping the job wouldn't turn out to be hell. However, when they arrived to see the school for the first time, some of the buildings looked as if they'd have been more at home in hell. Gothically ancient, with many of their walls half-hidden behind huge swathes of hanging ivy, they were more befitting of a horror film than a place of education.

"Crikey, you didn't mention the school we'd be working at was in Count Dracula's castle, Hunter," said Kelvin, finding a space and parking in the car park.

"I knew it was old, a long-established school, but not that it looked like this. You aren't worried, are you?"

"No, don't be silly. I survived squatting in that shop."

"Why, was that creepy too?"

"Not the shop, but hearing all the strange noises coming out of the graveyard opposite was a bit unnerving."

"There were noises coming from the graveyard?"

"Yeah, a lot of shrieking, and cries in the night. It happened mostly Friday and Saturday nights, probably explaining why you didn't hear any when you crept in and filled my wallet. It was on a Thursday night you did that. All the other times you only watched me on the hidden cameras I didn't know were just about everywhere. Oh, and that reminds me, thanks for deleting me getting off over that magazine."

Hunter laughed. "I think I was in danger of wearing out that section of the hard drive, I used to watch it every night and morning, but I don't need to anymore, not now I've got the real thing, do I? Did you ever get to find out who was making the shrieking noises?"

"Yeah, I got brave and crept over there one night. After the pubs chuck out, a lot of town boys take their girlfriend to the graveyard for a shag over the humps. I think they do it on the graves because it gives them such a magnificent orgasm that they can't help shrieking. I guess, really, people doing it over graves could be why we call it humping."

"You've just wound me up, haven't you?"

"Yeah, and I got you going, didn't I?" Kelvin giggled.

"You had me feeling grateful we didn't need a boneyard to make us squeal," laughed Hunter, thumping him.

"Yeah, I know, but talking of bones, can you believe the old gal who's come out to stand on the steps?"

"I think it's the head, Miss Felicity Trump. Greg said she looked like a living skeleton. I doubt we'll have much to do with her today, it's the caretaker who's supposed to show us around. It's gone nine, he should've been out here by now."

"He could be the bag of bones in the blue boiler suit on my side, having a quick drag round the corner. He looks like he's death warmed up too. I don't think anyone eats much here."

The gaunt man stamped out the cigarette butt, and barking a few times to clear his lungs, he ambled across and introduced himself as Bert Waldron, the school's caretaker for the past twenty-five years.

"So, there won't be much going on here you don't know about, then?" asked Hunter, as they scrambled out the car.

"Ah, that be true, and it all goes on at this school."

"All? How do you mean?"

"They may come from well-off families, but they ain't prim and proper angels we has here. Sluts, my missus calls 'em."

"Sluts? Really?"

"Last year the clap clinic came here, said to be for a health talk, but it was probably cos it'd have taken a double-decker bus to get all the whores needing treatment into town."

"Bloody hell!" Kelvin gasped.

"Ah, they'll be busy today, moving their stuff in, but when you comes back tonight to do your rounds, lest to want to go down with something, two good-looking guys like you might wanna be wearing a belt *and* braces."

"It's really that bad?" Hunter questioned, frowning. "Hasn't anyone here tried to stop it?"

"They's not gonna stop it. This is a small school by today's standards, only got two boarding houses, and even with the exorbitant fees it has to rely on prostitution to cover all the expenses and keep the place open. And it hasta stay open cos none of the old hags here would get a job anywhere else."

"You really believe that?"

"Talking proper and walking about with books balanced on yer head don't butter no parsnips today. But what the girls earn butters enough palms when it comes to qualifications."

"Are you saying the girls buy their exam passes?"

"How else would they pass 'em? It'll be an orgy tonight to celebrate being back. They'll get drink and drugs bought and earn a bit, and then many of 'em won't be proper sober again till they hasta go home for half-term. When it comes to rich bitches like we gets here, so long as they's got a bit of paper to say they's clever, it don't matter if they's stupid."

"But aren't the girls expected to go on to a university after they've been here?" Kelvin asked.

"Ah, and they does. It ain't like the old days. If a dog could write its name, there'd be a university that'd take it today, and it'd pass out with a list of diplomas as long as yer arm."

"Sadly, there's likely to be quite a lot of truth in that," said Hunter. "These days, they hand out degrees for subjects that are beyond the ridiculous. But being as you seem to know so much, Bert, do you know anything about Angelina Soames, the girl who went missing from here last term?"

"I know it's why you's here. Supposed to stop another one going missing, ain't yer? Some of the parents insisted on it. It won't do you no good, though. Police knew that, and that's why they's not doing it."

"How do you mean?"

"See that well-worn track in the grass?" Bert asked, turning to point to the adjoining sportsfield. "It's a public footpath, it's been tried afore, you can't stop people using it."

"And that's the way someone took her?"

"It's the way she done a runner with someone."

"She ran away? She wasn't abducted?"

"Ah, they couldn't tell the police, she be different from the others. When she got one in the oven, she be wanting to keep it, and she couldn't be taking a bairn home, could she?"

"Bloody hell!"

"Yeah, how the other half live, eh?" said Hunter. "Do you think any of the girls might know where Angelina went?"

"They'll all know, except today's intake. Rashid picked her up. He's the father, a young foreigner from up the smoke, so say with a donger on him that'd ring Big Ben. A lot of girls were jealous of her getting him. Apparently, he's promised to do the right thing and marry her when she's old enough."

"This is certainly some place!"

"Oh, you ain't seen nothing yet. This lot don't live by the same rules we does. One of them girls has twice come back off holiday and hadda get rid of one. Her father's a lord, and the rumour is, she's what you might call a daddy's girl."

"That's terrible!"

"Do you think we'll do any good here?" Kelvin asked.

"I don't know, I shall have to have a word with Greg, but I reckon something needs to be done," Hunter replied.

"Ah, you won't be able to do nothing. The families this lot comes from runs everything. It's no good going to the papers, if they don't own 'em they'll be hobnobbing with the people who do. There's a lot of places like this now. There's plenty of boys in boarding schools today who also spend more time putting it around than swatting. Never mind a lot of them do it cos they likes it, they makes big money."

"It all sounds so unbelievable."

"But it's true. Why do yer think most our big companies be run by foreigners now? Our lot ain't up to it. They comes out of our universities with degrees as long as yer arm, but they soon finds out that arm's only good enough to reach across a counter, serving coffees and burgers in a fast-food joint."

"But it can't be like that everywhere, surely?"

"Not everywhere, it ain't. We's still got some good places left, those like Eton, Winchester, Marlborough, Oxford and Cambridge, but this place ain't no exception nowadays."

"Well, it's certainly opened my eyes. I suppose you'd better show us where the boundaries are now and tell us about the security in operation."

"Security? Don't make me laugh. I'll show you around the grounds and that but there ain't no security. The front gates don't even get locked, there'd be no point. You can walk into here from any direction you want. It's countryside all around, and the only fences you'll find are to keep the cows out."

"You don't even lock the front gates of a night?"

"No, daren't do that. The teachers hasta have a door to door taxi service when they goes to the pub. It's a long driveway, and they wouldn't appreciate having to walk to and from the road if it was raining."

"They sometimes visit a local pub, then?"

"A people carrier picks 'em up, takes them into town and brings 'em back, Friday and Saturday nights. The local pub is too quiet for 'em; a one old man and his dog kinda place."

"A people carrier? Do they all go, then?"

"Course. It's okay, the head girl's got their numbers in case of an emergency."

"Like running out of booze, I suppose?" quipped Kelvin.

Bert gave them a guided tour, showing them all around the grounds and throughout the school's buildings. A few of the girls arrived while they were on this excursion, dropped off from cars by their parents. Bert explained how more than half of the girls would arrive later, after being met off their trains by a coach. Fielding Halt was two miles away, and the slow trains would stop when a ticket had been purchased to pick up or drop someone there. And then, handing Hunter a bunch of keys on a chain to cover everything, Bert wished them the best of luck and wandered off.

Chapter Three

Staring blankly through the windscreen at the road ahead, everything seemed to be passing Hunter by. He appeared to be buried deep in his thoughts as Kelvin drove them home.

After a few miles of this, Kelvin thumped Hunter's leg and asked, "What's up, angel features?"

"That's something I've been trying to work out."

"Eh?"

"I'd guessed there had to be something, playing the role of security guards isn't anything CoT would normally do, but even now, after seeing what the job entails, I can't for the life of me work out why Greg would want us there."

"I'm just hoping that at least half of what that caretaker told us is bullshit. I've an idea it isn't, though. Didn't you see the looks we were getting off those girls? Some were licking their lips, batting their eyelashes and thrusting their hooters at us. They had me hoping I was just a tossed salad."

"A tossed salad?"

"Yes, something dead boring that sometimes turns up with a meal. It's not you ordered it, want it, or even like it, but to be polite, you're supposed to pretend you do."

Hunter laughed, "You've no hope of being a tossed salad."

"No, nor have you, so I don't know why you're laughing. I thought you was going to ring Greg about the job?"

"I shall do, when we get home."

"Why not ring him now? I promise not to hit anything. I'll even slow down, if you want."

"I've no worries about your driving, I'm sure you must be almost as good as me already. You're a lot like Kamal in that book you read, you pick things up awful fast. One thing's for sure, I wouldn't want to fall out with you now. It took me a year to learn the Terror of the Dragon, it does for most, but in only a few weeks you're able to wipe the floor with me."

"Yeah, I'm sure half the time you let me win. But why not ring him now? It's a shit job, isn't it? If you tell him what it's like there, he might pull us off it."

"No, I swear I don't let you win, you are that good. And I can't ring him now because I need to be by our computer and my laptop when I do. It's not like Greg to get things wrong, so you can bet there'll be a reason we haven't thought of for why he wants us there. If I've got any hope of putting up an argument, I might need to be online, researching things while I'm talking to him."

Kelvin laughed, "I'm not the only one worried, then?"

"Hell, no. I'd rather take on a whole roomful of thugs than one girl. You're in with a chance, you can fight with thugs, do anything you need to, but even in this feminist age, where we're all supposed to be equal, a guy can find himself in real serious trouble if he so much as raises his voice at a female."

"Yeah, I know, it's not fair, is it? I'm convinced it's all to do with hormones and it'll never change."

Hunter turned to him, frowning. "Why would you think it's all to do with hormones?"

"Most men are straight, and knowing a man's dick rules his brain, women take advantage of it. They seem to get anything they want by showing off a cleavage plunging to their navel and legs that go so far up you can almost see what they had for breakfast. Why else would they be looking like that when they're reading the news, judging X Factor that many young kids watch, or talking politics on television? I mean, what's any of that got to do with a woman showing off her bits? I've never seen a man barely covering his bell-end and flashing a length on Question Time, but it seems even old prunes get away with showing nearly everything they've got in the hope it'll get them what they want."

"Blimey, I knew you went deep, but not that deep! Oh, and thanks for that about Question Time. I've now got a mental picture of David Dimbleby flashing his length at the camera and it could haunt me for the rest of my days."

"Sorry," Kelvin giggled. "I'm not a misogynist, and after so many years in care I couldn't be a prude, but I do believe in there being a proper time and place for everything. I really can't stand females who show off what they've got when it's not the right time and place. We had a girl who did that when I was at North End, and she was dangerous."

"Why was she dangerous?"

"She always had her tits and arse on show, and if she thrust either at Dave, the bloke in charge, he'd believe anything she said. Knowing that, whatever a boy had that she wanted, he'd no choice, he had to give it to her. No boy was going to risk being hauled up in front of a magistrate in the morning on a charge of attempted rape."

"She wouldn't have done that, would she?"

"Who knows? All the boys there were too frightened of her to find out, but she used to threaten them she would."

"Hell! As an inmate, I knew a few unpleasant girls who'd stamp their feet and scream, or have an epic crying fit to get their way or something they wanted, but thankfully I never met any as evil as that.

"I couldn't take it. I ran from there after only two days."

"I think I'd have run too."

"Did you ever run away?"

"I only ran four times, but like you, the first time it was at the magic age. It was why I was of interest to CoT too."

"Eight years old is a magic age?"

"I might be reading too much into it, but to my mind there's more than a coincidental amount to CoT that you can equate to MISIC and the Johnny Mo lot. By the time he was eight, Johnny Mo had met a headless body, seen his first bloody street battle, taken drugs, and joined a notorious street gang, the Mong Kok Warriors. And wasn't Kamal eight when his mother was murdered and he fled to Marrakesh and became a street urchin? Then there was Christian and Roger, they were about that age when life bowled them a googly. Might Kamal have done more than teach CoT the Terror of the Dragon?"

"Now that you've pointed it out, it certainly does look like he could have, doesn't it? Is MISIC still around?"

"No, and that's another coincidence. MI5 and MI6 are still around, of course, but although it was senior to them, MISIC was disbanded in the seventies, a few months before Kamal turned up to teach CoT the Terror of the Dragon. And if you want to chew on another one, also since the seventies, the same as it was with MISIC, nobody sends in their CV in the hope of getting a job. Only people who've been thoroughly checked out as suitable, watched for years if you like, stand any chance of being *invited* to join CoT."

"Bloody hell! So are you saying Britain's last defence if the shit really hits the fan is now CoT?"

"As they say, that's above our pay grade to know, but there will be those who do know. It does seem to operate the same way as MISIC did. Few know it exists, it has its officers, and like it was with MISIC, they pick agents for the field work."

"How about Greg? Would he know?"

"I'm pretty sure he would. I've not known him to consult with anyone before making a decision, so I'd say he's got to be way up near the top."

Kelvin laughed, "And I gave him a free hour of my time."

"Yes, but it wasn't a bad trade, was it? It was Greg who supplied the hundred thousand pounds I transferred into your bank account. You might like to know, when I joined he gave me fifty thousand. All the rest of my four million, that isn't really mine, I've made from jobs I've done for him."

"Fuck! Why would he have given me more than you?"

"I don't know, but I suppose it could be because of the two evenings a week you were spending with him and a bunch of old queens in that pub, wiggling your arse and talking about zips being faster."

"I don't wiggle my arse!"

"You wouldn't want to bet on it, would you?"

"Bog off! You just wait till I get you home. After you've made that phone call, you're mine."

"That's good," giggled Hunter. "It might solve a problem."

"What problem?"

"If we are on a late one tonight, we'll need to get our heads down for a couple of hours, not easy in the daytime, but after a session with you, I reckon I'll manage it."

Laughing, Kelvin thumped Hunter's leg again. "The way I'm feeling, angel features, you'd better set an alarm clock."

Back home, Hunter checked everything he might need was switched on and ready, and then, after putting his phone into speaker mode, he sat down at the computer desk and made the call. Kelvin pulled up a chair and sat alongside him, not wanting to miss a word.

"I was expecting this call hours ago," laughed Greg.

"You were? You know what it's like there?"

"It's different to the state schools you went to, isn't it?"

"Different? It's not so much a school as a knocking shop."

"Yes, and you might like to know it wasn't alone in finding a novel solution to its difficulties in our years of austerity. It comes as a surprise to some people that many private schools suffered a lot more than the state ones."

"A novel solution? Are you saying you're okay with it?"

"No, of course not, but using the word invention loosely, necessity is the mother of invention, and when it comes to inventions, you cannot uninvent them, you have to accept they now exist. It's not our problem, Hunter. Society will have to sort it out, and don't forget it's high society that uses that school. If you don't swan around in its circles, its morals can be somewhat surprising. Those girls are tomorrow's high society, and the only difference to the previous generation is they're getting paid to open their legs. Previously, it would rarely have happened at school, there wouldn't have been the opportunities, but if it had, it would've been for free."

"Really? Are you saying I've led a sheltered life?"

"No, but a different kind of life. You know as little about the privileged as they know about kids in care. They are two entirely different lifestyles that rarely cross."

"You mean it's quite normal for a rich girl to go looking for a good time at fourteen?"

"Something accepted but not spoken about in those circles, it's not unusual for a number of them. They get off at parties, during sleepovers, and as horsey people, often with a bit of rough in a stable. It's a fact, high society gets what it wants at any age. The girls at that school will all be on the pill."

"Not all of them. The caretaker reckons Angelina Soames did a runner because she was pregnant."

"According to Miss Trump, she'd have thought she was on the pill, but it looks like her pills were changed for duds. The girls found what were probably her real pills hidden under her bottom drawer after she'd gone. Presumably, they'd been swapped so she became pregnant. But did a spiteful girl do it, or someone else? That's why you're there, to find out. If it turns out to be the latter, we'll need to rescue the girl."

"Do they nobble toffee-nosed girls for the sex trade?"

"Yes, of course, why wouldn't they? A classy underage girl will be the fantasy of quite a few. You might like to know, the reward Angelina's parents are offering for her safe return is for whoever has her to name their own price."

"Bloody hell!" Kelvin gasped.

"What?" laughed Hunter. "Didn't the council do the same for you, when you ran away?"

Kelvin thumped him. "Don't be silly, they probably threw a party every time I did a runner."

"You don't know how near the truth that is," said Greg.

"Really?"

"Kids in care are a cost councils would rather not have, so for every one that goes missing there's a saving. Why do you think many kids' hostels are in seedy areas? Officially, it's because they can't afford to put them anywhere better, when really it's because if the kids get caught up in a life of crime and run, the council saves money. Of course, while the books look good for the council, the crime rates soar, but today it's all about public perception. Politics is an evil business."

"You don't like politicians, do you?" asked Kelvin.

"No, but I'm open to changing my mind, should I ever meet a good one. You might need to remember, when somebody says they became a politician to serve the people in the hope of making a difference, it was probably the first lie they told in a long career of telling lies."

"Wow, they hurt you really bad when they closed down the boys' homes. You had a crush on a boy in one, didn't you?"

"How would you know that? You cannot be so streetwise that you can read my mind over a phone, surely?"

"You once told me in the pub that most the large children's homes they started closing in the fifties were better than how they farm kids out today, and they were made to sound bad places, like some run by the church, so they could be closed and save money. But for you to know they were better, you'd have had to know a kid who lived in one pretty closely."

"If you keep that up, you'll have my job one day."

"He was correct?" Hunter questioned.

"Yes, Barry Pullman, a school chum and my first sort of er, let's say attraction. He loved his place, all the boys there did. Never mind it had a playground, a games room, a gym and a sportsfield, it was their home; somewhere they believed was permanent and where they belonged. No boys ran from there, they were like one huge family of brothers, and proud of their home, they'd fight anyone who'd a bad word to say about it."

"Unless you belong there, nowhere is home," said Kelvin.

"What happened to Barry?" Hunter asked.

Greg sniffed, and there was a pause, before, "They shut the home and farmed him out to a family in Sidcup. I only found out years later, he didn't survive a beating there."

"Bloody hell! Sorry, I shouldn't have said anything."

"No, it's me, I shouldn't have asked about Barry. Sorry."

"Don't be silly, you couldn't know that bit. Anyway, it was a long time ago, and though some scars stay with you for life, with everything you two suffered growing up in care, you'll already be hiding a lot more of them than I am."

"Yeah, I guess," Hunter sighed. "Tell me, why did you give
this job to us? I mean, two gay guys, what can we find out at
a place like that? We'll hardly be up for any pillow talk, will
we? Actually, the mere thought of that many schoolgirls was
so threatening, we were planning on camping it up."

Greg laughed. "Well, I hate having to inflate your egos, but
you two are the nearest we have to their ages for two hundred
miles and by far the best-looking. And yes, I think camping it
up might be a good idea."

"You reckon it'll put them off us, then?"

"Oh, no, quite the opposite. They'll see you as a challenge,
and believing it's their god-given duty to cure you, they'll be
on a mission. Don't worry, I doubt they'll be heartbroken if
you don't rise to the occasion."

Beyond gasping anything, Hunter and Kelvin momentarily
stared at each other, and then down at the phone.

"Hello? Hello? Are you still there?"

***

The Millicent Fielding School for Girls came with many
traditions, as do all long-established schools, and especially
the private ones. To break a tradition at that school was more
than any girl would do. Ostracised by all the other pupils, her
life would become so unbearable, she'd soon be searching for
a way to get herself expelled. Whatever shame an expulsion
might earn her at home, it could never be matched by what
she would receive there for staying on. Such was the way in
which tradition was held.

Not the usually accepted years for secondary education, the
school took girls in when they were aged thirteen and turned
them out aged eighteen, supposedly as refined young ladies
prepared for a university. In the first year they were known as
seeds, shoots in their second year, then they became saplings,
followed by blossoms, and finally they were splendours. It
was traditional that for a seed's first week a shoot would take

42

her under a wing and show her the ropes. And so, following the girls coming up with a novel way of saving the school, that way became included in those ropes. As tradition wasn't something to be messed with, the new girls had to accept the addition to the ropes, so ensuring the school's future should remain secure.

Originally, the main school building was intended to be a mansion, Fielding Hall, but George Fielding had died before it was completed, leaving Millicent and three daughters. Not wanting to rattle around in an enormous building on her own, as she would have done with her daughters being educated away for most of the year, Millicent had the plans changed to turn all of the building except for the top floor into a school for young ladies of the affluent, where she could have her daughters educated at home. The school opened in 1685, but as it grew, the additional classrooms it required saw the girls' accommodation being moved into two purposely-built houses in a similar style alongside the main school building, where over five storeys, every girl was given her own private room, albeit too small to swing the proverbial cat.

Not to anything like the same extent as in recent years, the girls having a room of their own had been a blessing to many a local youth. Since the school had opened all those long years back, like dogs sniffing round the door of a house with a bitch, boys from Upper Fielding and Lower Fielding had walked that footpath, taking the air, and there'd always been a few girls tempted by a bit of rough. Once, the two separate villages had been surrounded by farmland that was a part of the Fielding estate, Upper Fielding a mile to the north and Lower Fielding two miles to the south, but bit by bit, during hard times over the years, the estate's lands and farms had been sold off, until now it was only what was the school.

Hunter and Kelvin, arriving back there at seven-thirty, were surprised by the number of girls walking the grounds with a young man in tow, or sitting on the grass with one. They sat in the Volvo, doing no more than watch them for a while.

"I know you wouldn't expect to see boys like that in a girl's school, but don't they look more like they're boyfriends and girlfriends to you than prossies and punters?" asked Kelvin, eventually.

"I'm no expert, but now you've said it, they do. It looks as if all the guys have brought some alcohol, and they probably brought the spliffs being smoked too. It's the kind of thing they might do at a party where they were hoping to score, not what you'd expect if they were paying for it."

"Half those lads don't look like they could pay for much. I haven't seen any well-known brands of booze, it's got to be cheap supermarket stuff they're drinking."

"Yeah, they sure do know how to treat a girl well."

A girl neither of them had seen coming tapped on Hunter's side window, and they both jumped a little. Kelvin pressed the button to slide the window down and Hunter asked her what she wanted.

"Why are you watching everybody?" the girl asked.

"It's not against the law," Hunter replied. "Why would you want to know?"

"Because if you've come here to party, I was told you had to leave your car in the village and walk along the footpath to get here. Have you come to party? I'm looking for someone, if you have. Did you bring any drink with you?"

"No, we didn't. Why, is it compulsory to bring some?"

"You have to bring something to get off your head, don't you? How else you going to have a good time? Haven't you done this before?"

"Er, no, we've never been to a party here before."

"You look old enough to get drink from the village without being challenged. I was told they were very liberal. We could go and get some and then I could give you a good time. All the girls here have their own rooms, you know?"

"Why pick on us? Do we look like we want a good time?"

"You'd better. My shoot will be most unhappy if I don't get off tonight, and it seems all the other guys are taken."

"What's your name? Is it your first day here?"

"Summer Bell-hyphen-Anderson. I know, it's a really crap name, you have to say the hyphen. And yes, it's my first day, but I know the score, you'll have fun. I'm good at it."

"Well, we didn't come here to party tonight, I'm afraid. We only wanted to see what it was like. You see, we're not from the village or anywhere local, we've got a long drive home, and only an idiot would do it drunk these days."

"He could not drink," said Summer, nodding at Kelvin.

"Oh, thanks, I love you too," Kevin said, playing along.

"It's not what you'd call late," Hunter said. "There's plenty of time for more guys to turn up. Why don't you try your luck on the footpath?"

"You're no fun, are you? I suppose I'll have to," Summer said, stamping off in obvious disappointment.

"Bloody hell, Hunter, I don't think I've ever seen anyone so desperate for it."

Winking at him, Hunter chuckled, "Oh, I have."

"Bitch!" Kelvin thumped him, playfully.

"Actually, I don't think they look at it the same as we do, to them it's all about being off their heads and partying, as they call it, and a shag is just a part of it. They won't remember it tomorrow, but to them that's what a good time is about."

"Weird, or what? If they think that's having a good time, how will they ever find out what's really a good time?"

"Search me," chuckled Hunter. "Come on, we'd better put on our security blazers and have a stroll round the grounds. If I jangle the keys too, hopefully it will put any other girls off trying to accost us."

"I bloody hope so. I thought for a minute that Summer was going to get in and sit on your lap. If she had, we might never have got rid of her."

Hunter laughed. "You've got no worries there, I don't think even rigor mortis would work on it if a girl was around."

Contrasting nicely with the cavalry twill trousers they were wearing, the blazers were dark green, with a crescent label at the top of the arms that was neatly embroidered in gold with the word, 'SECURITY.' Dragons seemed to be a theme. On the top pocket one was threateningly breathing fire, and there was also one on a bronze-coloured lapel badge that Kelvin had questioned. It hadn't been pinned on or pushed through the buttonhole, with a much larger than expected backing plate, it seemed to have been fitted like a store's security tag that needed a special tool to remove it. Laughing, Hunter had told him not to worry about it, it looked good.

Sauntering the grounds, they'd taken a lot of stick from the girls and their companions, including wolf-whistles and jeers, when they happened to notice Summer had found someone who would probably satisfy her needs. He appeared to be of Indian or Pakistani origin, they couldn't be sure which, and while she hung on to his arm, it was obvious he'd come with four other guys; two white, two looking like him, and all five of them probably in their early twenties. And then, strangely, a lot of the other girls began to break free of their companion to run over to this bloke and excitedly crowd around him.

"What's the betting that's Rashid?" Hunter asked, aside.

"It's got to be real bad news if it is," replied Kelvin, as they walked over to check out the five guys.

From listening to the conversations, it soon became obvious it was Rashid, and he'd a sorry tale to tell about Angelina. If he was to be believed, they'd had a tiff and she'd run off with their baby boy for the bright lights, not to be seen again. The girls were lapping up the story, feeling sorry for him, while Hunter and Kelvin didn't believe a word of it. Having heard enough, they pushed through the crowd to confront him.

"I can't stop you using the footpath, but I can stop you from coming onto the school's grounds. You five need to return to the footpath," Hunter said.

Rashid laughed, turning to his mates to gather their laughs too, before turning back and saying, "Oh, yeah? And who's going to make us, then? You and whose army?"

And that saw the girls joining the guys in their laughter.

"I've already given you one warning, chum. I rarely give anyone two. I'd move it, if I was you."

Still laughing, Rashid took a swing at Hunter, and his mates moved in closer, ready to back him up. But long before the fist came into contact with Hunter's chin, he grabbed it, and holding on to it tightly while doing a forward somersault, he jerked it and dislocated the guy's shoulder. Not satisfied with that, in the deafening silence that had fallen all around, the sound of the crack was unmissable as he smartly brought the arm down onto his waiting taught raised-up leg, breaking it just above the wrist. Rashid screamed as if he was trying to wake the dead, until Hunter's pressure move saw him passing out. Almost filling their pants in shock, the two white blokes quickly ran back to the footpath, from there staring at them open-mouthed, while their two other friends were unable to join them. They were lying equally out of it at Kelvin's feet.

"You really ought to pick your friends more carefully," said Kelvin, aiming it at Summer. "If we hadn't been here tonight, you might've been the next one to go missing. The fact he's come back with four mates suggests Angelina was just a test run. They're here to groom girls for the sex trade."

There were many gasps from the girls.

"But Angelina only left because she was pregnant," piped up a girl from the back.

"Yes, Rashid made sure she became pregnant, and you can bet he told her in no uncertain terms she couldn't get rid of it because it was against his religion or way of life. That meant she couldn't stay here and she couldn't go home, she could only go with him. If she's still alive, she'll be in some hovel earning money for them on her back, and I wouldn't want to guarantee the baby survived."

The gasps were louder this time, and many of the girls ran off, crying, most of them forgetting all about their companion and heading for their accommodation block.

To shock those remaining, and Kelvin too, Hunter loudly said into his lapel, "Sky Cat, Sky Cat from Hotel Kilo."

"Hotel Kilo, go ahead. Sky Cat, over," came a reply.

"Sky Cat, Hotel Kilo has five for transporting, over."

"Hotel Kilo, e.t.a. three minutes. Sky Cat, over and out."

"And don't you two idiots even think of running," Hunter said, glaring it at the two on the footpath. "I could easily lose my temper if I had to chase you, and you wouldn't like that."

Still open-mouthed, the two guys appeared to be too scared to run, like they were frozen rigid.

"Jesus, you never told me the badges were radios," Kelvin said, aside to Hunter.

Hunter chuckled. "Yes, they go live when they recognise a call sign, but you didn't expect to know everything in a few weeks, did you? I didn't tell you they were radios because some of the calls can get a bit snotty if you don't observe our radio protocol, and I haven't had time to teach you it yet."

"Er, was it a helicopter you called, then?"

"CoT has several helicopters. Sky Cat's a Super Puma able to carry twenty-seven, including the two up front. It's said Greg bought it because he'd been involved in the design of one of its predecessors. It'll have been parked up somewhere nearby in case we needed it."

"And they'll take the guys away and torture them until they find out what's happened to Angelina, will they?"

"Do behave, torture is old hat. They'll use solotomin. It's a truth drug that was developed by CoT's boffins and it'll find out everything they want to know within minutes."

"Really?"

"Yes, and as you won't find it on Google, I've looked, and so say our security services haven't got it or even heard of it, I think it gives more strength to a MISIC connection. It too had stuff no one else had heard about."

"Bloody hell!"

Thump, thump, thump, thump . . . The sound of the rotors punching the air saw the grounds filling up again, as many of the girls came back out to watch the helicopter land. With no rain to speak of recently, some were passing thankful words that its nigh on six tons hadn't sunk into the grass to damage their hockey pitch.

A door on the side of the helicopter opened and five guys jumped out and ran over to collect the prisoners. Waiting in a line, they'd all recovered and had their hands securely bound behind their backs with cable-ties. Acknowledging Hunter and Kelvin with little more than nods, the CoT team grabbed the captives, taking them over to the helicopter and bundling them inside to put hoods over their heads and make them lie on the floor. However, there was something about the guys that had puzzled Kelvin, and as soon as the chopper took off, he questioned it.

"Didn't it seem to you as if those guys were smirking?" he asked, frowning. "Like there was a joke at our expense?"

"They had a reason to be smirking," said Hunter.

"Huh? Why?"

"There's something else I didn't tell you in case you got a bit self-conscious and it affected how you'd perform, should the need to perform arise, as it did. The eye of the dragon on your top pocket is the lens of a video camera, and you don't always have to switch it on, a jolt or a sudden movement will do it. When they came on, they'll have seen me putting down one of those idiots while you, only with us a few weeks, put down two and in a lot less time."

"Bloody hell! Sorry, Hunter, I wouldn't have done it if I'd known they were watching us."

"You've nothing to be sorry about, you only did what you were expected to do and what you're paid to do. You might be wearing laurels for being that good, but don't you think I'm wearing them too? After all, wasn't it me who taught you how to be that good?"

"You're not just saying that?"

"No, I told you I'd never lie to you. Come on, there's not going to be any more threats here tonight, you can drive us back to Puffney Bigshot and we'll pop into a club I know in town. We can celebrate your fame with a drink."

"Our fame, but we've got drink at home."

"I know we have, but it's a special club; members only. As they say, you ain't seen nothing yet."

"I haven't? What's special about it?"

"You'll see when we get there, won't you?" said Hunter, sporting the grin of a Cheshire cat high on a naughty trip.

Chapter Four

Puffney Bigshot was an old and heavily leaning towards the conservative type of town where everything had to be just so; done correctly, in other words. It was one of only a very few towns in the country not to suffer from drunk and stupefied youths on its streets of a night, not even at weekends. Hunter had taken Kelvin there a couple of times for him to buy his clothes, but too excited by being able to shop, the lad hadn't taken any notice of the street names, so he had to be directed to the car park in Corporation Street. A sign at its entrance, a few yards before an automatic barrier, warned it was strictly only for members of Bangers, the club opposite. Turning into it to drive up to the barrier, Kelvin was surprised as it lifted to allow them in.

"Don't tell me, it recognised the car's number plate?"

"Of course it did. Why else would it have lifted?"

With only a dozen or so cars in there parked up, there were plenty of free spaces. Kelvin parked in one near the entrance.

As they crossed the road to the club, Kelvin said, "Crikey, there's a doorman in a top hat and tails at the top of the steps, he'll never let us in dressed in security jackets."

"He will. He's only standing there to stop anyone who's not a member trying to get in."

"What, that old-timer? He doesn't look to me like he'd be able to stop anyone."

"I know, but if somebody was to push past him, anything happening to them would be their own fault, wouldn't it?"

Kelvin laughed, "Don't tell me the floor opens up and they fall into a tank of sharks or piranhas?"

"You're awful close, I'll give you that. It opens up and they fall onto a mattress in a locked room below the floor, where a dust on the mattress fills the air and sends them into a deep sleep until someone has the time to deal with them."

"Bloody hell! So, the club's owned by CoT, is it?"

"Yes, it has several around the country where members can socialise and hold meetings. Many of them, the same as this one does, come with a lot of secrets."

"Like what?"

With a smile, the doorman doffed his hat and opened one of the two glass doors, allowing them into a narrow vestibule where another two glass doors, leading into the club, were a few yards to their right and not straight ahead as one might have expected. Flashing a polite smile, Hunter thanked the old boy, acknowledging him as Charles. Kelvin smiled too, before staring down at the polished wooden floorboards and walking on them as lightly as he could manage.

"You can stop worrying," laughed Hunter. "If he hadn't got the green light, Charles wouldn't have opened the door. The floor won't open up and swallow us."

"There's a green light?"

"Yes, there are light-emitting-diodes he can see up in the void above the entrance. A red light tells him someone hasn't been recognised by any of the three cameras trained on them as they come up the steps."

"The cameras know me?"

"There's an awful lot of both of us on file, but don't worry, it's for our protection as much as it is for CoT."

"Crikey!"

Through the doors and they were in the club. With thickly-piled wall-to-wall patterned carpeting and polished wooden tables surrounded by red-leather bench seating in alcoves, it looked every bit as conservative as Kelvin had expected. A bar ran the full length of the left wall, with many gaps in the counter to suggest it wasn't a secure arrangement, especially as he couldn't see a barman.

"What are you having?" Hunter asked.

"I'd better just have an orange-juice, please. I don't want to lose my driving licence before I've got it, do I? I can catch up with you on the drink later, at home, if you want."

"We'll both catch up later, I'll just have coke for now. He's waving at us like a lunatic, you'd better go over and say hello to Greg while I get the drinks."

Spinning his head, looking around, Kelvin asked, "Where? Oh, over there. What's he doing in here? It's a long way from Chestnut Dale. Um, I think you might as well come with me, it looks like the barman's on a break."

"There is no barman, only somebody to ensure nothing runs out. You serve yourself and the drinks are free. And knowing Greg, it wouldn't surprise me if he didn't take advantage of his favourite chopper going up today and piloted it himself."

"The drinks are free?"

"Yes, why not? Anybody who'd abuse it and get bladdered wouldn't be in here, would they?"

"No, I suppose not, silly me," laughed Kelvin, walking off to join Greg and ask, "What you doing here, Bo . . . Greg? Sorry, I nearly said Bob then."

Greg laughed. "Yes, I'm sometimes frightened of getting it wrong myself if I've had a few. I'm here because I made sure we had a shortage of pilots today. Sit down, then, there's no charge. You two need to update me on a few things."

Hunter arrived with their drinks, bringing an extra one. "I hope you've got someone to get you home," he said, putting a gin and tonic in front of Greg and sitting next to Kelvin.

"Yes, it's all arranged, you needn't worry, I wasn't going to ask you. I'd an idea you'd be having a hard one tonight."

"Steady on there, Greg. You don't want make yourself cry, do you?" Hunter quipped, as quick as a flash, to have Kelvin spluttering orange juice back into his glass.

"Yes, I could have put that a bit better, couldn't I?"

"Did you manage to get enough out of Rashid and the other four guys to find the girl?" Hunter asked.

"No, annoyingly, we didn't. That's why I was hoping to see you. We didn't pick up on anything until the cameras came on, when you started putting them down. Did they have much to say before that?"

"No, next to nothing. Rashid taunted us because I'd told them to return to the footpath. Apart from that, we listened to him telling some girls that he and Angelina had had a tiff, she'd left with the baby, and he'd not seen them since. Why, didn't the truth drug work?"

"It worked, but none of them could tell us where Angelina is now, only that she'd moved on. I was hoping you might've picked up on a loose thread we could pull."

"Um, there might be something," Kelvin said. "When he told the girls she'd left, he said it was for the bright lights."

"For the bright lights? Some people refer to the West End as the bright lights, but if they had known she'd been taken to somewhere like that, why didn't any of them reveal it under the influence of the drug?"

"It could be because you were asking them *where* the bright lights were when they aren't a place," suggested Kelvin.

"What would they be if they're not a place?"

"Lights that could be just about anywhere, and a camera so she could put on a show and someone make a film or a video of her. If she was tricked into leaving school, and she's being forced to work in the sex trade, I can't see her being put out on the streets. She's posh totty and underage. I reckon they'd advertise her on the internet."

"Jumping Jehoshaphat! I'm not joking, I reckon you really could land up with my job one day. Come on, quickly," said Greg, leaping up out of his seat.

"Where we going?" Kelvin asked, as they followed Greg.

"I don't know, but my guess is we're off to visit the bowels of the earth. It's where Bangers hides quite a number of its secrets," Hunter replied, grinning madly.

"Huh?"

"There's a whole world hidden deep beneath the club. You see, the town of Puffney had Bigshot added to its name when centuries ago people came here to develop gunpowder, guns and cannons, and later other explosives. And as in those days things often went bang unexpectedly, they stored and worked on them in caves and tunnels deep underground. Back then, this building would've mainly been used as accommodation, with an office at the front where people could come to place an order for the latest weapons of mass destruction."

"I didn't know its name had to do with weapons."

"No, nor did I, once. Apart from where there's been huge factories, mills or mines, not many do know the full working history of most towns. I doubt if we will tonight, but if we do go along the tunnel to the airport, I hope you like funfairs."

Kelvin's face screwed up. "An airport and funfairs?"

"It was one of many airports built for the war, but now it's only used by a gliding club and as somewhere to store or get a helicopter serviced. It's the way they would've brought the five blokes here, via the airport the other side of the ringroad, and so they'd no idea of which direction they were heading, they'd have gone down the lift which spins so fast, it's like one of the rides in a funfair where you're thrown up against the wall. There is a spiral staircase, but as the steps seem to go on forever, no one uses it."

"Bloody hell! A spinning lift? And so fast it throws you up against the wall? I've not even heard of that in James Bond."

"The truth is often stranger than fiction."

"You can say that again!"

Hunter giggled, "The truth is . . ."

Kelvin thumped him.

At the opposite end to where they'd come in, there was a central double door with another door about twelve feet away on either side of it, and the labels on them said the left was for 'Ladies' and the right one 'Gents.' Greg went into the one on the right, and suspecting he'd gone in there to answer a call of nature, Kelvin was about to wait outside when Hunter pushed him through the door.

"Don't panic, we're not going cottaging," laughed Hunter.

Kelvin could see a row of cubicles faced a long urinal, and Greg was busy unlocking the last cubicle with a key, where a notice on its door said it was out of service.

"Come along, quickly," said Greg, tugging them inside, and squeezing past them to relock the door before squeezing back and pulling the flush handle sharply upwards.

"Whoa!" gasped Kelvin, a steadying hand flying out, trying to hold on to the wall. "It's awfully fast, isn't it?"

"Yes, but you're okay, this one doesn't spin," Hunter said.

With the speed of the lift, Kelvin concluded they'd gone down a hell of a long way when a door at the bottom simply needed sliding open. Leaving the lift and looking around, he could see they were in a large flagstoned cave with walls of painted-white rock from which five tunnels led off. Greg was heading down the furthest right of them like a greyhound out of the traps, and in the time it took for Hunter to shut the lift door, they needed to run to catch up with him.

"What's behind all the doors we ran past?" Kelvin asked.

They'd arrived at what, by its barred door, seemed like the entrance to a small prison in a cave. Beyond it, there were six cells on either side before you couldn't go any further. Greg told them the guard behind the desk was phoning for Doc, and they'd have to wait for him to turn up.

"I've no idea what's behind some of the doors, and as I've not been down this tunnel before, none along here," Hunter replied, to answer Kelvin's earlier question. "I know there's a rarely used mini-hospital in the next one, and the one after that's got an armoury, a combat training area and a shooting range, the one after that has lots of laboratories where boffins work, and the next one's mainly used for storing things, but don't ask me what. The last one is by far the longest tunnel as it goes all the way to the airport. That has a lot of rooms off it where our mega-brains perform miracles on more computers than you could shake a stick at. They reckon there's not a computer system in the world they couldn't get into, and I believe them. After all, they came up with everything needed to sort Royston out in next to no time, didn't they?"

"Yeah, that was incredible. I couldn't believe how you just ran a program somebody sent you and a few seconds later a gold debit card popped out of that thingamajig like a huge printer. And even then, I didn't expect it to work, but it did."

"Apparently, the thingamajigs were developed behind one of the doors down here, and though mine's had to be updated once for a new security measure, it hasn't let me down yet."

"Is that how CoT gets its money, it prints off bank cards?"

"No, apart from having an anonymous benefactor who for decades has annually donated untold money, it imposes a tax on some worldwide internet companies. Some that, while not doing anything illegal, aren't morally paying the UK a fair amount of tax. It's a sizeable whack it takes, but as it goes to help some of those who'd have benefitted if they had paid the morally correct amount, it doesn't feel guilty about it."

"How does CoT manage to tax these companies?"

"They aren't like a corner shop that shuts its doors, counts the cash in the till, checks it against the stock sold and what's remaining, sets aside money for the staff wages and whatever else it needs to cover the running costs, and works out how much money it actually has that day. Big internet companies, those with turnovers measured in the billions, have countless thousands of transactions going on around the clock on every day of the year, meaning there is never a time when they can tally up their money, stock and costs with any accuracy, they have to rely on what a computer tells them. And, as you have seen, computers are like putty in some people's hands. With the fluidness of such a setup, the few millions being creamed off here and there are impossible to see, never mind find. So, as long as that computer keeps telling them they are making money hand over fist, they're never going to stop to question it. Stopping something of the size they've grown to be, just to *physically* check a small amount of their turnover isn't going astray, would be at a price they couldn't consider paying."

"Bloody hell, you make it sound so easy."

"It is, for our mega-brains. Of course, to make the money skimmed off untraceable, there has to be a merry-go-round of fictitious people and flyby firms in business with off-shore banks, investment schemes and the suchlike, but with money coming in every week from them, it gets to us eventually.”

“It sounds like CoT needs it if it’s got several helicopters to run and all what you’ve said is down here. But why does it have things like that? Why would it need a shooting range and an armoury? It almost sounds like it’s a private army.”

“It’s not an army in the military sense, but because of what it does, some agents have to be proficient in using firearms.”

“Bloody hell, that makes it sound even more like CoT is really MISIC under another name. MISIC gave Johnny Mo and his oppos guns and taught them how to use them.”

“And there were times they needed them, weren’t there?”

Greg, feeling that he ought to put them right, joined in the conversation, explaining, “CoT isn’t MISIC with a different name. We don’t have command over the police, the security services or the armed forces, we’ve no hot case or a means of seeing the Letters of Last Resort are destroyed, and we don’t have legal access to the country’s coffers. The differences far outweigh any similarities. If you must liken us, then liken us to Johnny Mo and his motley team, not to MISIC.”

“Oh, I get it,” Kelvin said.

“You do? Then tell me,” said Hunter.

“The similarities are to do with helping people who need to be helped. Like CoT does, Johnny Mo made the rich pay so he could do jobs for the poor. And the biggest difference will be, no matter what, MISIC was primarily there to protect the establishment, while like Johnny and his team, CoT couldn’t give a toss about the establishment.”

“You are simply amazing,” Greg said, plainly impressed.

“Yes, I think he’s amazing too, but are you saying he got it right?” Hunter asked,

“Spot on. And as he’s quite plainly a fan of Johnny Mo and his team, I’m sure he’ll be pleased to know they have more than one finger in the pie when it comes to CoT. There’s not only Kamal who still keeps an eye on us, there’s the kid who almost breaks your heart at the end of the book he must have read. Do you remember the name of Sandra and Tony's boy, Kelvin? He was nine years old when the book ended."

"Tobias Bellingham-Topps? Toby?"

"Today, Toby is CoT's top dog, the UK's pack leader."

"Bloody hell!"

"He took over when his father retired in 2001."

"So Tony joined CoT too?"

"Tony was in charge of MISIC when it was disbanded, and as he wasn't known for his love of the establishment, he was invited to join CoT. Within days, he reckoned our agents in the field should be taught the Terror of the Dragon, and so along came Kamal to teach them. Not unexpectedly, as there was something going on between them, when CoT's top job became vacant the following year, Kamal convinced us Tony would be good at it, and voting for him turned out to be the best thing CoT's members ever did. We've come a long way since then. Having our own aircraft, scientists and a team of computer geniuses? We hadn't even dreamed of it."

"Crikey! Um, so, do Tony and Kamal still have something going on, and is Johnny still banging Tony's ex-wife?"

Greg laughed. "None of them are spring chickens anymore, they're knocking back the years, so I couldn't say about the banging, but the setup has remained exactly as the book left it. Johnny and his crew are a commune with unconventional ideas, living together as one big happy family."

"Cor, I like a happy end."

"Er, you're not by any chance trying to win the pun of the year award, are you?" Hunter asked, grinning manically.

Kelvin frowned and then, realising what he'd said, punched Hunter's arm, giggling. Greg, however, lost it completely and dived through a nearby door.

Ten minutes passed slowly, and they'd recovered from the merriment by the time Doc turned up and they finally got to see Rashid in his cell. Kelvin learned Doc was a consultant at the local hospital with an alphabet after his name. CoT kept him on a retainer so he'd be available as and when he was required, though not, of course, at the expense of the life of a hospital patient. Apparently, he'd administered the truth drug to their prisoners earlier, and as he didn't appear in any way annoyed at being called back, Kelvin guessed his retainer had to be a pretty big screw. Although 'screw' was a word none of them wanted to enter their mind, once they were inside the cell. From floor to ceiling it was in white tiles, including the low intrusion that was the bed, and in the corner over a drain there was a hose attached to a tap that Rashid would plainly need to use later. Asleep on the bed, apart from a plaster cast on his arm, he was wearing nothing but an adult nappy, and there was a bit of a whiff to him. Greg explained it was an unfortunate side-effect to the drug, it did more than loosen a tongue. Doc shook Rashid, waking him, and then seeing his eyes, he proclaimed the guy didn't need another dose, he was still up there somewhere, flying with the cuckoos.

"What bright lights has Angelina gone to see?" Greg asked, shaking Rashid to keep him awake.

"Speshal wuns dat makes yer look betta," he slurred.

"Where are these lights?"

"I dunno, dooweye? Dey coobee anywhere."

Greg sighed deeply, seemingly stumped, so Kelvin decided he'd have a go. "Who took Angelina to the lights?" he asked.

"Arty-farty, o' course."

"What's Arty-farty's real name?"

"Petty . . . Petty . . . Petty Goo Willyums."

"What's Pettigrew Williams' address?"

"I dunno, dooweye?"

"Do you know where Pettigrew spends a lot of his time?"

"They says he's always at de arty-farty fing in town."

"And which town is that?"

"Slapper's town, o' course."

"So, he often goes to the Arts Centre in Slapperton, then?"

"Yah, dats it, de arty-farty sender, always there."

"Is Pettigrew involved in making pornos?"

"Only za bestest ever!"

Greg shook his head. Kelvin had got more out of Rashid in a minute than he had earlier in half an hour.

Turning to Greg, Kelvin said, "An Arts Centre is sure to have a website. If you've a computer handy, maybe we ought to check it out? If he's always there, Pettigrew could be listed on it with a phone number."

"I can't see it being likely," Greg said. "If he's involved in porno films and the sex trade, he'll be on big money. Why would he work for an Arts Centre that'd only be paying him peanuts?"

"He doesn't have to work for it, he could belong to a club or organisation that meets there and uses its facilities. These days, some Arts Centres can provide all the equipment you'd need to shoot and edit a pretty good feature film. It has to be hired, of course, and it doesn't come cheap, but it'll do the job. If he's making pornos and runs the risk of being raided and having the equipment confiscated, it's got to be a better option than buying his own."

"I can feel my neck on the chopping block already," sighed Greg, shaking his head again. "Come on, follow me."

A few minutes later, down the opposite tunnel, in the room used by computer geniuses Kent and Taylor, just two who worked the nightshift, up popped the website. It soon became obvious to them, Slapperton's Arts Centre was popular. With something going on every day of the week, there were a few clubs and organisations on a page for 'Arts Centre Friends.'

"You could try that one," said Kelvin, pointing to a link for the Slapperton Filmmakers' Club.

Kent clicked on the link and the club's website opened in a new window. The posters for a selection of films that could be bought and downloaded came with a short description and a link to watch a trailer. Far more interesting, though, was the link on the menu at the top for 'Who We Are.' Clicking it brought up six 'senior' members, whatever that meant, each with their photograph and an email address. The top one was Pettigrew Williams, proudly standing alongside a Porsche.

Greg shook his head yet again, sighing, "Do you know, I think I might be getting too old for this job? The Arts Centres I remember were worse than the old fleapits. They'd only put something on a couple of times a year. If you were lucky it'd be the local amateur dramatic society murdering a play, and if you were unlucky it'd be the operatic society doing its best to inflict death by screaming. They didn't have friends."

"Things do change," said Kelvin. "And sometimes it's for the better."

"Yes, well, I suppose I should find something consoling in you not being infallible."

"Huh?"

"Public perception again, and you've fallen for it. You've not considered how they've come to be better; the cost of it."

"What cost?"

"The community centres, youth clubs, and public libraries many councils closed down so the few able to afford it, and had a way of getting there, were forced to pay them through the nose for some of the things they once had for free or at a minimal cost, while the majority were left with nothing. Ever heard of divide and conquer? If you divide a community, you can do whatever you like, no one will stop you. People didn't always say, 'Ring the bell, I'm on the bus!' There was a time they'd shout, 'Stop! There's people running for the bus!'"

Kelvin laughed, "Wow, you have got a really big chip on your shoulder."

"If it's fishy, you'll find it often comes with chips. Haven't you ever run for a bus?" Hunter asked, frowning at Kelvin.

Kelvin thought about it. "Sorry, Greg. You're right to have a chip. I've been running for busses all my life, and now I've caught one, I ought to be shouting for it to wait for anybody who's running. I will in future. I won't get it wrong again."

"I'm pleased to hear it. We all lived in a much better world when everybody could get on the bus," Greg said, smiling at Kelvin for seeing the light.

"That's strange," said Kent, moving his mouse around.

"What's strange?" Greg asked.

Kent moved the mouse again. "See how the address that the link goes to comes up at the bottom of the screen?"

"That's normal, isn't it? My computer does that."

"Yes, but not in red. It can be red on ours because of some software we have running in the background, and when it is, it means we're on a magical mystery tour. But why would an innocuous website for some filmmakers want to do that?"

"A magical mystery tour?" questioned Greg.

"The website is hiding. It's using like what you could think of as an exchange to pass us on to a host that has the website, but which host we get, and what far-flung country it's in, is often difficult to find out. It's totally illegal to have the same website name hosted by different hosts all around the world, but with a bit of jiggery-pokery, it is in effect what some of the really bad porn sites manage to do to keep their money flowing in. If the website should be shut down or blocked on one host, the exchange will simply send you to another one."

"We think the bloke at the top of the screen has at least one porn site," said Kelvin.

"That explains it, then," Kent said. "He's not very clever."

"He's not?"

"No, he obviously has one big website with any other sites running as subs from folders in it. If he didn't have it set up that way, we wouldn't see anything wrong on this site. Well, Pettigrew, let's see just how petty you like your porn."

Kent opened a folder that was pinned to the taskbar and ran one of the programs in it. Within seconds, a screen opened up listing all the folders and everything else the site contained.

"Crikey, some of the folders look real dodgy," Kelvin said, staring at them. "Teen Todgers and Teenage Twats? There's even one for Toddlers Tinkling. I mean, really?"

"Do you want to see any of them?" asked Kent.

"I suppose we'll have to see what at least a couple of them are about," replied Greg. "You could try the one titled Latest Jail Bait. Maybe if it's underage it won't be too explicit."

"I wouldn't bet on it," Kent said, opening up the folder and clicking on '*index.html*' so the website appeared.

"Bloody hell! Isn't that Angelina?" gasped Kelvin, pointing at the last of twelve pictures in four rows of three. "That girl sure looks like the one in the photo you showed me."

"Yes, it does look like her, and they're saying she's a bit of posh called Angel, aged twelve," Hunter said. "It's close, but hasn't Angelina turned fourteen?"

"Yes, fourteen last May," Greg confirmed. "But no doubt being twelve makes her more appealing for some. I suppose you'd better follow the link, Kent."

Kent clicked on the girl's photo and they were taken to her page, where they found more photos of her and a video. Greg told Kent to play the video, while suggesting they didn't see it in full screen. Clicking on it revealed the first minute was taken up with Angelina seductively stripping off, and then a minute was of her flaunting herself, teasing an up and ready for it young stud. As they didn't get down to doing anything more than touching, it appeared to be a case of leaving the audience wanting for more, with the reason for it becoming apparent at the end, where an advertisement told them that anyone wanting to see the full video had to be a member or sign up and pay a fee.

"Do you want to see the full video?" Kent asked. "We can get around the signing up bit and be watching it in a matter of minutes, if you want."

"No, I think we can guess what it'll be like, but you really could get to it in minutes?"

"Yes, we made a program that gets us past user names and passwords. It's the biggest secret in the world. Put simply, it doesn't matter how elaborate you make a security system, at some point after it's satisfied everything is okay and you're allowed access, one or more small pieces of code have to run to move you on. Our program finds and interrogates those pieces of code, even at another destination, and once it knows what they're looking for, it can make them run."

"It's that easy?"

"Yes. Fortunately for us, there isn't a computer system in the world that can ever be totally secure."

"Really? Not one?"

"The money NATO's system cost, and what it costs now in an attempt to keep it secure, will be beyond our imagination, and yet just for the hell of it, a few years ago a boy got into it on his home computer. It's not the nuclear bombs you should fear, it's the operating systems controlling them. What if that boy had been a terrorist out to make cockroaches happy?"

"You have a lovely way with words, Kent."

Taylor, who'd been sitting at his computer, quietly working on something, sat back and said, "Pettigrew Williams lives at 11 Buckingham Road, Slapperton, but according to the Land Registry he doesn't own the property. It's a detached house with five bedrooms, nevertheless, council tax records have him as sole occupant. And not that there'd likely be another in a hundred miles, I've checked the DVLC database and the Pettigrew Williams at that address is the registered keeper of the same model of Porsche as in the photo. Also doubtless of interest, he's got an old Astra and a prehistoric van too."

"Efficient, or what?" Kelvin gasped, impressed by how the guy had effortlessly waded through what had to be protected records. "That has to be him if it's the same model. How far is Slapperton? Are we going after him tonight?"

"I'll need to give it a lot of thought before we do anything, but when we do, you won't be going after him," Greg said.

"Why not?"

"As none of the idiots you captured know where Pettigrew lives, he's likely close to the centre of things. And depending on how close is how much protection he'll have. Those five you caught will be expendable minions, working for peanuts with a few free drugs and all the shags they can get thrown in, but Pettigrew is in a different league. If he should know the head honcho and where he lives, we could be talking of blood and bodies on the streets."

"What head honcho?"

"Pettigrew may be getting the girls, making the videos and running the website, but he isn't the boss."

"How do you know he isn't?"

"He doesn't own his house, and he's got two old bangers. If he was the top dog, with the money that sex makes, he would own his house and he wouldn't have those old bangers."

"He's got a Porsche, though."

"Being the registered keeper doesn't mean he owns it. I'd give a pound to a penny he only owns those old bangers. It's how big underground organisations work. The boss sees to it those close to him enjoy a good lifestyle, they can have pretty much anything they want, but when it comes to money, he'll pay them little more than their expenses. By paying them in kind rather than cash, he doesn't have to worry about any of them having the money to start up in competition to him."

"How big is the organisation likely to be?"

"That, we shall need to find out before we do anything. As Pettigrew obviously has a boss, the Slapperton outfit could be merely a small part of a much bigger operation, and possibly even one run by one of the crime lords of London."

"Crime lords of London?"

"Yes, and when the police refuse to admit they exist in case they should be asked to take them on, we shall need to think carefully before we make our move, won't we?"

"Bloody hell!"

"It's not all bad news, though. Now we know the score, the school can hire a real security firm, which means you won't need to go back there."

"So, we're off the case?" Hunter asked.

"I'm afraid so. Whatever we do next, we're going to need armed agents. All the armed-to-the-teeth gangs killing people will be selling a crime lord's drugs. If a gang was asked to take us out, it would have to try to do it, and some of those gangs are pretty damn good with their weapons."

Chapter Five

Pettigrew checked the time on his watch before placing it on the bedside cabinet and sliding into bed. It told him it was nearly one-thirty. He suspected none of the lads ringing him was probably good news. It meant they'd all managed to get boxed off and no doubt he'd receive an update from them in the morning. Feeling pleased about that, he reached out and turned off the bedside lamp, snuggling down and soon falling asleep to dream about a holiday in the Bahamas. It was what the boss had promised him if he could come up with another five girls as good as the last one.

Like all the houses in Buckingham Road, number eleven lie back from the road. That particular one lie way back behind a privet hedge, where after a long front garden with a driveway down the right-hand side, there was enough space in front of the house to park several cars. The driveway continued on past the side of the house to disappear behind it, and outside what looked as if it was the backdoor but on the side, parked up was the Porsche. They guessed if they were there, the two old bangers were hidden behind the house.

They, in this case, were the four in a people carrier quietly backing down the driveway at two-thirty that morning. It was being driven by Teresa Baron, who not because of weight but for her love of speed was often called Ton-up Tess. Sitting in the shotgun seat, her husband, Dennis, was otherwise known as Daredevil Den, his nickname coming from the ariel act he performed at the circus where they'd met. Behind these two sat Trevor Watts, more commonly called Curly. He'd earned his nickname for what had become like his trademark. No matter whether it be by his fists, boots or bullets, if it was a guy and a case of child sexual abuse, it was a pretty safe bet at least one of them would land up in the bloke's short and curlies. Sitting next to him, Richard Tennyson was known by the others as Dead-eye Dick, and not for no good reason. He was two years older than Den, and they'd been best mates at that circus. A crack shot, better than shooting a cigarette out of a girl's mouth from across the circus ring, he could shuck your peanuts for you with a rifle at a thousand yards. With all of them around the mid-forties, they lived on the outskirts of Puffney Bigshot, in adjacent streets, and they made up one of CoT's armed teams, trotted out when more than the usual amount of resistance might be met.

The first thing Pettigrew knew about having intruders was when Curly pulled off the duvet and belted his testicles with several hard left and right punches. He immediately shot bolt upright in excruciating pain, with a desperate need to cry out for relief, but the involuntary movement only went to help a ball of rag being shoved into his open mouth going in more easily, before his mouth was sealed shut with gaffer tape. As soon as his hands and feet were securely bound by cable ties, the others began to search the house, while with a menacing grin on her face and a gun in her hand, Ton-up Tess stayed behind to watch he didn't try to do anything stupid. However, Pettigrew hadn't a hope in hell of doing anything, stupid or otherwise. Unable to bellow out his pain, or even cup a hand down there in an attempt to relieve some of the agony, a cold sweat crept up on him and he fell into unconsciousness.

***

Waking first, Rashid leapt to his feet, his head complaining about the sudden move. Not wanting to believe it, he looked down at his mates in horror. The same as he was, they were all completely naked, but even worse, not something guys normally like seeing of each other, each of them was adding their own piece of glory to the already glorious morning. He kicked Ali, yelping when it hurt his toe.

Ali sat up, squinting all around. "What is it going on? I do not know where I am. Where the fuck are we?"

68

Though you'd be unable to detect Rashid's origins without seeing him, the same could not be said about his two closest friends, Ali and Naveed. There were times when they were so stereotypical, anyone would have to be forgiven for thinking they were listening to a seventies comedy show.

"You're not a bloody African," Rashid replied.

"I am not African?" questioned Ali, shaking his head.

"Yeah, there's this tribe of short-arses in Africa called the Fkaahwees. Some famous explorer git is said to have named them that because they spend all day jumping up and down in the long grass, shouting, 'Where the fuck are we? Where the fuck are we?' I think it's supposed to be a joke."

"Oh, it is the strange English humour. Why is it we are not clothed? Where has all our clothes gone?"

"I'm not a bloody encyclopaedia. How would I know?"

Naveed sat up, rubbing his eyes, and then opening them, he did a double-take, gasping, "Oh, my goodness me! Please do not be telling me Graham and Clive have been doing what it is it looks like they have been doing."

"What, those two? I would hardly think so. Leaving them like that was probably another English joke."

"That is not a joke."

"I know, but I wish I had my phone with me. You'd better give them a dig before they get to like it."

"Or it is one of them does choke himself."

Naveed leant over and shook them, and on waking up, they leapt up, spitting, spluttering, and wiping their mouths.

"What the fuck's going on here?" demanded Clive. "Where the fuck are we?"

"I'm not going through all that again," Rashid sighed. "We don't have a bloody clue where we are. You can see for miles in every direction, but there's not a house or even a road to be seen anywhere."

Graham looked all around. "I'd say we're somewhere in the middle of Salisbury Plain."

"Salisbury Plain? Are you sure?" Clive asked.

"No, but the way some of the ground's messed up, it looks to me as if a tank could have done it, and they do a lot of tank training there."

"But that's gotta be eighty miles away. How the hell are we going to get back if we're naked? No clothes, no phone, no money, and no way to get home. Fuck!"

"Did anyone work out who that fucking lot were?" Rashid asked. "They can't be the feds, not to leave us like this."

"But they must be something like them if they had a bloody great chopper," said Graham. "Those security guards weren't supplied by a normal security firm, no normal one would've had a chopper hanging about, and what security guards have you ever known able to fight like that?"

"Please do not be talking about choppers," sighed Ali. "I do not want to be hearing it."

"I do not want to be talking about last night at all," Naveed said. "Once I be taken to a cell, they stripped me naked and they held me down, and then I be feeling a big prick. I am not remembering much after that."

"You are a big prick, Naveed. I think they must've injected us with something to make us answer questions. Oh, and give us the shits. Didn't you wake up in a nappy and have to use the hose?" asked Rashid.

"That is what I do not want to be talking about."

"I remember somebody came in after that, and very kindly they gave me a mug of cocoa. I do not like cocoa, but my mouth be feeling like a budgie's bottom and I drank it, and then I am not remembering anything," Ali said.

"It's the bottom of a budgie's cage, you idiot! I suspect we all drank the cocoa, I know I did. It's how they managed to get us here without us knowing, it was drugged."

"So, how are we going to get home?" Graham asked.

"We'll have to walk, at least a part of the way, and if you're right about this being Salisbury Plain, as it looks like early morning, we'll need to walk into the sun," Rashid said. "At some point, we're sure to come across a house or a cottage or something, and then we'll just have to steal some clothes and money. Come on, we'd better be making a move. The sooner we start walking, the sooner we'll be home."

"Okay, we will be walking, but I will not be happy unless it is you who is leading the way," said Ali, hesitating. "I do not want you behind me when I am walking in the altogether. It is the stories I have to think about."

"What stories?"

"The things I hear people saying about you and Sonia's gay brother. They be telling me you give him one."

"Don't be stupid! That happened a long time ago. We were underage, still at school, and one day he threatened to tell his parents about me and Sonia doing it if I didn't fuck him. So, I fucked him. I knocked his bloody lights out. We didn't have sex, you idiot!"

"Okay, I am believing you, Rashid, but I am still thinking we will all be happier if you are walking in front of us."

"Yeah, Rashid, if you go first, it'll mean we won't have to worry about being attacked by any wild animals. The chat-up line you got from Tipping Point, 'It's a little bit bigger but a whole lot better,' don't cover it, mate. That ought to be flying a flag to warn low-flying aircraft," Clive quipped.

"You watch Tipping Point?" questioned Graham.

Rashid snarled, "Shut your fucking mouths, the lot of you, you're only jealous! Come on, follow me!"

***

Greg hadn't returned home last night. Realising he'd only have to come back, and not wanting to be the gooseberry for anything Hunter and Kelvin might want to get up to in their young relationship, he'd declined their offer of a room and booked into a hotel. Knowing that, and expecting they would receive a call, Hunter and Kelvin were showered and dressed early that morning. Greg didn't disappoint them, he called at nine o'clock, and they entered the cell to see him questioning

Pettigrew at nine-thirty. The armed team who'd brought him in were there too, making it a little crowded.

"Jesus!" Kelvin gasped, looking down at Pettigrew. "I bet that bloody hurts."

Although the bloke was wearing an adult nappy to cater for any accidents, he wasn't entirely in it. Packed in ice cubes, so swollen did his scrotum look, it had all the appearance of an overfilled shopping bag about to explode.

"Yeah, I'll bet it does. Curly certainly didn't hold back on having a ball with him," laughed Hunter.

"Those who prey on youngsters deserve all they get," Curly said. "If I'd had my way, I'd have cut 'em off."

"I bet you grew up in care too," Kelvin said.

"How did you guess?" laughed Hunter. "You might like to know, it's courtesy of Curly that Benny Fulford, one of your foster dads when you were four, doesn't have his two best mates anymore. He fed Ding and Dong to the Fulford's dog."

"Bloody hell!"

"Loved 'em, he did," Curly said, grinning madly. "Scoffed 'em back and asked for more."

"Change the subject, please," moaned Greg. "I've not long had breakfast. Here, you'd better try your luck again, Kelvin, I think I might be losing it. I still haven't managed to find out where they're keeping Angelina."

Sauntering over and shaking Pettigrew to gain his attention, Kelvin asked, "Where's Angel?"

"Bobbysocks' top floor, I expect," Pettigrew replied, with a spaced-out look. "It's where the best ones usually go."

Greg shook his head. Of course, she was Angel now.

"Is Bobbysocks a hotel?"

"Everyone knows it's a hotel on Leckington Rye Road. It's world famous. People from all over the world goes there."

"It's got a reputation, then?"

"As the best. It's the poshest, cleanest and best run sporting house in London. It'll cost you an arm and a leg, but when it comes to underage, anything you want can be got there."

"How much will Angel be costing anyone?"

"I don't know. About a monkey, I expect."

"Five hundred pounds a night?" gasped Kelvin.

"No, an hour. That's only peanuts for the people who go to the Bobbysocks. Some of the sheiks earns money faster than you can count it, and there's billionaire Russians now."

"Bloody hell! Er, who owns the hotel?"

"An island company in the South Seas, Paradol Hotels."

"Really? So, who owns Paradol Hotels?"

"The General."

"Do you know the General's real name?"

"Giorgio Paramana."

"And he lives on that island, does he?"

"The General's got houses all round the world, but a lot of the time he's at his big house on Leckington Rye."

"What happened to Angel's baby?"

"I don't know, it's probably in the nursery. It's where they usually keeps babies. Keeping them there stops the mothers running. If they run or go to the police, the baby gets put in a bin bag and taken to the tip."

"Bloody hell! Um, where is this nursery?"

"In a room of an extension to the General's house."

"Where is his house? I mean, what's the postal address?"

"Leckington Rye House, Leckington Rye Road. No idea of the post code, but it's the only one on the common."

Turning to Greg, grinning, Kelvin asked, "Is there anything else you need to know?"

"I don't think so. I'd call for a round of applause, if I didn't think it might go to your head."

"Oh, I've thought of something," Kelvin said, turning back to Pettigrew to shake him again and ask, "How many look after Giorgio and the hotel? How big is the heavy mob?"

"Giorgio's got a dozen armed security men on shifts around the clock to look after him and the house, and the Leckington Louts get drugs at a special price as part of a deal where they look after the hotel and sell some of them there."

"Are the Leckington Louts a street gang, then?"

"Yes, they're the law around Leckington Rye."

"How many of them are there?"

"I don't know, about a hundred, I suppose. They're a really ruthless lot. No other gangs mess with them or go onto their patch, they'd have their heads blown off."

"They've got guns, then?"

"Guns, knives, machetes, acid, they've got everything, and some of it's a lot better than what the police have. There has not been a copper seen on their patch in donkey's years, not since one of the gang squirted acid through the window of a police car."

"That's what I feared," sighed Greg. "With no safe option, it'll have to be blood and bodies on the streets."

"You're still going after them?" Kelvin asked, wide-eyed.

"Yes, of course. We've never given up on a job before, and it's not going to happen on my watch."

"Will you be doing any blowjobs?" asked Curly.

"With those odds, I may have to blow a few, if not all. No rush, though. I'll give it some thought first."

Kelvin turned and frowned at Hunter, questioning it. "Greg may be doing blowjobs? Really?"

Hunter laughed. "It's just an expression we use. It comes from a time when there were many more police per head of population. So many that if a copper got into trouble, he only had to blow a whistle and other coppers would hear it and run to help him. These days, Greg wouldn't even need to get on the blower, he'd just send one email to all UK units."

"You mean the whole of CoT would turn up?"

"Only the active officers and agents from around the UK, but yes, if he called for them to assist, just about all of it. It's not happened yet, but should we need help from units abroad too, the expression then is 'mooning off the castle tower.' It would be like letting those across the moat know we'd landed up with an arsehole of a job and hadn't got it covered."

"Weird, or what?"

"There's a lot of expressions like that we use, but don't go worrying about it, you won't have to learn them, you'll just pick them up. They're forever changing, anyway."

"Like what? Give me an example."

"Well, back in the days when people fried bacon, and it was risky because it spat hot fat everywhere, if we were watching someone in a crowded pub and I wasn't sure if you'd seen a load of guys come in who were his mates, meaning we were outnumbered, I'd have told you I thought I could smell bacon frying, so anyone who overheard wouldn't understand. Now we normally grill bacon and it no longer spits hot fat over you, I might say I hoped I wasn't becoming a woman, I was sure I was having a hot flush. Frying bacon or a hot flush, the suggestion is we might need to get out of there in a hurry."

"Crikey, it's not easy, is it?"

"It's easier than you think. You just listen for something unusual in the conversation, something you wouldn't expect to hear, and then it comes to you straightaway."

"I think we've got everything we need out of Pettigrew, so unless you can think of anything else, Teresa, you'd better do a wipe-out and dump," Greg said, walking out of the cell.

Kelvin turned to Hunter again, shocked. "A wipe-out and dump? Please tell me that's only one of those expressions. I know Pettigrew liked the sound of his voice, but it did mean he helped us a lot. He told us more than we asked."

"It is, don't panic, Teresa's not going to bump him off. She trained to be a nurse before joining CoT. She'll be injecting him with an experimental drug the boffins haven't managed to perfect yet. It has a long name no one can say, so everyone calls it wipe-out. He'll fall asleep and then they'll dump him back home in his bed, and when in a few hours he wakes up, he won't remember us."

"An experimental drug?"

"Yes, it's safe, but still a bit of a hit and miss thing. It wipes out your recent memories, but with the difference in dosage needed only minute and dependent a lot on the patient, when he wakes up, Pettigrew may not be able to remember the last twenty-four hours, or it could be anything up to a week."

Kelvin laughed, "Those swollen nuts won't half come as a surprise when he wakes up, then. He'll be wondering what the hell he was doing in the night."

Hunter thumped him. "Trust you to think of that! Come on, we'd better find Greg again. If I know him, he's gone to the cafe for a natter with Grace and Favour."

"Who are Grace and Favour?"

"A lesbian couple in their forties. In the mornings, Grace makes sure the cafe is clean and the pantry, fridge and freezer are well-stocked. The cafe is a do-it-yourself job, like the bar, and Grace's partner is Liz, but as she always comes with her to help out, doing her and us a favour, we sometimes call her Favour. Grace and Favour seem to go together, don't they?"

"Weird."

Kelvin learned the cafe was down the passageway behind the double doors that they hadn't gone through off the club's bar last night. It was off the left of the corridor, through more double doors, while three doors on the right and a facing one at the end sported nameplates to suggest offices. Like the bar area, the cafe had alcoves with seating around a table, and the counter had gaps to allow access to the kitchen, but unlike in the bar area, although everything looked new, with a red and black theme that extended to the floor tiles, it was a tribute to a long bygone age of chrome and Formica.

"Don't worry, we haven't gone through a time warp," joked Hunter. "Apparently, it's like this because there's never been anything so easy to keep clean as the milk bars of the sixties, and as it's a do-it-yourself job in here, and we're expected to clean up after ourselves, having nothing that needs more than a quick spray and a wipe comes in handy."

"Curiouser and curiouser cried Alice," Kelvin giggled. "For a moment there, I was half-expecting to see an old-fashioned jukebox. I guess it's Grace and Favour that Greg's drinking a cup of something with over there, but what's going on in the three alcoves behind them? It looks like a load of kids doing their school work."

"It is. Grace and Liz were disillusioned teachers before they gave it up and came here. Now they private tutor some of the members' kids, so say doing the job properly, and as nobody has ever complained about the results, I guess they are doing it right. They adopted the mixed-race one in the corner when he was a toddler, renaming him Justin, which is a misnomer if ever there was one."

"It is? How do you know?"

"Grace and Liz live only a couple of streets away, but in a house too small for a birthday party, so since I arrived here, he's had his at ours. He's a great kid, do anything for anyone, but I think they've brought him up to be far too innocent. He was thirteen last July, and he hasn't realised, he of all people shouldn't be wearing budgie smugglers around a pool."

"Bloody hell, Hunter!"

"I know, but how do you tell a thirteen-year-old something like that? I couldn't do it, I was too embarrassed."

Kelvin giggled, "You don't, you buy him some swimming shorts for his next birthday. As they're a present, he's going to have to wear them, isn't he?"

"You, are just a genius. Why didn't I think of that?"

"I don't know. I hope it wasn't because you were too busy ogling. What is he, part Caribbean?"

"Don't be silly, never mind he's far too young, I don't do ogling. And as for his origins, nobody knows, but if I had to pick something, I'd have to say part elephant."

"It can't be that bad, surely?"

"You'll see for yourself next year. Shorts might turn it into a mystery, but they could never hide what I saw."

"Jesus, if it is that bad, one day it could be a hell of a cross for him to carry."

"Let's just hope he turns out to be gay, then, eh? It might be his only hope of finding someone to help him with his load."

"Is that really true, then?"

"It is according to everything I've read, and supposedly by a lot more than a hop, skip and a jump. I'm not kidding, some of the claims made are mindboggling."

"You researched it?"

"Yeah, well, there's something you've not worked out yet."

"What?"

"Humour acts like a suit of armour for CoT. Its members are forever winding one another up. Until I got the link to see you on video, they had me believing you were an elephant, and a bit worried about that, I researched it."

"You're not disappointed, are you?"

"Do behave, you'll never know what a relief it was to see you on video and find out it wasn't true."

"Hmm . . ."

"Hmm? What do you mean, hmm?"

"If they like winding people up, they might have had Justin wind you up. Unless it was obvious at his previous parties, it could easily have been a case of strapadicktome."

"Strapadicktome?"

"Yeah, if there is such a thing as an innocent thirteen-year-old boy today, which I doubt, I bet it's not one with same-sex parents. There are private shops and online sources selling all kinds of phallic things, including huge strap-ons. If Justin's parents are lesbians, they might have already had something like that. If you were being wound up about me at the time of that birthday party, it could easily have been part of the same wind-up. So, how do the dates match up?"

"Oh, no, they match up to prove I'm a prize idiot, and also explain why I didn't see a lot of Grace and Liz that day. They were all in on it. It was me who the kids were giggling about, not Justin. I've been had big style, haven't I?"

"It does look like it. We'll need to make certain first, but if you have, you ought to get your own back."

"And how would I do that?"

"I'm sure we'd be able to think of something. And maybe do it for Justin's birthday party next year, eh?"

"How did I ever survive without you?"
"You'll never know, not now I'm with you forever."
"That's got to be the best thing I've heard today."

***

There were whisperings around Leckington Rye House that morning. Gorgeous George, what the staff called the General behind his back, was having a lie-in. At some point he'd ring for his breakfast to be served to him in bed, and waiting for him on the tray was a note from Mario, who as well as acting like his personal assistant was in charge of security. That the breakfast would hit the wall, once he'd read the note, was in little doubt. Something Mario had preferred not to tell him personally, the note said, '*All websites went offline overnight. Call Gal went down and they've no idea why. Said they'll get back to us when they've found the fault. - Mario – 8.25am.*'

Gorgeous George rang for his breakfast at eleven o'clock, and Lottie, who was convinced she always won the lottery to cover the bad jobs because of her name, carried it up to his room fifteen minutes later. True to form, he read the note, the breakfast hit the wall, he leapt out of bed half naked, she fled screaming, and he bellowed from the door.

"Mario! Get your fucking arse up here!"

"Yes, boss?" asked Mario, entering the room seconds later.

"Are the sites back online yet?"

"No, boss, I tried a little while ago, I rang Call Gal again. It seems they can't find the fault, and it's worse than that now, all the hosts they've been using have ditched them."

"Ditched them? What do you mean, ditched them?"

"The hosts think now it must be a virus nobody's heard of because their drives have been wiped clean. They've lost all their backups, and not just ours, everything. Call Gal reckons they aren't happy."

"*They're* not happy? *They're* not happy? How the fuck do they think I feel? How did they lose their backups?"

"I don't know, boss. I suppose they tried copying them over after they lost the others and something got to them."

"So, let me get this right. Are you telling me we're paying Call Gal a fucking king's ransom every month for five hosts around the world and none of them has or now wants to have our websites?"

"It looks like it, boss. Pettigrew will have the latest versions on his computer, of course, and I've been ringing him almost non-stop to see if he can find someone else like Call Gal, but he isn't answering his phone. I've left lots of messages."

"Fuck!"

Mario's phone rang in his pocket. He took it out, looked at the screen, and frowned. "What the . . ?"

"Is that him? Is that Pettigrew?"

"No, boss. It says it's Samael, spelt like Samuel but with an a instead of the u. How can it be, though? I haven't a Samael in my contacts. I don't even have a Sam or a Samuel."

"Sam-a-el?"

"Yes, boss. Look." Mario turned the screen towards him.

"You've not upset a stranger lately, have you?"

"Not that I can remember, boss. Why?"

"If you can't remember, you'd better hope some smart-arse who knows how to hack a phone is having a joke, then."

"A joke, boss?"

"The only Samael I've heard of is a fallen angel, and I'm not too sure he's real. Hadn't you better answer it?"

Mario accepted the call, and his boss moved closer and put an ear up to the phone too.

"Is that someone called Mario who works for the General at Leckington Rye House?" a deep voice enquired.

"Er, yes, but who are you? How did you get this number?"

"I'm the General's worst nightmare. I'd like you to pass on a message for me. You can tell the General, not only have his websites gone, his number will soon be up too. I'm coming to get him, and all the evil ones who work for him."

"Get him? Who the fucking hell are you?"

"Let my name tintinnabulate in your ear, Mario, for I am Samael. Many know me as the grim reaper, while others call me the angel of death. Be afraid, Mario, be very afraid. It is time for you to put your affairs in order. All of you."

The call ended, and the two men did no more than stare at each other for a few moments, ashen faced, with neither of them wanting to admit to the other, the call had spooked him more than a little.

"It's got to be an attack, Mario. Someone's trying to shit us up. Rally the boys, it's war!"

"Righto, boss. Er, the Louts too?"

"Yes, we'll need every fucker we can get. This time, we're going to obliterate that bloody band of shirtlifters!"

"But how do we know who Samael is, or who he's working for, boss? He could be anyone."

"Not to use a word like tintinnabulate, he isn't. He's got to be one of Claude's funny boys. The others wouldn't have a clue what tintinnabulate meant, nor would anyone in a street gang. Most of those morons can't even speak proper English, never mind understand each other. Knows like what I means, man? S'all about blud and fam and having a bag and being real badders in bed, innit? And respect, man. Mustn't forget the respect. Mandem gotta have respect or he gets shanked, yana? Bloody load of idiots, if you ask me."

"So, we're going north of the river tonight? We're going to take on Claude's gangs and hit a load of his places? But what about the agreement?"

"Bollocks to the agreement! We hit him before he sends his lot south of the river and hits us."

"Righto, boss. Er, what *does* tintinnabulate mean?"

***

Hunter handed back the phone. "It's a fraction bigger and a little heavier than most of the phones you'll see around, but that's a really neat bit of equipment, Greg."

81

"Yes, once they've perfected another add-on, everyone will be getting one next year."

"What's the add-on?"

"Voice distortion, for when it's needed. With everything on the market today to disguise a voice, if you're clever enough, the disguise can be removed. Once our boffins have finished testing our version, that won't be the case for us."

"CoT must have the cleverest boffins in the world," said Kelvin. "I mean, never mind the debit card maker, you've got things like the truth drug and wipe-out that nobody else has heard of. How come?"

"We do have amongst the best in the world, and they work for CoT because they're people of conscience. It's the same with our computer geniuses, officers and field agents, they're all amongst the best in the world."

"People of conscience?"

"Yes, they have immutable values, and what they do for us is worth more to them than all the beans and glory they could get elsewhere. We also give them more freedom to pursue their own ideas here than anywhere else would. Because in the real world companies have to balance their books and pay out dividends to shareholders, they restrict their people to working only on what's likely to make them a lot of money."

"Makes sense, I suppose."

"What doesn't, though, is how you would know a word like tintinnabulate. Where did you pick that up? And how did you come up with an idea that might set gang on gang and leave us with fewer to tackle?"

Kelvin laughed. "I didn't know tintinnabulate, I once came across it in a book I was reading and had to look it up. And as for having the idea, I guess when you're brought up in care, being able to work things out and manipulate people comes as natural, like a part of the package."

"And what about you, Hunter? How did you learn to alter your voice like that? Was that a part of the package too? You were entirely different, sounding like a much older person."

"Yes, it's just another bit of the package. I used to take a lot of time off school. In your schooldays, I expect you'd have had to forge a letter, but for years now a parent or guardian has had to phone the school."

"You really are a remarkable couple. What are you doing for the rest of the day?"

"After lunch, Kelvin wants to visit the shooting range."

"He'll have to go some to beat you."

"You didn't tell me you could shoot," Kelvin said, turning quickly to frown at Hunter.

"Him shoot? Hunter's won our combat trophy for the past three years running, that's every year he's been with us."

"Bloody hell!"

"Oh, thanks, Greg. Now I'll never be able to talk him out of wanting a gun, will I?"

"Sorry."

***

Rashid's idea of them walking into the sun, until they came across somewhere to rob, was not without its problems. The ground making up much of Salisbury Plain doesn't lend itself kindly to being walked on in bare feet. Unevenly tufted, the grassy terrain hides many perils. Never mind it is heaven for snakes and lizards, there are things like thistles, nettles, and earth-hugging brambles hidden in the grass, and there are also many sharp stones. They were forever stopping for one of them to attend to the latest assault on a swollen and bloody foot. Any glory that they might have been adding earlier to the glorious morning had long been lost.

Although they weren't in the slightest amused, looking like swimmers coming out of the sea to prance idiotically up a stony beach, bending over with their heads forward, arms out and knees splaying wide as they performed a peculiar dance, if anyone had been there to see them, they would have made a comical sight. It was with quite some relief they eventually came across a tarmac road. Crossing their direction of travel from left to right, it was little more than a country lane, but a whole lot less challenging. They decided to follow it to the left, what they worked out to be the more northerly direction and up country, rather than risk heading for the coast.

It turned out to be a quiet lane, with seemingly next to no traffic. So when, after ten minutes of much easier progress, they heard a vehicle approaching from behind, they got into walking in single file, with thumbs outstretched to beg for a lift. It was not a sensible move for them to make, they'd have done far better had they hidden in the ditch.

The car that passed them, not stopping, was full to capacity; a family on an outing, with the mother leaning over from her front seat to scream at her two young daughters and son in the back. While they knelt up on their seat to gawp out of the rear window at the naked blokes, she unsuccessfully fought to cover their three pairs of eyes with two hands. Although it was, it really shouldn't have come as a surprise when, after another ten minutes, the next vehicle they heard approaching turned out to be a police car, followed by a pick-up van.

"Oh, not the fucking feds!" Rashid groaned, loudly. "Now we really are in the shit!"

"We are really in the shit?" Ali questioned.

"Yes, you fucking idiot! You can bet being naked will be a Section Five of the Public fucking Order Act, and as we've no way of proving who the fuck we are, they'll be taking our fingerprints. It ain't like we've not got form, is it?"

"Once they see we've got previous for drugs, they'll think we got to be naked because of drugs, and that'll give them the right to search our homes and computers," Clive said.

"And then we'll all be going down," sighed Graham.

"My fucking arse still hasn't got over the last time," Rashid groaned. "You should've seen the black bloke I had to share a cell with, that fucker would've made horses scream."

The police car and pick-up van stopped, and not long after that, there was much wailing and gnashing of teeth.

Chapter Six

Ask those who purport to know how many gangs there are in London and some will come up with a figure closing on two hundred, while others will tell you it's just four, and in a way, both answers are correct. Without the four, it's unlikely we'd be calling the others gangs. They'd be little more than a throwback to the nineteen-fifties; groups of extremely bored youths who congregate on street corners and occasionally get up to mischief.

There are close on two hundred known *street* gangs in and around London today; the hooded youths and kids that arm themselves to the teeth and go around doing things such as selling drugs, mugging old ladies, stealing cars, and killing each other over territory and matters of respect. According to an official database of street gang members in the capital, 78.2% are black, 12.8% white, 6.5% Asian, 2.2% Middle Eastern/Arabs, and under 1% are East Asian or of unknown ethnicity. And as many of these members are easily offended, or dissed in their terminology, anyone falling foul of them, no matter how unwittingly, risks being killed for it. However, what you won't find an official mention of anywhere are the four gangs of notably fewer though more mature people that protect London's four crime lords.

Most people are inclined to believe that areas of our capital city being ruled over by criminals ended with the Kray twins and the Richardson gang, but nothing could be further from the truth. There has always been an undesirable element like that, it's likely there always will be, with the only difference being their extent of evilness. Without the money, extensive contacts and know-how of the crime lords today, there'd be very few drugs available on the streets, illegal firearms would become almost impossible to get hold of, and the sex-slave trade would be so small that it could easily be crushed. For all those things to be available as readily as they are today, it takes huge investments of money that'll occasionally be lost, and a hell of a lot of organisation; far in excess of anything a street gang could manage. If you could follow all the major illegal activities you encounter back, and this applies to just about everywhere, the chances are you'd find a crime lord involved in it somewhere, and often unknown about by those performing the actual activity you meet. Street gangs neither know nor care where the drugs they buy come from, or how their contacts get to have them. So long as they can get hold of them and they're good enough to make money, they aren't worried about piffling matters like that. It's the same when it comes to illegal firearms and easy young girls, for as long as they're out there, readily available, why would anyone bother to stop and question how? How is only important if you plan on tackling one of those crime lords.

So explained Greg at a much greater length, while watching the time as they enjoyed lunch on him at the Queen's Legs. If he could keep them there until two o'clock, he knew Kelvin would be unlikely to get on the shooting range for hours and probably give up, hopefully making Hunter happier. He was annoyed for not realising, it hadn't mattered when he was on his own, but now he'd found a partner, the last thing Hunter would want to see was Kelvin being good enough with a gun to be called to action and going down in a gunfight. It seeded an awful suspicion in Greg. Not only might he not be gaining another armed agent, with the two of them being closer than a wall to wallpaper, he could be about to lose one.

"What I don't understand is, though I've read about gangs in the past, like the thieving kids in Oliver Twist, I've never read about any who went around like they do today, killing each other and forcing young kids to have guns and knives and deliver drugs," said Kelvin. "Why is it different now?"

Greg sniffed. "It's because of politicians, of course."

"Politicians? What, do you mean because they closed down so many youth clubs and sportsfields?"

"That hasn't helped, but no, it's because some politicians in the sixties were either stupid beyond belief, or so greedy that they didn't care who lined their pockets."

"They took bribes? To do what?"

"I cannot believe even a politician could be so stupid, so I can only suspect some undesirables saw an opportunity with the coming of hippies and the thousands of youngsters who wanted to be like them. They found enough politicians with a bit of clout who were only too pleased to have their palms greased. With all the hell America suffered with prohibition still alive in people's memories, for what other reason would anyone risk something like it happening again?"

"You mean Al Capone?"

"He's the one you remember because the cinema made him famous, but there were plenty of others with gangs too. And after all what it led to, you wouldn't have needed a degree to know what'd happen if you banned God's bountiful gifts."

"God's bountiful gifts?"

"Since the dawn of man, people of all ages and from every background had enjoyed nature's recreational gifts, and they had never been a problem. But using the excuse of it being a way to deal with hippies, many governments started to make those gifts illegal. Not unexpectedly, underground markets began springing up, giving rise to crime lords, gun-toting and knife-wielding street gangs, and the whole host of chemical concoctions that pass for recreational drugs on the streets today. Before those new laws, nobody turned into a zombie and frightened kids by smoking a reefer or ingesting a few magic mushrooms, but today our towns and cities are overrun by mindless people staggering around until they fall down and become corpselike, or turn aggressive and want to fight the world. Those politicians of the sixties knew what would happen, prohibition had shown them that, so can you think of any reason other than financial gain why they would have inflicted on their nations what so many of us have to put up with today?"

"No, and I don't think I like politicians now either."

"It's long been known that nothing corrupts like power, so it's only sensible not to trust them. Incidentally, it might be hard to believe, but the only *genuine* hippies most people saw were on television. The free love, and running about naked to contemplate your navel, was just a small part of the swinging sixties and hard to find outside a few areas of London."

"You looked for it, then?" Kelvin giggled.

"I knew about it because it was on television, but I was too young then to go looking. Many people did, though, and as I said, hardly finding real hippies existed outside London."

"All the psychedelic stuff, the dancing naked in the parks, passing the spliffs and shagging whoever you fancied, didn't last for long, anyway, did it?" said Hunter.

"Nobody expected it would. The weather wouldn't let you roll about naked on the grass for long in most of the countries that had hippies, and if you're sharing everything, you soon start to run out of it and the novelty begins to wear off. What thousands wanted to be, they'd have hated had they managed to achieve it. The genuine hippies couldn't find employment, most of them lived in communes in dilapidated squats, and they were often so filthy that they stunk to high heaven. The female ones soon got fed up with it."

"They complained?" Kelvin questioned.

"The hippy lifestyle worked well for the guys, but it wasn't so good for the girls. As well as being expected to do all the chores, they'd be passed around for a bite to eat or the chance of a spliff. It wasn't long before they rebelled, joining various movements and marching for women's rights."

"If the girls were being passed around for a meal, it wasn't exactly free love, was it?" laughed Hunter.

"No, they soon tumbled being a hippy was all about guys getting as much sex as they could with as many girls as they could manage. The thousands of working young people, who only *played* being hippies at weekends and at pop concerts, had a much better life. They had jobs, money and style."

Kelvin laughed.

"What?" Hunter asked.

"Wally, a guy at Nellie's, must be older than Greg. He once told me he'd been to couple of hippy love-ins. He said if they couldn't get it with a girl, like there wasn't enough girls to go round, a lot of the guys didn't stay straight. He reckoned he'd never known the like of it since."

"Yes, that sounds like Wally," Greg laughed. "Did he also tell you the difference between a straight guy and a gay one can often be measured in pints? Wally's always liked straight men. In his day, he turned getting them into an art."

"Yeah, he did, almost crying into his beer. It must be really horrible getting old and past it."

"I'm sure I wouldn't know," said Greg, aloofly.

Kelvin laughed, but it was a bell ringing that Hunter heard in his head. "Come along, we'd better hurry, fruit drop," he said, quickly standing up. "If we don't, you won't get a place on the shooting range for hours."

"Really? From what you said earlier about talking me out of wanting a gun, I thought you didn't want me to learn about firearms and how to shoot."

"I didn't, and then I remembered why I learned."

"Why was that?"

"Sykes, an old schoolteacher, was always going on about, 'Come the revolution.' He could put up a very convincing argument for it not being a case of if but when, and he said we should do everything we wanted to do in life, it was better than lying on our deathbed regretting we hadn't done it. I've learned about guns and I choose to have one, so how do you think I'd feel if the revolution came, and you didn't have the gun you'd wanted because I'd not wanted you to have it?"

"You daft ape, I'd make bloody sure I didn't get shot. I'm nothing like James Dean."

"What's James Dean got to do with anything?"

"He took chances, and he died chancing his luck, speeding in his sports car. He's well-known for a quote he stole and adapted about living fast, dying young, and leaving a good-looking corpse. In the original, it was a *beautiful* corpse.”

“You must’ve done a lot of reading in those libraries.”

“I did. Knowing things opens doors. You wouldn’t believe the half of what I’ve read. If you’re able to recite a few lines of Shakespeare, people start to take you seriously, they don’t think of you as a scrote.”

“You’ve read Shakespeare?”

“Yeah, why wouldn’t I? I’ve had a Puck about with Bottom in A Midsummer Night’s Dream, and I’ve read Romeo and Juliet. O Romeo, Romeo, wherefore art thou Romeo? Deny thy father and refuse thy name. Or if thou wilt not . . .”

“Alright, alright, I believe you!”

“Well, now that’s settled,” Greg chuckled, standing up and feeling much happier now. “We’d better go and see just how good you are with a gun, Kelvin.”

“You don’t expect me to be good straightaway, do you?”

“He will be hoping you are,” Hunter said, grinning as they followed Greg, heading for the door. “You see, being good with a gun is similar to being good at darts. If you cannot hit the board after a couple of goes, with all the practising in the world, you’re never going to win a trophy playing darts.”

“Practicing doesn’t make you get better?”

“You might become better, but it’ll never be enough to get you in the first team. When it comes to guns, you are either a crack shot or you’re not.”

“Crikey!”

“In the Life and Times of Johnny Mo – Private Eye, didn’t you question why Johnny, Karl and Tel should be given guns and licences within only hours of first handling a gun? Didn’t that seem strange to you?”

“No, I merely thought it was a case of the author employing a bit of literary licence. Are you saying all three of them were good shots straightaway?”

“It seems everyone who’s good at the Terror of the Dragon is also good with a gun. It’s probably to do with learning how to focus your mind and training to have fast reactions. Don't worry, you're by far the best at it I've ever met. Nobody else has managed to wipe the floor with me."

"Bloody hell! No pressure, then?"

"The pressure comes later, in Combat Alley," said Greg.

"Combat Alley? What's that?"

"A mock up street where all sorts of people appear at doors and windows. It has to be changed around every few months, a completely different set up so no one becomes familiar with it. Every agent we issue with a firearm is required to pass an annual test there with an electronic gun. They're expected to gun down all the bad guys, not to be gunned down themself, and to do it without any of the good people being hit."

"Oh, wicked!"

"Well, I reckon there goes my trophy for next year," Hunter laughed. "You sure you aren't like James Dean, fruit drop?"

"I'm sure. Sal Mineo would have done nothing for me, not even after twenty pints, which I couldn't drink, anyway."

"You really have done a lot of reading, haven't you?" Greg said, plainly impressed. "There were rumours to suggest they were more than just good friends, but as far as I'm aware, no one found out if the rumours were true."

"Yeah, well, that'd have been because even back then there were people working on public perception. In the fifties, film studios as good as owned their film stars, and they couldn't have one of their heartthrobs being thought of as anything but a hundred percent straight at that time in history, could they? I read they gave any male stars who preferred men what they called arm-furniture; females to be seen with in public."

"That's likely true," said Hunter. "They reckon nobody had a clue about Rock Hudson until he came out in the eighties, not long before he died from AIDS, and apparently he was a massive film star in the fifties and sixties, always seen with a voluptuous female in tow."

"Er, yakking away, haven't we just walked out the pub and not paid the bill?" Kelvin asked, suddenly coming to a stop.

"No, we haven't," Greg replied. "Come on, keep walking. I don't go there often, but when I do, I don't have to pay."

Kelvin laughed, "Not another pub with a cheque?"

"No . . . Well, yes, I suppose there could've been a cheque at some point. CoT bought it a long time ago. It's run by one our members."

"Why would CoT want to buy a pub?"

"Hidden behind wood panelling in the cellar is a way down to one of our caves, and as we couldn't have anybody finding it, we had to buy the pub. In case it should be needed, it now acts as a handy emergency exit."

"Aren't the tunnels safe, then?"

"Yes, of course they're safe, but it's a myth we don't get hit by severe earthquakes. There's been several severe ones over the centuries, a couple of them felt from Scotland to the south coast. One in the eleventh century, felt as far away as France and Denmark, did so much damage, people thought the devil was involved."

"The devil?"

"Oh, don't knock it. In another severe one, in 1275, people in all three places swore oaths to say they had witnessed the devil laughing after an earthquake badly damaged the Abbey in Glastonbury, brought down the Church of St Michael up on the Tor, and destroyed the priory church on St Michael's Mount as far away as Cornwall. Incidentally, there have been several churches of St Michael built on Glastonbury Tor and they've all come to grief. But then, the Archangel Michael and the devil are said to have history, aren't they? Maybe it's only to be expected."

"Yeah, right!" laughed Kelvin.

Back inside the club, Greg told Hunter to show Kelvin the maze and explain how the more commonly used route to the tunnels worked while he, avoiding stairs when he could, used the lift in the cubicle and went on ahead to arrange things.

"There's a maze in here?" Kelvin questioned, being pushed by Hunter through a door behind the bar.

"A myriad of passages, empty rooms, and narrow staircases on either side. This was originally two properties, though not mirror images of each other, and only on this floor has there been any joining of the two, leaving the other floors as still separate. And because it's built on a hill, the room you could fall into from the entrance, and the storeroom for the cafe and the bar's cellar, aren't really in a basement, they're at ground level for the back of the properties, where for both there are double doors to a backyard and the service road behind for deliveries. Except, that's not exactly true."

"Huh? It isn't?"

"No, the doors on the right work, it's the way stock comes in, and there's a couple of dumb waiters so nothing has to be carried along passages and up stairs, but the doors on the left side are blocked off with a load of old crates overgrown with brambles on the outside, and although they look like they are, they aren't the doors you can see on the inside."

"They're not?"

"Because either side's different and not a mirror image, and there's no windows on that floor, after negotiating the maze, nobody could know they're not seeing the building's outside wall but another wall built several feet into the room from it, where behind the locked double doors there are stairs on the left to the tunnels, and on the right there's a conventional lift, complete with electric sliding doors, buttons and a full-length mirror, and it's large enough to take twenty people."

"Devious, or what?"

"Well, we don't want to be competing with Wookey Hole, do we? It'd be quite a headache having to relocate everything there is down there."

"Not half!"

Kelvin discovered the lift, and the staircase, where he tried not to imagine how many steps it might have, emerged in a cave up the tunnel used for storage. A short walk, and in the tunnel leading to the shooting gallery, Hunter took him into a room on the left. It was like a small warehouse with a counter where you could order stuff, and waiting for them there, Greg introduced Kelvin to the bloke behind the counter, William Smith, or Billy Guns as he was commonly known, explaining he was one of their top arms experts.

After shaking Kelvin's hand, Billy Guns didn't let go of it straightaway, instead he inspected it, turning it over to worry Kelvin for a moment as he seemingly fondled it.

"Hmm . . . I think a Glock 19 should do you fine," he said, finally letting go of Kelvin's hand.

"A Glock 19?"

"It's a reliable gun, versatile, compact, and easily concealed with fifteen rounds, and bonus, if you should find you've got a party, it'll happily take thirty-three round magazines. It also comes with an integrated picatinny rail as standard for fitting flashlights, lasers and many other accessories. You can forget about buying yourself a dog, it's a Glock 19 that'll be your best friend."

"Crikey!"

"I swear by mine, never at it," said Hunter, grinning.

"Okay, I'd better have one, then," Kelvin said.

Billy Guns spent a while breaking it down, reassembling it, and explaining how the gun worked and the correct way to use it, having Kelvin copy everything that he did until he felt familiar with it, and then he took him out of the room and further up the tunnel to the shooting range, commandeering an alley for him.

"Take your time and fire off six shots. See if you can hit the centre spot," Billy Guns said.

Greg and Hunter looked on attentively, and as soon as he felt happy with his aim, which was in no time at all, Kelvin squeezed the trigger six times in rapid succession.

"Well, you managed to hit the dead centre of the bull's eye with the first shot," Greg said, laughing as he walked over to Kelvin. "That takes some doing when you've never fired a gun before. If you had taken your time, like you were told to, I reckon you might have hit it again."

"Oh, sorry, I didn't realise Billy meant I had to re-aim the gun *between* shots."

With a shocked look, Billy Guns said, "You've nothing to be sorry about, lad. All six went through the same hole, dead centre of the bull's eye. I've been here for twenty years and I've not known anyone do that before."

"Are you sure?" asked Greg, blinking stupidly.

"The safety board's never taken a hit, and it's still not got a mark on it. So, where else *could* they have gone?"

"Jumping Jehoshaphat!"

"How did you *do* that?" asked Hunter.

"Um, I don't know. I was always a pretty good shot with a water pistol, though. If it wasn't a fluke, maybe that helped."

"Try it again, son. Another six shots, the same as you did it the last time," said Billy Guns.

Greg, Hunter and Billy Guns took a step back, Kelvin took aim at the hole he'd made the first time, squeezed the trigger six times in rapid succession again, and when no more holes showed up, it told them it wasn't a fluke.

"I reckon you might as well take that trophy to be engraved now, Greg," said Hunter, laughingly shaking his head. "And to think the other night I told him he'd no sense of direction."

The howl that produced, as they all fell about in hysterical mirth, said that was the end of Kelvin's shooting practice for the day, not that he needed any. Once they'd recovered from the merriment, Billy Guns took him to Combat Alley, where after completing the test perfectly, there was just the matter of some paperwork and Kelvin became only the second CoT member to be issued with a gun at the age of seventeen. The first, little more than three years ago, had been Hunter.

***

Pettigrew didn't wake up until a little after four o'clock that afternoon, and then fearing the worst, and not wanting to flop them out in front of his female doctor, he began searching the internet for a reason why his testicles should have swollen up and become painful overnight. He couldn't remember they'd been even more swollen earlier, but after a while it did dawn on him that the swelling was slowly going down and the pain considerably receding. Finding nothing on the internet that might account for their condition apart from an accident or overdoing rough sex, and he couldn't see how it could have been either of them, he decided he would leave it for now and see if they went back to normal on their own.

It was only then, when he abandoned his searching to check on his emails and social media presence, that he realised the time according to his computer. Frowning, he checked it was the correct time on his phone, and in doing that he saw how many calls he had missed from Mario. Guessing he could be in a hell of a lot of trouble after reading one of the messages the guy had left, he didn't phone back.

"Fuck the General!" he cried, out loud.

Pulling two suitcases down off the top of his wardrobe, he began filling them with some of his clothes. Pettigrew didn't much like the General or his setup, and he reckoned now was as good a time as any for him to do a runner. So what if he lost a flash car and a house? Once he was free of the General, with the money he would be able to make from producing pornographic videos of the quality he churned out, he'd soon see the like of them again. And this time none of the videos would have to be of eight-year-olds or toddlers being abused, just so the General could advertise that they were available for abusing and could be hired by the hour.

Pettigrew didn't have a problem with age, providing the kid had gone through puberty and wanted to become a porn star, it was forcing kids who hadn't got that far in life and weren't given any say about it, he couldn't stomach. A few weeks of suffering his mother, while he got back on his feet, would be well worth it. He could start again somewhere else, and not know any of that guilt.

Chapter Seven

The plans had been made by eight o'clock, when the first of the groups of Leckington Louts slunk off, bending forwards slightly with hoods up in readiness to turn their heads away from the street cameras they'd have to pass. As the youngest and most unimportant members of the gang, some not having yet proved themselves, they were required to make their own way, meeting up with the more senior members in the multi-storey car park opposite the Man Club in Queen's Square at ten-thirty. The senior members would arrive in cars, and once they'd checked there were no feds hanging around, the least important ones would hit the club, maiming and killing as many as they could. Then, as soon as they'd made an escape, the senior ones would do a drive past, showering the club in a hail of bullets and lobbing fire bombs. Once they'd taken out that club, the plan was to meet up again, half-a-mile away, in the service road behind Happy Boys and do the same to that club, before moving on to another of Claude's venues.

In case they should encounter a formidable response at any of the targets, shadowing them on their night of destruction would be six of the General's personal security guards armed with Heckler & Kotch MP7 rifles, and six no-nonsense guys from those who looked after his clubs, four with Colt M4 Carbines and two with IWI Tavor X95s, the latter weapons intended as part of a major update for the Israeli army, but instead having found their way into the General's hands.

It was known the General didn't do things by halves. All his men were ex-army, fully combat trained and experienced in deploying firearms in all kinds of situations. Added to the number of Leckington Louts there'd be, all armed to the teeth too, it was a redoubtable force he'd have out on the streets that night. Only a fool or a madman would expect one or two police armed response units to take them on. If they weren't going to be wiped out or suffer unthinkable casualties, for the tactics the police would need to employ, they'd have to wait for many more armed units to turn up, giving plenty of time for his men and the Leckington Louts to have it away on their toes and disappear into the night.

However, in accordance with the old adage concerning the best-laid plans of mice and men going awry, it didn't exactly work out like that. The less important Leckington Louts, who were having to find their own way to the meeting point, were doing it in groups of twos and threes, hoping like that they wouldn't be noticed passing through different territories. But many were noticed, and neither two nor three is a number a gang member is safe being in if they're found trespassing on another gang's territory. Within minutes of an encroachment getting a mention on social media, a dissed gang will saturate the area. Barely half of the less important members made it to the meeting point, and of those that did, many were in a sorry state. Beaten up and badly bruised, some suffering cuts too, they'd all had their weapons taken off them.

***

As proof of all the extra virility and vitality that comes with being young, Hunter and Kelvin often turned in early. It was a little after eleven o'clock, and they had just gone to bed for some romantic stuff, when Hunter's phone rang and began to dance around madly on the bedside cabinet. Reaching out for it in a contortion that would have had a circus performer feel proud, he managed to catch it.

"It's Greg," he said, showing Kelvin the phone's face. "I'll have to answer it."

"I know," Kelvin giggled. "But he's awfully good with his timing, isn't he? I hope he doesn't have a camera in here we don't know about."

Hunter laughed, and accepting the call in speaker mode, he said, "It's a real bad time, Greg. Is it important?"

"Oh, sorry, yes, it is rather important. I haven't caught you on the job, have I?"

"Let's just say if it hadn't been you, I wouldn't have heard the phone. So, what's rather important?"

"There seems to be a news blackout on radio and television, but videos of it are all over social media, going up faster than they can be taken down and replaced with notices about fake news, but it isn't fake, agents have rung in to confirm a lot of it. Parts of London are like a bloodbath. Two nightclubs have been hit and hundreds of people killed, many of the dead said to be armed police, according to one report."

"Blimey! You said parts of London. Does that mean it's not limited to one area?"

"It looks like it may be limited to one now, but there's been victims of serious attacks popping up all over the place, and if the social media know-alls are to be believed, most of them are Leckington Louts."

"And you want us to take advantage of it? You want us to rush over to Leckington Rye, hit the hotel and the house and grab Angelina and the baby?" Kelvin asked, excitedly.

"You're not far off, but not exactly right. Two armed crews will hopefully do that, but I'd like you to be on hand."

"If they're going in, why would you want us there?" Hunter asked, frowning.

"We don't know what they'll find. There'll likely be others in the hotel they can't leave behind. More underage, possibly boys as well as girls, and if you ever thought Ton-up Tess' crew could be a little uncouth at times, it'll only be because you've never met Happy Harry and his crew."

"Happy Harry?"

"When Harry and his lot get going, they're the real McCoy of uncouth. Castration barely makes it on their scale. If they should do some of the things they've done in the past, I doubt if any young kids would want to go with them."

"Like what?" asked Kelvin.

"You don't want to know."

"But I do, that's why I asked."

"Well, three years ago, they rescued a young backpacker in Columbia, and just to leave a message, they decapitated the six who had her and left them naked, with their bodies ripped apart so their heads were staring out of their stomachs."

"Bloody hell!"

"And they work for CoT?"

"They have excellent morals, but over many years they've learned, if you don't want a fire to reignite after you've gone, you need to leave behind the aftermath of an inferno."

"Makes sense, I guess," said Kelvin. "So, you want us to be babysitters for whoever they find?"

"After all what they'll have been through, they'll hardly be needing babysitters, but they could do with being with people who they haven't seen act like monsters in a horror film."

"Really? Maybe I ought to tell you, if there are any tinkling toddlers, my nursery rhymes leave a lot to be desired."

"They do?" questioned Hunter, frowning.

"You judge it. Our carer said he loved us, it was an awful lot. It's why he put us in his bed, and got us smoking pot. He kept a baby's bottle, and in it he'd put gin. And while we sucked it out the teat, he'd try and force it . . ."

"Okay, okay, I believe you! They aren't good."

"You haven't heard it all. There are more verses."

"Don't bother, I think we get the gist."

Kelvin laughed. "I remember the rhymes we made up better than any real ones. I was ten when I made up that one and it gave me a lot of grief."

"The carer heard you saying it?"

"No, I only put it in because it rhymed, but the other boys wouldn't believe me, they were convinced I was being given gin. They liked smoking the pot, but he couldn't get me to do it, so he wasn't getting off me what he was off them, and I told them so, but they refused to believe it. So, convinced I was being given gin, they started to become more and more adventurous with the carer in the hope of getting some."

"Strewth! You must have made his day with that rhyme."

"I know, I felt rotten about it for a long time."

"Talking of time, it's passing," Greg reminded them. "I told Aunty to expect you within the hour, and that was about five minutes ago."

"Aunty?" questioned Kelvin.

"Our vehicle pool in Central London," Hunter revealed. "If we're transporting an unknown number of kids, I guess we'll need to pick up something more capable of carrying them."

"But Central London in less than a hour? We've still got to get dressed," Kelvin said, as they both scrambled out of the bed and made a start on it.

"Don't worry, we'll make it. You haven't seen what the Jag can do yet. It's had a few mods."

"Mods? It was flying the day you brought me here!"

Hunter laughed, before asking, "A bow tie job, is it, Greg?"

"The party should be over by the time you arrive, but yes, it would be prudent to go dressed for the occasion. Oh, and all doggie bags will need to be skinned sausages. Keep in touch, won't you?" Greg said, ending the call.

"Bow ties, doggie bags and skinned sausages? What was all that about?" Kelvin asked, tying his shoelaces.

"A bow tie job means tooled up, doggie bags are what we'll be taking out of there, in this case kids, and skinned sausages says they have to go to Bangers for questioning. Simples."

"Crikey! Um, I'm ready."

***

Harold Hawkins was a well-built man, tall and rugged, and like some others in his crew, he was fast running out of his forties. People called him Happy Harry because it was as if he'd never learned how to laugh; a smile or a grin was the best anyone had seen. Back in nineteen-eighty, he'd escaped his tough upbringing with regular beatings and stowed away to America, where in the early nineties, he started to bum his way across the country on a motorbike, doing cash-in-hand jobs in order to survive. It was while doing one of the jobs in Wyoming that he found the love of his life. However, Asha was a native American, one of the Cheyenne, and her parents were dead set against them having a relationship. Unable to gain their blessings, after they had been secretly seeing each other for two years, they eloped, marrying in Las Vegas, and it was there, a few years later, while risking a few dollars on the tables one night, it seemed Lady Luck chose to smile on Harold. Having enough money to do it, at last, he found a way to sneak back into England in 1998, bringing Asha and their two sons with him in the hope the mixed-race marriage might be better received there. It hadn't gone down too well with a lot of people in the States. He'd met some so nasty, they'd told him they would rather have seen him married to a Mexican than a Red Indian squaw, and they'd spat at him and cursed before walking away.

But on arriving safely back in England, Harold was greeted by a man who told him that he, and subsequently all of them, had been watched, and it was CoT that had arranged for his way back into England, and also for Lady Luck to smile on him that night. It was interested in him and his wife, and the skills they'd shown with guns and rifles whilst working for a Wild West Show. The man asked them what they planned to do now they'd arrived in England, and apart from signing-on in the hope of getting dole money and some benefits to help out with the boys, neither of them knew. So, the man then asked them if they'd like Lady Luck to smile again. As soon as he mentioned they could have a large house in the suburbs with a garden for the kids, a car for each of them, and a bank account to keep it all going, they were sold on the spot.

Their two sons, Kuckunniwi and Ohcumgache, both names meaning Little Wolf in Cheyenne, grew up to work for CoT too, as part of Happy Harry's crew. Looking much younger than in their mid-twenties, with Kuckunniwi the oldest by a year, they'd inherited all the skills of their parents.

The two others making up Happy Harry's crew were Alvin and Connie Smart, a brother and sister. In their late forties, they'd been in care as children, dumped on a farmer and his wife out in the wilds of Hampshire, there to be half-starved, worked to their bones, and seemingly forgotten about. They had run away from there many times, but they'd always been caught the same day. With so few people about, to their utter annoyance, little escaped a country eye. It seemed the few local yokels there were, most of them able to tell you when the last cow had taken a dump, had nothing better to do than be nosey.

Brought up like that, they'd learned little about life, and not conditioned to going out, meeting people, and all that that led to, when they became old enough and had to leave the farm to be replaced by two more unfortunate kids, they'd no idea what to do or how they'd survive. In their desperation, they crept back and stole a load of ammunition and the two rifles they'd had to use to shoot any rats, rabbits or wild birds seen around the farm, in the hope they'd be able to find some shelter and feed themselves. And that is how a CoT member, taking a day out in the country with his dogs, found them. Or, more accurately, his dogs did. Way past being described as grubby, with their clothes now little more than rags falling off them, they were holed up in a shelter they'd made out of branches and leaves in the woods, ripping the corpses of wild animals apart to eat.

Fortunately, the CoT member had enough sense to realise, they had to be really good shots with their rifles to be able to survive like that, and instead of notifying the authorities, he phoned Boris, Greg's predecessor. The waifs were picked up within the hour, and once they were clean, and they'd been fed, watered and clothed, Boris had them tested to see just how good they were with their rifles. Discovering they were both what is technically known as shit-hot and then some, after a few enquiries had been made into their backgrounds, with the promise of their own house and a substantial bank account, Boris invited them to join CoT, fully aware they'd hardly turn him down. And they didn't turn him down. In fact, they were so grateful, in his most embarrassing moment, they'd leapt on him. The fact neither of them got married, and they stayed together, is likely because of their isolation as children, they didn't acquire any of the necessary social skills, but it doesn't bother them in the slightest. Living how they do now, and doing the things they do for CoT, they are happier than pigs wallowing in the proverbial.

All who join CoT have a story, and in a nutshell, that's the stories of Happy Harry and his crew. And, it's a fact, people with stories like that are invariably reliable. If it is asked for by those who have been good to them, there is nothing they wouldn't do. So, when Greg had asked them to leave behind the biggest message ever, it hadn't been a problem, they'd told him they would be happy to oblige.

Happy Harry's crew, in two cars and a Transit van, carried on along Leckington Rye Road, heading for the General's house, when Ton-up Tess turned the people carrier, with her crew aboard, left into the car park outside the Bobbysocks. A number of flashy cars were parked within space markings around the car park, most of them with a dozing or a bored chauffeur inside, and there were lights on behind the curtains of many of the hotel's windows, possibly proof that business was good. Apart from two youngsters in hoods hanging about outside the hotel entrance, probably there to push drugs, as they'd expected in the circumstances, there appeared to be a distinct lack of security. Not bothering to look for a suitable space to park in, Ton-up Tess stopped outside the front doors, and she and her crew climbed out.

The two hooded youngsters looked them over, and then one of them swaggered across, drawling, "You fucking twats lost, is ya? This ain't your fuckin' kinda hotel."

Curly's fist seemed faster than the speed of light. The boy's feet left the ground, literally, and he flew backwards through the air to knock his mate over and land on top of him.

"And this ain't your fuckin' day, boy," said Curly, opening up his long coat to reveal an arsenal.

The boys scrambled to their feet, and like frightened rabbits seeing a fox, they bounded off into the darkness.

"The oldest of those two couldn't have been any more than eleven," Teresa sighed.

"Yes, I'm afraid it's a sign of the times," said her husband, Daredevil Den. "We ought to get a move on, love. If all the phones suddenly in use in the cars now are anything to go by, I doubt we'll find anyone on the job."

"We're not to frighten any young ones, remember?"

"I know, but it won't be the arses of any young ones I'll be sticking the barrel of my gun up, will it?"

Dead-eye Dick laughed, "The last guy I did that to thanked me for the best orgasm he'd ever known, and to prove it was, he keeled over and died of a heart attack."

"You lot do like to play, don't you?" Teresa sighed, leading them through the doors.

With its concealed uplighting, thick-pile carpeting, flocked wallpaper and large smoky mirrors, the foyer held a promise of it being plush inside. It was quite small, though, little more than the size of a double-width corridor leading to the stairs and lifts. On the right, open doors led into an equally nice lounge with a bar, empty at the time, and on the left was a reception counter, like an oversized serving hatch through from an office. Realising they weren't their normal clientele, two guys in suits behind the counter froze at first, and then one of them went for something inside his jacket, while the other dived for something beneath the counter.

They'd both made a bad move. Teresa put a bullet through the centre of each one's forehead, the only sound from her gun fitted with a Reading silencer in the soft surroundings, a barely perceivable, 'Thup! Thup!' The brainchild of Thomas Reading, one of CoT's boffins, the silencer was said to be the most efficient ever made. And now there were two more who would never be able to argue the point.

"No, don't bother getting up, guys, I'm sure we can find our own way," laughed Teresa, walking off to lead the others over to one of the lifts.

They went to the top floor, and when the lift doors opened, it immediately became evident, gun barrels being shoved up jacksies wouldn't be on the menu. The doors to the six rooms were all open, and six scantily clad youngsters, three boys in only underpants, two girls in loose robes, and another with a sheet wrapped around her, were huddled together and staring down out of the Fire Exit. Cars could be heard outside in the car park, their tyres mournfully squealing on the tarmac and throwing up stones as they sped off into the night.

"Have all of them done a runner?" Teresa asked, hurrying over with her crew to join the youngsters.

The kids spun round, shocked silent for a moment, and then one of the girls replied, "Yes, but who are you? Are you why they ran away? We're going to be in terrible trouble now."

"You can think of us as your angels without wings, come to save you. You're Angelina Soames, aren't you?"

The girl gasped, "How did you know?"

"We were sent to find you. Your parents want you back."

"No, no, I'm not going! They'd never accept Ibraham, and I wouldn't go anywhere without him."

"Is Ibraham your baby?"

"Yes, but he's mixed-race, and they don't like that."

"Well, they do now, they've changed, and it's already been discussed. They'd accept being turned into lepers, if it would get you back. Your parents can't wait to meet him."

"Really? You're not trying to trick me?"

"Have you ever known an angel to lie?"

"I've never met an angel."

"Oh, I doubt that very much. So, this lot obviously are, but how many more here are under the legal age for sex, or are being forced to sell their bodies?"

"All of them, except the staff, and most of them are only here because the General has something on them."

"What about the blokes we found on the way up, the two on the reception counter?" Teresa asked, hesitantly.

"If they were in suits, it'll have been Trent and Connor, and they're monsters."

"Monsters?"

"We have to put up with them abusing us, and not only us girls, Trent's bisexual, into boys too, the younger the better."

"Thank Mary Duck for that!" Teresa sighed.

Angelina frowned. "You're pleased about it?"

"No, I'm relieved. I'm afraid, in our business, if somebody looks like they're going for a gun, you don't wait to see if it's only an address book so you can be on their Christmas list."

"You killed them?"

"I sent them back to their maker for judgement."

"Gosh! They did both have guns, and you couldn't imagine some of the things they liked doing with them in bed."

"Oh, I think I could," sighed Teresa. "So, you were going to tell me how many more there are here."

"There's four underage girls on the floor below, and there were two eight-year-old boys, but they got sold to the Middle East last week and haven't been replaced yet. The next floor down has what we call the gullible. Six girls who someone paid for to get into the country illegally and they landed up here, and there's four a bit older on the floor below that, but one of them only looks after our two toddlers because she's a bit naff to look at. We did have another two boys until about a month ago, nine-year-olds, but we heard they were done-in and buried on the council tip. They were forever playing up, crying and trying to fight the clients off."

"Good God! And there's two toddlers?"

"No one knows their real names, but the General calls them Bill and Ben, his potty men."

"Do you think we could cut to the chase, love? I feel more than ready to blow a few bloody heads off, now I've heard that lot," said Den.

"Language, dear!"

"What do you mean, language? You can bet your arse this lot swear as much as I do when no one's around."

Looking at each other and grinning, the youngsters as good as confirmed it.

"Maybe you all ought to get dressed," said Teresa.

Stopping one of the boys going, Den asked, "What's your name, son? How old are you?"

"Andrew Saunders, but everyone calls me Sandy instead of Andy for obvious reasons. I'm nearly fourteen. Why?"

"If you're not going to change your underpants, would you mind if we looked round your room while you get dressed?"

"They're apartments, like little flats, not rooms, and they're all exactly the same, but no, I don't mind. The pants are clean on, I'm not changing them, but it wouldn't have mattered if I was. Why would it, with what I do?"

"Correction, son. What you used to do," Den said.

The apartment consisted of a well-furnished lounge with a bar in one corner and facilities in another to make snacks and hot drinks; a bedroom with a dressing table, a wardrobe, a tallboy, and with its bedside cabinets, a king-size divan bed that faced a huge flat-screen television showing gay porn; a good sized bathroom that was actually a wet room with a few unusual shower attachments; and one other room.

"You might not want to look in there," Sandy said, just as Curly was about to enter the one other room.

"Why not?" Curly frowned.

"It's what they call a dungeon."

Den pushed in and opened the door, took a look all around, and quickly shut it again.

"Is it bad?" questioned Teresa.

"Certainly nothing you should see, my love. If you were to get any ideas, I couldn't keep up with the likes of that. It has to be on par with a medieval torture chamber in there."

"Really?"

"Whips, rubber gloves, all kinds of restraints, and a whole lot of mind-blowing phallic things. There's even a sling with stirrups hanging in the centre of the room. I reckon a woman could use it for giving birth in, except I think in there things are supposed to go the other way."

"Good God! You've got no fears of me wanting anything like that, love, I can assure you. Come on, the lad's dressed now, we need to get this bloody job finished."

"Er, language?" chuckled Sandy.

Teresa laughed, "Touché, but don't you gloat!"

It took them the best part of an hour to collect all the others and reach the ground floor, where with Curly watching over them, they were stored in the bar for the time being. It turned out there wasn't a barman, it was for one of the two reception blokes to serve any clients if they turned up early and wanted a drink while they waited.

Sandy showed the others the way down to the laundry and linen stores in the basement, where the only other members of staff on duty then would be. Eight women who understood very little English, they were there because they had to be, the General had something on them, and it was their job to change the sheets between clients. With the women knowing so little English, it proved a challenge telling them they had to leave and never come back. It wasn't until Dead-eye Dick pointed his gun at them that they finally got the message, quickly grabbing their coats and handbags and fleeing, with their hands flapping in the air as only women can do it.

Once the women had gone, and everybody had managed to stop laughing at the sight of them trotting across the road to disappear on the common, the youngsters were ushered out into the car park. And then with keys he'd found while doing one or two other things, Curly locked all the doors, so that any further punters turning up couldn't get in.

"Where are you taking us?" Angelina asked.

"We've transport coming to take you somewhere safe, and there it'll be decided where each of you needs to go. You'll have to walk along the outside of the common, until about halfway to the General's house, to wait for it."

"I'm not going anywhere without Ibraham!"

"You won't have to, we've another crew of angels sorting out the General, they'll get Ibraham to us safely."

"They'd better!"

"Why don't we wait in the hotel for the transport?" Sandy asked. "It would be a darn sight warmer."

"Oh, it'll be more than warm in a minute. Once we're all a safe distance away, the hotel's going sky high. Right, now you lot walk with my guys to the waiting point, while I drive Berty Bus there. I'd give you all a lift, but there isn't room, we keep a lot of stuff in it."

"Berty Bus?" laughed Sandy. "Really?"

Teresa smacked him round his head, playfully. "You can go off people, you know?"

"Nah, not you. Angels don't go off people."

"You're a cheeky one, aren't you?"

"Best cheeks in the business, but you been peeping?"

"Go on, get off with you, you scallywag!" Teresa laughed.

Chapter Eight

Happy Harry and his crew had spent the time reconnoitring Leckington Rye House and its extensions. In the course of doing that, they'd also disabled all its vehicles, most of them classy models doubtless costing a fortune. They'd discovered the General was in his study on the ground floor of the main building, where one of his men was helping him to keep up with the social media reports. Another man was staring at CCTV monitors in what had to be the security office on the ground floor. In the room next to that, in two sets of bunk beds, three of the bunks had men sleeping in them, their gun in a holster by their pillow, and one bunk was vacant. Yet another man was wandering around in the main building, seemingly so aimlessly that he frequently passed through the kitchen stores to raid a biscuit tin. And they were the only threats. The left-hand extension merely contained household staff in their accommodation, most in bed asleep. One other member of staff, a middle-aged woman in a nursery on the ground floor, was asleep too, as was the baby in a cot. It was abundantly obvious, in his desperation to hit someone hard, the General had left himself on a wing and a prayer.

The explosion two hundred or so yards away briefly lit up the sky, and in the same instant, with night-sights on his rifle, Happy Harry shot out the cable that carried electricity to the house. With a few bright sparks and flashes at the top of the pole, the building plunged into darkness. It was also the same instant that Kuckunniwi and Ohcumgache crashed through the window, coming back out only a few moments later, one having told the middle-aged woman to run and never come back, the other with the still sleeping baby wrapped up in its bedclothes. Inside, the house was in pandemonium.

"What the fuck's going on?" yelled the General, leaping up, and in rushing in darkness to the door, knocking over Mario.

"I think it's a power cut, boss," Mario said, getting up.

"A power cut? We don't get power cuts." A hail of bullets took out one of the floor to ceiling windows. "For fucksake! I suppose that's a fucking power cut too!"

Mario didn't answer him, though he did gurgle a bit before he died, not that the General would have heard it. A rifle butt to the back of his head had seen him crumple to the floor.

The window to the room where the three men in bunk beds were sleeping went the same way. Immediately leaping out of their bunks in shock, they became unmissable targets, their reaching out for them hands never to feel a gun again.

Possibly as a result of the amount of sugar he'd consumed, the biscuit-loving man's ringpiece had clamped tighter than a camel's arse in a sandstorm. He was wound up so much that, feeling his way along a corridor, with his eyes only slowly becoming accustomed to the darkness, he was firing his gun at the slightest suggestion of something. He had just killed a reflection of himself, destroying a full length mirror, when the man who'd been watching the CCTV monitors came out of that room, and he killed him too.

Wearing night-vision glasses, and seeing it happen, Connie and Alvin couldn't help but snigger. And hearing sniggering behind him, the man spun round, but he didn't get to squeeze the trigger again. A shot from each of them and his ringpiece relaxed.

The household staff, most of them in their nightclothes, but some with the sense to bring torches, were hammering on the double doors, trying to get into the main part of the building to find out what was going on. Happy Harry waited until the floodlight that ran off a car battery had been brought in and was working, and then he removed the bar they'd put through the door handles to keep the staff out. They burst in, and then stopped to stare at him, his crew, and their guns.

"You all need to get dressed and pack a case with anything you want to take with you," Happy Harry told them. "Very shortly, there won't be a Leckington Rye House."

In what could only be described as a mass panic, the staff raced back up their staircase to do just that, madly jabbering away and falling over one another. It wasn't long before they were back down, most of them with two suitcases and some with one that was empty. Those with the empty cases began pushing their luck, heading off up dark corridors to gather a few treasures to take with them. Many returned hardly able to carry their case, and to have some of the crew chuckling, one of the women, almost bent over double, was struggling with two heavy suitcases, and a golden unicorn hanging from her neck in a sling that she'd made from a tablecloth. They didn't know it, but she'd been polishing that unicorn for the past ten years, and if everything was about to be destroyed, there was no way she was going to leave it there.

Once it appeared everyone had gone, to be sure, the crew conducted a search of the building. While doing this, Happy Harry discovered the General's bedroom, spending a minute or two in there rifling through his personal stuff. Collecting information, he did the same in the study, there needing to go out to his car to fetch a gizmo that gave him the combination number for the electronic wall safe. He took photos with his phone of all the important stuff, and before destroying it, he forwarded the pictures to Kent, on night duty under Bangers, suggesting he ask Greg what to do with it. He was pretty sure the bank accounts would be emptied, but perhaps only after a load of investments had been cashed in. Then, happy that part of the job was done, he conferred with the others, deciding on the finishing touches to the message they'd leave behind.

***

Arriving in Leckington Rye Road to collect Angelina and her baby, and any others who needed rescuing, Hunter and Kelvin were far later than they wanted to be. Traffic had been heavy, with roads blocked and blue light activity seemingly everywhere. Many times they'd had to find a different route.

113

"Crikey, look at that! Do you reckon that could've been the Bobbysocks?" Kelvin asked, as they passed by a huge pile of rubble with flames roaring their way out of it to lick high into the night sky through mountains of billowing smoke.

"It's easily possible. If the police won't come here, I doubt if any of the other emergency services do. The natives will be awful fire conscious, you can bet they don't have many. Oh, look, there's Berty Bus, up there on the right."

"Berty Bus?"

"Yes, I was told that Ton-up Tess gave it a name because it does what she says better than her husband does."

"Weird."

Hunter slowed down and drove the minibus across the road, to park behind Berty Bus. There was nobody in it, but within seconds, Teresa appeared from behind one of the many Plane trees in amongst the bushes that bordered the dark common.

"Twenty-three charges, I'm afraid," she said, coming up to Hunter's open window. "Including two toddlers and a baby, but they're as good as gold. You'd best go down the road and turn round before they get on board."

"Actually, the traffic's hell the way we came, I was hoping we could find a better route home by leaving that way. Is that the Bobbysocks alight back there?"

"Yes, Curly excelled himself. The whole place lifted into the air, severing the gas pipe before it collapsed in on itself. If I know him, he'll try doing the same with the General's house, once that lot have finished enjoying themselves. You wouldn't believe what was going on when I had to go down there. Men being men, they'd brought us the baby, but they hadn't thought of things like nappies and formula."

"Oh, they're leaving a message, you mean? Is that why you said we'd better turn round? You can see what they're doing from the road?"

"Messages, not a message. They've got six blokes, and one of them, the General I think, is still alive. I saw two of them being strung up in the trees, and that was enough for me."

"They're putting the bodies in the trees?"

"Yes, naked, and tied up like trussed chickens. They've cut off their right arms and stuck them up their arses, like they're fisting themselves. They're leaving spray-paint messages too, telling the Louts to go or we'll be back to do it to them."

"Bloody hell!" gasped Kelvin.

"Yeah, I know, they don't do things by halves, do they?"

"I see you've got blinds. If you want to try going back that way, you could pull them down," said Teresa.

"No, it's probably best we turn round. Kids are kids, if they think there's something we don't want them to see, they'll be looking all the more. They certainly know how to batten the hatches round here, don't they? An explosion, an inferno, and no doubt gunfire, and there's not a soul to be seen."

"In an I know nothing area like this, I doubt if anyone risks looking out of their windows. They'll merely have thought it was the Louts up to something, and the less they knew about it the better."

"Strange place, isn't it? It's got an air of affluence, and yet it has a notorious street gang."

"A lot of Hooray Henries live along here, overlooking the common. It serves their needs; good links to Central London and the City, and a drug delivery service without equal."

"Well, let's just hope the bottom is about to drop out of the housing market around here, eh?" laughed Hunter. "I'd better go and turn this boneshaker round."

To turn round easily, Hunter drove down to the entrance to Leckington Rye House, to do it there, and seeing what was in those trees was beyond belief, but as like nothing to what was happening on the ground. An almighty scream told them he was alive when one of Happy Harry's crew chopped off a naked man's arm with one blow of a butcher's chopper, but for how much longer had to be anyone's guess. He was still alive when they cauterised the stump afterwards, using a tool that they'd kept red-hot with a blowlamp, his bloodcurdling screams the proof. They looked on horrified as Connie spread grease on the hand of the severed arm, and then the men took over, forcing it up inside the guy, and not stopping with their twisting and pushing until they'd reached its elbow. That was when the screaming trailed off, though with his body lunging around frantically, the bloke still didn't appear to be dead. As they drove away, having completed their turning round, the crew were hauling him up on ropes that they'd thrown over a bough of the nearest tree.

"Remind me never to upset any of that lot," Kelvin said.

"Yeah, they're more than uncouth," said Hunter. "Though, saying that, being that guy's obviously just found his second motor, I reckon they could at least have left him with a bottle of poppers to sniff."

"Eh? He'd never get the top off with only one hand."

"I know. Just as he thought his life couldn't get any worse, it would do."

"Oh, that's wicked!" Kelvin laughed, thumping him.

"Not feeling sorry for him, are you?"

"Hell, no! As long as we're sure they're guilty, and we are about this lot, I just look on it as hedging our bets."

"Hedging our bets?"

"Yeah, in case Hell doesn't exist, we're just making sure they get to pay their dues."

Hunter laughed. "Don't let Teresa hear you've doubts about Hell existing, she'll bend your ear for hours."

"She's religious?"

"She has her beliefs. In her eyes, anybody who listens to a confession and forgives someone in the name of God, so they can keep on doing wicked things again and again and again, and they only have to confess them each time to be given a clean slate, is a servant of the devil. She reckons the Pope's destined for Hell, where he'll meet all his predecessors."

"Bloody hell!"

"I know, but if there is a good god, you try coming up with a rational argument against her reasoning. I couldn't."

"There isn't one, is there? Do you believe?"

"I haven't entirely ruled it out."

"Crikey!"

The youngsters were all waiting by the roadside, when they arrived back at the picking up point. Hunter opened the door, and they scrambled aboard, filling the back of the boneshaker first as if they were going on a school trip. They had to wait for Sandy. He was having his ears bent about something by Teresa and Den, and when he finally got on board to sit in the only seat available, up the front next to Kelvin, who was next to Hunter, he looked flushed, as if he'd been embarrassed.

"Giving you a hard time, were they?" Kelvin joked.

"More like the third degree. They were asking me a hell of a lot of questions," Sandy replied.

"Like what?"

"They wanted to know everything about me. Did I have a family, like parents, or anybody hoping to see me again? Had I ever been in trouble with the law? Was I really gay? Had I done anything I was ashamed about? They went on and on."

"But you like them, don't you?" Hunter asked, grinning.

"They're alright, but how did you know I liked them?"

"Because if you didn't, you'd have told them to piss off and got on the bus earlier. You could do a hell of a lot worse, you know?" said Hunter, before turning round and shouting to the others, "All put your seatbelts on, and I want no tongues out or any funny faces at the windows, or you'll regret it!"

There was laughter, and a jeer went up. Ignoring it, with a toot, and a wave out the window, Hunter drove off.

"I could do a lot worse?" asked Sandy, frowning. "What do you mean by doing a lot worse?"

"I reckon they would only have asked you all those other questions after you'd told them you had nobody, and if that's the way it went, I'd say they were after you."

"After me?"

"Was the second thing they asked about whether or not you liked motorbikes, and you said no, you didn't like them?"

"Yes, but how could you know that?"

"Donny, their son, was killed in a motorbike accident about five years ago. He was nineteen, still living with them, and they wouldn't want it happening again."

"You mean they want to adopt me?"

"It couldn't be a proper adoption, not with the kind of work they do, but I reckon that's what it is. So, how would you feel about having adoptive parents who risk their necks to make a living, sorting things out with guns?"

"Oh, wow, that'd be whacky! Angels for parents!"

"Angels?"

"I know they were only joking, but it's what they said they were when they burst in on us. Angels without wings."

"Well, Donny grew up to become an angel, and if there are such things, he might even be a real one now. Play your cards right, and you never know, there could come a day when you are one of us too."

"Really? You think so?"

Hunter nodded. "Enough to put a wager on it."

"Oh, it only gets better!"

The boneshaker was more like a badly converted removal van than anything that should have been made for ferrying people about in. With an inadequate suspension, like many of the small busses now found on less popular routes, it lacked a lot in comfort. So, finding most of their passengers were fast asleep when they pulled up outside Bangers took quite some believing. And after they'd woken them up and ushered them into the club, that took some believing too. More CoT people than Hunter had ever seen before were sitting or standing at the tables in the lounge. It was like Greg had found a whole army to deal with the youngsters.

"Bloody hell! I've seen old newsreels from the war that looked like this," said Kelvin, staring at the scene. "The men who got called-up had to go through something like it, being passed on from table to table. They'd have to cough and have their balls checked at one, get an eyesight test at another, and at the next one. . ."

Standing right behind them, Greg put a hand on Kelvin's shoulder, making him jump

"Crikey, I didn't see you there!"

Laughing, Greg said, "Don't worry, it won't be as bad as call-up here, but we do need to find out exactly who they are and where they live so they can be taken home. And as some of them won't want their parents knowing everything, if they so wish, they can be checked for the diseases associated with what they've been doing, and if it's needed, receive treatment before they go home. I promise you, they'll be alright."

"Yeah, but not all of them. What about any who haven't got a home? They won't be alright if they land up going back into council care."

"We'd never put any youngster into council care. Have you forgotten about Benjamin Court?"

"The boy who got eaten?"

"Yes, and after he'd found out, didn't Johnny Mo set up the Benjamin Court Children's Foundation? You aren't allowed to have large children's homes like we had years ago in the UK, but for any we can't find a good home, there are four on that island where Johnny lives. Those who we can't find a decent home could easily come off best. They'll be enjoying all the fun of a tropical island, and having the best education money can buy. An above average number from those homes get into Oxford and Cambridge."

"Bloody hell!"

"Johnny Mo again," laughed Hunter. "Are you sure that CoT isn't his baby, Greg?"

"Oh, I'm sure. CoT was around before Johnny Mo, but it has been run by someone in his family since the seventies."

Kelvin laughed. "Yeah, and as the most senior member of it, I bet Johnny gives the family an awful lot of advice."

"Well, being you can't buy an island of that size in the sun unless you've done exceedingly well, you'd have to be a fool not to take it, wouldn't you? And when it comes to Johnny's family, it does have a lack of fools," Greg said, winking.

"It's a big island?"

"About a third of the size of the Isle of Wight, I'd say."

"Bloody hell!"

"I was hoping you could help me with a little problem."

"What kind of problem?" Hunter asked.

"One of the boys here, Andrew Saunders, or Sandy. Teresa and Den phoned me. They've taken a shining to him."

"We thought they had. But why is it a problem? He doesn't have a family, does he? He told us he didn't."

"Obviously we'll check all that, make sure his story stands up, but if he is free and is happy to be with them, there's the security aspect to consider. They're pretty sure he'd be happy to be with them, but they're worried about him being given wipe-out, like we'll have to give it to the others. If he can't remember them or how they met, will he still feel the same?"

"That's a toughie."

"No, it isn't," Kelvin said. "If they do hit it off, just don't give him the wipe-out."

"And what if he blabs about what he's seen here?"

"Who would he blab to? The friends he'll make at any new school wouldn't believe him, and he'll know if anyone else did, he could lose his home and be put into council care. He wouldn't be that silly, he wants to be an angel."

"An angel?"

Hunter elucidated. "When they burst in on the kids, Teresa explained themselves as being angels without wings."

"And Sandy wants to be one, as soon as he's old enough."

"Yeah, well, we'd better stop talking about him, Greg, he's left the queue and that's him coming over here," said Hunter.

"I wouldn't blab anything to anyone," Sandy said, walking up to them. "I promise I wouldn't."

"You couldn't have heard what we were talking about from over there," Hunter said, frowning. "It's not possible."

Sandy grinned. "But it *was* what you were talking about, me blabbing, wasn't it?"

"Yes, but how do you know? Do you have super hearing?"

"No, just good eyes. I learned how to lip-read."

"Crikey, you must know a lot of secrets."

"Why would you have learned how to lip-read? You aren't deaf, are you?" Greg asked, mumbling it softly, with a hand across his mouth as if in thought, but in reality to check.

Sandy laughed. "You don't trust anybody, do you? No, I'm not deaf. I was once, though, for nearly two years, er, after an accident. When I was seven, I fell down the stairs."

"Yeah, but are you sure you didn't only fall down them to keep a dog, cat or rabbit alive?" asked Kelvin.

Frowning, Sandy cautiously asked, "You were in care?"

"We both were," Hunter replied. "You aren't alone. Most of the people you can see in here would have had a tough childhood. It's why they're angels."

"And it's why you can trust me not to blab. I've seen what some of those angels can do, and I wouldn't want something like it happening to me. I don't want to be found dead with my arm chopped off and stuck up me in a tree."

"You saw the bodies in the trees?" gasped Hunter.

"Yeah, one, and they were pulling another one up. Teresa had been gone for a long time getting some baby stuff, and I crept off to see if she was alright, but I had to turn back or else that other lot of angels would've seen me. I reckon the one who was cutting off their arms might've thought he was the Archangel Michael. He's got a big sword, hasn't he?"

"Yes, but only in one hand," said Greg.

"Huh?"

"It's said he holds the hand of God with the other."

"Oh, yeah, I'd forgotten that."

"You knew it?" asked Kelvin.

"Yes, he holds the hand of God to do his will. I spent some time at a place where they were religious. I had to read a bit of the Bible every night, and become a choirboy at the local church. Thankfully, it was Church of England, so it shouldn't have messed up my chances with Den and Teresa."

"How did you know they weren't keen on Catholics?"

"They'd seen me earlier wearing only my underpants and a crucifix, so when Teresa said on the common that she hoped to God I wasn't a Roman Catholic, it sort of said it wasn't Christians she didn't like, only Roman Catholics. Anyway, I told her I wasn't one, and she seemed happy for me."

"You really *do* like them, don't you?"

"Yeah, the more I think about it, the more I do. They don't hide anything, what you see is what you get, and that's it. I really hope they want me."

Greg's phone rang. He took it out of his pocket, answered it, and then a look he gave Sandy said something. It was one those pictures that painted a thousand words.

With all the colour leaving his face, Sandy blurted, "No! No! Something's happened to them, hasn't it?"

"I have to go," Greg said, aiming it at Hunter and Kelvin, his face growing more sombre by the second. "Will you two look after Sandy? Take him home with you for tonight?"

Chapter Nine

Hunter had parked the boneshaker next to his Jaguar, as his passengers were being bundled into the club earlier. Seeing both vehicles were still there, he knew the guy from Aunty's, who'd brought his car down to swap back, hadn't started the return journey yet. Thankfully, with modern cars being like computers on wheels, Aunty's blokes never needed the keys, a gadget no bigger than a cigarette packet met all their needs, so he didn't have to go looking for them, they were where they normally lived, in his pocket. They put Sandy inside, on the back seat of the Jag, and Hunter drove them home.

Sandy had stared out of the window in silence throughout the short journey, and feeling he ought to say something, as they turned into the drive, and the headlights revealed where he was going, he said, "Smart house!"

"We like it," Hunter replied. "Look, if I leave you here with Kelvin, you won't run off or do anything silly, will you?"

"No, of course not. I swear it, I won't."

"Where you going, angel features?"

"I thought I'd go back to the club. I'll find out what's going on a lot easier there than on the phone."

"Okay, but don't go off doing anything silly, will you?"

"Would I?"

"You'd better not, and don't call me Wood Eye."

Hunter punched Kelvin playfully, as they got out, and he waited until they were safely indoors before driving off.

"Blinking heck! It's smart inside too, isn't it?"

"It's one of the perks of being an angel. I thought I'd died and gone to heaven, the first time I saw it. Would you like a drink or something? Off the top of my head, we should have coffee, all kinds of silly teas, hot chocolate, orange juice, and there's sure to be cans of coke."

"Have you got any vodka to go with the orange juice?"

"Crikey, yes, we have, but you drink? Alcohol, I mean?"

"I'm a working boy, or I was one, and working boys need something to take the edge off things. You ought to see some of the ogres I've had to entertain. As long as I didn't go mad, a vodka and orange juice was a lot better for me than some of the other stuff I could've taken."

"Drugs?"

"You name it, it was there."

"Bloody hell! Okay, a vodka and orange juice it is. I'll have one too. Er, you haven't got to entertain me, you know?"

A smile crept in, refusing not to be seen as it spread across Sandy's face. "I know, I'd already worked that one out, and anyway, you're not an ogre."

"Thank goodness for that! Right, go through there, into the lounge. We can have a settee each, and you can put on what you want, the television, or we could listen to music."

"Thanks, I'm not in the mood for anything on, though."

Kelvin poured the drinks, placed them on the coffee table between the settees, and said, "I won't be a mo."

Sandy didn't question it, suspecting he'd gone to spend a penny, until Kelvin came back and popped a pill, swallowing it down with a sip of his drink.

"Was that a happy pill?"

"No, just something special that'll stop me getting drunk. I haven't got my full licence yet, and if we've got to go out looking for Hunter later, I don't want to crash the car."

"You think he'll do something silly?"

"No, not really, I doubt if there's anything to do, they've probably had nothing more than a prang or something, but if there is, he does like to play the hero."

"I really hope it's nothing. Are you two married?"

"Not yet, we've only been together a few weeks, but we're working on it. It'll be sometime next summer, and there'll be a big do around our pool afterwards. We've a few surprises planned for someone. You can come, if you want."

"I will, if I can. But you've got a pool here?"

"Two. In England, you need one indoors and one out."

"Blinking heck!"

"Yeah, I know. Things still pop up to surprise me. So, how long were you working at the Bobbysocks?"

"Coming up to four years."

"Didn't you ever think of running away?"

"Only at first. Free meals and a decent bed was better than being in a squat, and if you haven't had much of it, it is kinda nice when you know a client really loves you. Some paid all that money, and all they wanted was to have a cuddle."

"Crikey! Are you gay, or did you have to pretend?"

"No, thank God, I'm gay, but a few of the punters liked me to make out I was straight."

"They get off on straight boys?"

"Yeah, the Arabs are a bit funny. Gay is taboo for them. So is alcohol, but that doesn't stop some knocking it back."

"Bloody hell!"

Sandy laughed. "There was a regular Arab who liked me to fight him off, while he kept saying, 'If you're going to have one, have a big one, bitch!' And when he got there, I had to cry and be ever so grateful. He always gave me a big tip."

"Jesus!"

"Oh, they weren't all good like that. One brought his so say son with him for a sandwich, a straight lad who wanted to experiment. I had to be the sandwich filling, with the bloke top slice. But the trouble with straights is, very few have any idea about housekeeping, and that one sure didn't."

"Oh, gross!"

"I know. The time I took in the shower afterwards must've doubled the water bill."

"I think I'd still be in it. How did you get to be in care?"

"My mother was a druggie, on the needle, dad couldn't take it and did a runner when I was three, and one day she overdid it. They found my old man, but he was up to his eyes in debt with another woman and in no position to look after me, so he had it away again. I heard he topped himself, in the end."

"Crikey! I was too young to know my story, but from what I've been told, it's almost the same. And you really wouldn't want to know the number of bad places I stayed."

"I only knew one good one, and don't laugh, but that only happened by luck or divine intervention."

"Eh? Divine intervention? What do you mean?"

"You were right, I didn't fall down the stairs. I went deaf when our foster dad came home from work drunk and belted me so hard my head hit the wall. He was always hitting me, and it wasn't until I was older, after I'd run from there, that I realised why. He'd rather I'd been a girl."

"A girl? You think he didn't like boys?"

"Well, he certainly liked girls. My foster sister didn't get hit once. She never got told off. He'd have her cuddled up on his lap for hours, and though she could do it for herself, he'd always bath her and put her to bed, and be ages about it."

"You reckon he's a Captain Birdseye?"

"I don't know, but I wouldn't put it past him."

"Jesus! So, where's the divine bit come into it?"

"Don't laugh, but suddenly going stone-deaf frightened me so much, I may only have been seven, but that night I made a bargain with God. If he'd give me my hearing back, I would do anything he wanted. Actually, I tried making that bargain many times. And then about a year after I went deaf, slowly my hearing began to return. Not wanting to risk it happening again, as soon as it became good enough to hear what people were saying without having to watch their lips, I ran, and it was on the night I ran that Uncle Ben found me."

"Uncle Ben?"

"The Bible basher who made me join the church choir. He found me sleeping in a doorway, and he was going to call the police so I'd be picked up, but my story and all the pleading I did must've been awfully good because he didn't, he took me home to his wife and they decided to keep me. The only good home I ever had was with Uncle Ben and Aunty Betty."

"Bloody hell! So, why did you leave there?"

"I didn't want to, but I think the story given to the school of me being a nephew, and my parents had been killed, stopped holding water. An hour after I came home from school one day, some official turned up on the front doorstep with two coppers to take me away. Once it started to get heated, and it looked like I'd be going, I ran out the backdoor and I didn't stop running until I'd hit Leckington Rye."

"Crikey! And that's where the General found you?"

"Some Leckington Louts did. They told me not worry, they knew where to find me a good home, and then they took me to the General's house and he bought me."

"They sold you?"

"Yeah, and argued over the price. I didn't know it then, but in the underage sex game, boys are worth more than girls."

"Did you find out why?"

"Girls are easier to get, they're a lot more gullible. Out on the streets, most boys are straight, and one's got to be really down on his luck to go along with anything like that, but tell pretty much any girl she's gorgeous these days and she'll be a pushover. So many girls just giving it away now, and doing it younger and younger every year, was a big worry for the General. He was frightened it wouldn't be long before no one would pay his prices. Trade was down again for the girls last year. It's been falling off for years."

"Bloody hell!"

"Do you want to know a funny?"

"Go on."

"The General was the biggest homophobe on the planet, but that didn't stop him making money out of gay boys. The fact there were fewer of us, and we were making more money for him than the girls, must have hurt."

"Really? If the girls weren't making so much, why did he want Angelina? Why didn't he go for another boy?"

"I think having another one would've been too much for his homophobia. The silly duffer was hoping an influx of quality young girls, some really posh nosh, might see trade pick up."

"And you don't think it would've worked?"

"Nah, not a chance. There's no shortage of underage posh nosh, it can be found everywhere. The pubs and clubs are full of affluent young girls flashing fake I.D. cards. Once they've got that warpaint on, with a lot of them, it's impossible to tell if they're twelve or twenty."

Kelvin laughed.

"What?"

"Warpaint. It's a good description."

"I know. It's always puzzled me why straight guys chase a mask. There could be anything under it. I've *had* to go to bed with frogs, but why do they take a chance of one being on the pillow in the morning? It doesn't make sense to me."

"A lot of frogs, was it?"

"Yeah, and not one turned into a prince."

"Don't worry, one day your prince will come. Mine did."

Another smile crept in. "I'm not looking for a prince, but if I was, he'd have to come more than one day."

Kelvin laughed again. "You've got a really wicked sense of humour, haven't you?"

"The world can be really wicked, not my jokes. I've always found it better to laugh at what it can throw at you than cry about it. If you can laugh, you've won that battle."

"Crikey, that was deep!"

"I know, there's times I surprise myself. I think it probably comes from when I went deaf. Though it suddenly became a frightening world, I refused to let it beat me. I taught myself how to lip-read and laughed at it."

"And then your hearing came back and you had that divine intervention. Of all the places you could've landed up, you landed up with a Bible basher. That's weird."

"Yes, but it's not proof it was divine intervention. Don't forget, the Bible basher was taken from me and I landed up being a working boy. That probably happened because there cannot be proof. If there was proof, we wouldn't need faith, would we? And having faith is what it's all about."

"Crikey, that's more than deep, that's pit mining! Keep on like that and you'll be hitting magma."

"I didn't dig that pit, it comes with the religion."

"You've got a lot of faith, haven't you?"

"Yes, it seems sensible to me. I've lost nothing if there isn't a heaven, and if there is . . . Whoopee! I've got a ticket."

"It's difficult to believe you're only thirteen. The way you can talk about things, if they couldn't see you, anyone would think you were at the very least my age."

"I'm *nearly* fourteen, but blame Uncle Ben. He taught me the value of learning, and it stayed with me. Any spare time I had, and working boys do get quite a lot of it, I'd be reading a book or on my computer, learning something."

"The General allowed you to have a computer?"

"We all had one, except the toddlers. They had other things to amuse them. You don't get that in a squat, do you? It may be difficult to believe, but it was like a home. We were safe, and we had a lot of freedom. If we didn't have a booking, as long as it wasn't all of us, we could go out during the day."

"Wasn't the General frightened you'd run?"

"Not really. Apart from knowing what we'd get if we were caught running, where else could we live like that?"

"But think what you had to do."

"I know that's debateable, but not everybody I entertained was an ogre. There were some drool factor tens."

"Really? Drool factor tens?"

Sandy forced a smile this time, and it was noticed. "Cracker was a drool factor in the millions. He was the youngest of the Louts who found me that day, only a year older than me, and he would sneak in to see me whenever he could because it wouldn't have done for the others to know he was gay."

Kelvin frowned. "Somebody in a street gang?"

"Everyone is a victim of circumstances. In another world, I wouldn't have been a working boy, he wouldn't have been in a street gang, and we would've been each other's prince."

"So, it was more than sex between you?"

"A hell of a lot more. We've blubbed enough tears to fill a swimming pool because we couldn't be those princes. It'd be weeks sometimes before he could sneak in again."

"Crikey!"

Sandy sniffed, wiping his eyes. "I hope you can believe me now. Nothing anyone said or joked about could come close to how wicked the world can be. From what I overheard in that club before we left, half the Leckington Louts have been killed, and Cracker might've been one of them."

Kelvin leapt to his feet, shocked, and grabbing the glasses, he said, "I'll get us another drink. I think I need a strong one, and I wish now I hadn't taken that pill."

"It's okay, I don't need another. One drink is useful to dull a pain, but no amount of it has ever made anything better."

"But I need one, and you will too. You're going to hate me, but you deserve to know, it was my idea to set gang on gang so it'd be easier for them to rescue Angelina and any others. I didn't expect it to kick-off so soon, though, or be so bad."

"I don't hate you. It's not in me to hate anyone. We always knew something like it might happen one day. It's Cracker I fell in love with, not what he had to be or anything he had to do. I'm against that just as much as you."

"He had to join the street gang?"

"If the Leckington Louts tell you they want you, you don't say no. Anyone who says no lands up dead and buried under tons of rubbish on the tip. Cracker was only nine when they got their hooks into him."

"Bloody hell!"

"People have no idea how bad it is out there on some of the streets today. He told me he'd known ten go up the tip, all of them young kids, the mules who take the biggest risks. So bad is it, when the parents reported them missing, frightened for their own safety, they said they'd expected the kid to run away, they'd tried running before, and then they just became another statistic, one of the thousands that go missing every year, with many of them never to be heard of again."

"I've spent a lot of time on the streets, and I knew it had got really bad lately, but you've researched it?"

"One day, and I don't know why, I started to wonder how many other kids had run from care, like I had. Apparently, as a percentage, I found a lot more ran away from being in care than from their family, but then to confuse that, I found a site that said an unknown number of kids from broken homes and dysfunctional families ran away every year and nobody took it upon themself to report them missing. Confusing, eh?"

"Yeah, and especially when you consider how many broken homes and dysfunctional families there are today. It might be thousands more go missing, or even tens of thousands."

"Have you ever wondered what it would be like to be a part of a normal loving family?"

"Hell, no. I've found love now, not the family type, it's a different kind of love, but in the past, that wicked world you go on about was more than enough for me to cope with, why would I have wanted to pile anything on top of that? Why did you ask? Was it because you wonder?"

"I think I probably knew something like it for a while with Uncle Ben and Aunty Betty, they really cared about me, and it was a million times better than sleeping rough, but I'm not convinced it's everything it's cracked up to be."

"Huh? You're not?"

"No, if I'd been there much longer, I reckon I'd have turned into one of those snowflakes you're always hearing about."

"Would that have been so bad?"

"Yeah, I think so. I'd have hated to find out about the world like snowflakes do. They're so protected from everything."

"Like what?"

"Sex is a big one. When I used to go to school, all the older boys watched porn, they'd no idea it wasn't love, and while a few reckoned their girlfriend was okay re-enacting the porn, others got wound up by their tactics being rejected. One even went and topped himself after his girlfriend made fun of him on social media. I'm glad I didn't learn about sex that way."

"I know the way I learned wasn't good, but it was better than that. It taught me that sex wasn't love, and one of you getting your end away doesn't automatically mean it's good for the other. And, being as I wasn't a snowflake, there was nothing anyone could've said or done that would've had me topping myself. Parents who shield their kids so much that they can even think of doing it ought to be locked up."

"I'll second that. I was nine, nearly ten, when the General had some of the other boys teach me about sex and explain what I was expected to do. Were you that young?"

"Sorry if it knocks the wind out of your sails, but I was four years old the first time something happened to me."

"Blinking heck!"

"I didn't know it was sex then, I only knew it hurt like hell, but I was soon brought up to speed."

"I suppose I was lucky, really. I was already finding boys attractive, so everything they said I'd be expected to do only went to blow my mind away. And I was eased into it slowly, I didn't meet any ogres for a long time."

"You and your ogres," Kelvin said, doing his best to fight off a grin. "Is an ogre somebody old and ugly? We all get old and lose our looks, one day. Hell, what made me say that? I must've spent too much time in Nellie's Inn."

"No, an ogre's a dirty great big fat blob of lard. Twenty or more stone of blubber, as slippery with sweat as an oil slick, with a dick you can't find under the rolls of fat, and usually with breath that'd kill a canary. Having that going to town on you isn't good at any age, but if you're ten years old, and it's the first one you've met, it's terrifying."

"Okay, that is an ogre. That is most definitely an ogre. And I'm so grateful now I've never had to make one happy."

"They made the General happy. Knowing they'd not get it anywhere else easily, he made any ogres pay double. Fifteen hundred an hour instead of seven-fifty."

Kelvin gasped, "You made fifteen hundred for the General if you entertained an ogre for an hour? That's insane!"

"But it was worth it to the ogre. No matter what we did, he didn't need to murder me, or take the risk I'd run home and spill the beans. If you're not involved in a criminal setup, a body isn't easy to get rid of so it won't be found. It's why the clients paid ridiculous money. They could satisfy their illegal yearnings with no comeback and no worries."

"Bloody hell! What did they pay to have you all night?"

"The price of an all-nighter depended on the time it started, but it'd usually be from about four grand upwards. Although, ogres weren't allowed to book an all-nighter, not since one of them woke up to find his boy dead in the bed. Drugged-up to oblivion, as they'd both been, they think the boy died from not realising he couldn't breathe with the weight of an ogre collapsed on top of him. But should he have been put in that situation? The boys earned enough for him as it was, did they really need to entertain ogres overnight?"

"Jesus!"

"Yeah, I know. Most of the people who say they live in the real world don't have a clue what goes on in it. If the body of a murdered kid is found and it hits the headlines, people will throw their arms in the air, saying how terrible it is, but what about all the others that don't hit the headlines? There will be people who know what happened to them, but do they care or do anything about it?"

"I recently learned about that. It costs the authorities money to do something, and they're mainly concerned in how much they can save. If it's not in the public eye, it's forgotten."

"I find it amazing, there's over sixty million people in the UK, and most of them don't have any idea what's going on around them, they live in their own cosy little world."

"I think they do know but prefer not to face up to it. In that cosy world, their kid doesn't have anything to do with drugs, they wouldn't bully anyone, they don't belong to a gang, they don't rob and steal, they wouldn't force anybody into doing anything, and they definitely wouldn't hurt anyone, they're a good and well-mannered kid. So, it isn't their problem."

"Yeah, and I'm sure half of what they don't want to face up to is their own past; the things they got up to when they were dragging the streets."

Kelvin laughed. "I've heard about some of that. There were no sext messages in those days, youngsters got it out down a back alley or behind a bike shed. And their parents probably said they wouldn't do that, having done it themselves in their day. Not accepting what goes on could be inbuilt. Oh, that's good, it sounds like Hunter's back."

"I hope it's good."

Moments later, Hunter came into the room, and looking at Sandy first, he said, "Teresa and Den are okay, you can stop your worrying." And then he turned to Kelvin, to add, "It seems there's a couple of things none of us knew about."

"Like what?"

"Number one, the Galaxy Bar, a cafe come wine bar further up Leckington Rye Road. The Louts use the basement as a meeting place, and to cut and distribute their drugs. If any of them make it back there, all hell will break loose because of number two, which is the venues the General had hit belong to Claudius Capisto, or Claude, and he's got connections to Family with a capital F."

"Why a capital F?"

"It's the Mafia. Claude is linked on his mother's side, and that's enough for Cibero Romero to be in the area now with a hit squad. Our crews are keeping an eye on them. It's mainly residential, as we saw, but that might not stop Cibero. If he gets bored waiting for revenge and they start shooting out the windows, a lot of innocent people could die."

"Bloody hell!"

"Greg's after talking to Cibero, but he'd need us too. How do you feel about that? We don't have to do it."

"Yes, we bloody-well do, you don't know the half of it!"

"Really? I'll ring Mary and Andy, then. With a bit of luck, they won't be too mad about being woken up."

Chapter Ten

Knowing there would have to be a good reason for it, Mary and Andy were okay about being woken up in the early hours to babysit. Sandy wasn't so okay, though.

"I don't need a babysitter," he complained. "I can look after myself. Don't you trust me? I won't nick anything."

"We trust you, but it's not that. Most of the time we have to be law-abiding people. They'll only be here so we comply with the law in case there's a fire or something, not to really look after you. Don't give them a bad time, eh?" Hunter said.

"Okay, but they'd better not try putting me to bed."

"They won't. You'll like them, anyway, they're magic."

"They're magic?"

"You'll see. If you do get tired, there's four spare bedrooms to choose from upstairs, help yourself."

"But whatever you do, just don't go pressing button nought if you take a shower," Kelvin added, grinning.

"Why not?"

"Your tackle might never forgive you. Hunter's little joke, I found out the hard way. It's ice mode, and like being stabbed by a thousand needles."

"Blinking heck!"

"You should've heard him scream," laughed Hunter.

Sandy shook his head. "You two are something else."

"We are, and you will be soon," Kelvin said, winking.

It wasn't long before Mary and Andy arrived, using one of their keys to let themselves in, as they always did.

Coming into the room, Mary said, "Don't worry yourselves about anything, now. We've brought plenty of wet-wipes and nappies with us for the little one. I'm quite looking forward to this, I haven't changed a baby in years."

Wide-eyed in disbelief, Sandy sat bolt upright, from where he'd been slumped on the settee.

"Didn't Hunter say they're magic?" laughed Kelvin. "You aren't alone, Andy knew a few frogs before he met Mary."

"I did, and as they weren't having mine, if I couldn't find them a suitable frog, I'd get them a toadstool to sit on. They don't like toadstools, you see, they're too much for a frog, so it soon got rid of them."

"A toads . . ? Oh, I get it! Yeah, okay, they're magic. We'll get on, I won't give them a bad time."

With Sandy feeling better about his not babysitters, Kelvin and Hunter raided their arms safe to grab a few extra bow ties before leaving. Thirty minutes later, they were in the air, flying towards Leckington Rye. Not the chopper's pilot this time, Greg was in the back with them and some others.

"Oh, what was that earlier I didn't know the half of?" asked Hunter. "I didn't ask then because of the look you gave me."

"Yeah, I'm on a guilt trip about it. The love of Sandy's life is a secret because he's a Leckington Lout. A year older, he's called Cracker, and he was in the group that found him and took him to the General. I'll be feeling bloody awful about it if he's one of the dead ones."

"You mustn't hold yourself responsible for anything a Lout chooses to do," said Greg, trying to look sympathetic.

"But that's it, most of them don't choose, they're told what to do, and if they don't do it, they're up the tip, buried under tons of rubbish. If I'd known that, I wouldn't have come up with that gang on gang stupid idea, and I didn't imagine for a moment they'd hit any nightspots. I'm wondering now how many innocent club-goers might have been killed."

"None, both clubs they hit had been evacuated. They either had very good radar, or it's possible the Louts had a mole."

"Crikey!"

The sun wasn't up, but dawn had begun to creep over the horizon when they landed on the common half an hour later, near the ruins of the General's house. Seeing someone in the distance flashing a torch, once, and then twice, then once, and then twice again, continuously repeating the pattern, the pilot hopped the helicopter a good bit closer to the flashing light. Greg opened the door and Teresa climb aboard.

"There's been some movement since it became obvious the chopper was landing, but once they'd found the Galaxy Bar, it seemed as if they were prepared to wait it out. There were a dozen hanging about in the line of trees opposite the bar, but they're now by various cars parked on the street, talking with perhaps another dozen in them. We know the first two cars, nearest the bar, have automatic rifles," she said.

"It looks as if you were correct," said Greg. "They're after finishing off any Louts who make it back. Ones and twos being gunned down by the men in the trees, and should a load turn up, the guys with the automatics spraying them in a drive-past. Is Cibero in one of the cars?"

"Yes, he's in the back of a big blue Mercedes, parked a safe distance behind the others. None of them can be familiar with the area. We've seen a dozen Louts creeping in the back way, entering the cellar by a door down some steps, and not one of them looking old enough to buy a packet of fags legally. It's possible there could be others in there who managed to get back before we started to watch the place."

Greg frowned. "Cibero's men missed the back alley?"

"There isn't one. The houses behind, in Gribble Road, are a lot less prestigious, a mixture of terraced and semis converted into flats and bed-sits. The Louts have been coming down the side of one of the semis and over the back fence. The low wire fence behind the bar is the only one you could cock a leg over, all the rest have high wooden ones to block out the riff-raff, so it looks as if it's deliberately low for that reason."

"With the Louts going in the back way, they wouldn't have seen it, so I hope they know the General's house and the Bobbysocks have gone. If we have to get between them and Cibero's lot, I wouldn't want to be shot at from both sides."

"They'll know. We sent two packing who'd been outside the Bobbysocks, and kids today are never off their phones."

"I really hope so. I've brought Grant and his team to back you up. Where's Happy Harry and his crew?"

"In the trees now, watching Cibero's cars. One or two at a time, they staggered past the cars earlier, doing the soft shoe shuffle, and as soon as they were out of sight, they crept back along the common."

"That's a relief! I feel a bit happier now."

"What's the soft shoe shuffle?" asked Kelvin.

Hunter explained, "Acting like a sop staggering home, that everyone goes out of their way to avoid, you drop something down a trouser leg and kick it somewhere. In this case, a safe bet is under a car."

"They've kicked bombs under those cars?"

"Well, they wouldn't have been ham sandwiches."

"Crikey!"

Teresa left, taking Grant and his team with her and heading off into the trees and bushes, and a moment afterwards, Greg, accompanied by Hunter and Kelvin, headed in the opposite direction, following the line of trees and shrubbery until they were level with the big blue Mercedes.

Greg, a little too long in the teeth to undertake mad dashes across roads, stayed hidden in the bushes. Hunter and Kelvin made it safely into the Mercedes, one sitting on either side of Cibero, while his driver counted clouds in La-La Land as the bump on his bloodied head grew larger.

"Hello, old bean. Nice day for it, don't you think?" Hunter said, his gun pressing into Cibero's chest.

Kelvin's gun was pressing into him on the other side.

"Who the fuck are you? What do you want? Our business here has nothing to do with you."

"Oh, it has more to do with us than you could ever imagine, chum. I hope you saw the General as you came past. If you did, you'll be pleased to know the blokes who did that are still here. How do you feel about your arm going up your jacksie? The General was alive when they did that, and it's a shame, really. It was wasted on him. He wasn't into fisting."

"I've got twenty men here, you won't get away this!"

"Really? How many do you think we have? They've been watching you since you arrived, and that chopper has brought more. The fact you haven't seen any of them should tell you they're a lot better at this game than yours, chum. Or, if you are actually paying yours, maybe that should be chump."

"Who are you? What setup?"

"My partner is going to search you. I'm afraid by necessity it'll be more than a little personal, we don't take chances, and then you'll find out who we are."

"If you've got a sweaty arse or bollocks, mate, I won't be happy," said Kelvin, starting on the task.

"I'll have you know, I take pride in my personal hygiene."

"You'd bloody better!"

Completing the task, and nodding the confirmation that he wasn't carrying any arms to Hunter, Kelvin wiped his hands on the bloke's suit, leaving white marks all over it. "Jesus, he's got more talc on him than you'd find in a ton of coke."

Holding back a laugh, while feeling sorry for Kelvin having had to go there, Hunter raised a thumb at the window.

Greg emerged from the trees, and crossing the road, he got into the vacant shotgun seat.

"Oh, for fucksake, not you!" Cibero groaned, loudly. "I was told you'd popped them years ago."

"I do love to disappoint people, especially you, don't I? So, what's it going to be? Are you and your men walking out of here weaponless, giving me your word you won't return, or do we send you off on a journey? I hear it's still summer in Hell; blazing hot. You'll be needing more than that talcum powder I can smell on you."

"I'm not stupid. We'll go, and you have my word we won't be back, but you're going to make us walk?"

"What's the cost of a few cars to you, Cibero? You won't have far to walk, the tube station's at the end of the road. So, what's the allee-allee-in signal?"

Cibero groaned again. "Three long blasts on the horn."

Being it was a Mercedes, the three long blasts couldn't be confused with a bout of flatulence. All the men further up the road in their cars got out, and with those who'd been standing by them talking, they hurried down the road towards their boss. Coming out from behind the trees and bushes to follow, still unseen by Cibero's men, the CoT crews had firearms aimed squarely at the men's backs.

The men crowded around the Mercedes, and on seeing the driver slumped at the wheel, one frowned, popping his head through the window to ask, "What's up, boss?"

"Not you, you worthless bunch of idiots, you aren't up to much! If you don't want to be leaving the planet in the next few seconds, I suggest you don't turn round before you throw your weapons on the ground. And don't try to be clever, all of them. I can guarantee it, this lot won't tolerate clever."

It was a comical sight. White-faced, and feeling stupid, the men dropped the weapons in their hands, and finding various others that had been hidden around their bodies, they dropped those too. Turning round slowly, they gasped on seeing the number of guns trained on them from only a few feet away.

Greg, Hunter and Kelvin emerged from the nearest house's hedge they'd been hiding behind, grinning, and the latter two kicked the weapons into a pile away from the men.

"Toodle-pip, old beans. The tube station's about half a mile thataway," Hunter said, pointing. "You will watch out for the funny men hanging from trees, wont you?"

Scowling, Cibero got out of the Mercedes, two of his men retrieved the driver, and with the driver having to be held up to walk, they set off down the road together, with the men suffering nagging reminders of their worth. Greg gave them a few moments, and once they too had moved a safe distance away, he nodded at who he knew to be the button-pusher. If he was there, and he was, it would have to be Curly. He had a thing about pushing the button.

Curly took a tiny box out of his pocket, opened the lid, and with all the anticipation on his face of a child waking up on

Christmas morning, he pressed the button with his thumb. In simultaneous explosions, eight cars, including the Mercedes, flew high into the air, skilfully blown across the road and not towards the properties, to come crashing down on their roofs or sides, ruining them enough to be a write-off. It let Cibero and his men know, they could have been taken out at anytime without one of them even realising they were there.

"Muppets," said Greg, shaking his head despairingly at the bunch of losers who'd stopped to look back in horror. "How the mighty have fallen."

"An old foe?" Hunter asked.

"We have history."

The tone of Greg's voice suggested his reply wasn't to be pursued. Wondering why, Hunter didn't pursue it, but then to send his mind off on a riot, Teresa mouthed at him that she'd tell him later. Plainly, it had to be some history.

Teresa had Den run back to Berty Bus, to collect a pair of wire-cutters, before they wandered off to check out the Louts who'd made it back to the basement. With the bar closed at that time of the day, if they weren't to be heard, they needed to walk there the long way, to the end of the road, turn left and then first left into Gribble Road and go in the back way, over the wire fence, and whether or not Greg could still cock a leg high enough to get over it was, to her mind, a matter for debate. Hunter and Kelvin hung back a little, until they were walking with Teresa's group, as the column slowly made its way along the road.

Turning to Teresa, Hunter asked, "So, Greg's history with Cibero, what was it he didn't want to talk about?"

"I don't know how much you know about Greg, he's good at keeping things bottled up, or if you can appreciate just how difficult it was for a gay man to find somebody years ago, but he didn't have much luck in finding a partner."

"We know he was attracted to a boy in a home once, when they were at school together, but he landed up being fostered out and beaten to death," Kelvin said.

"Yes, Barry, and even at that tender age, they'd a great deal more going on than he'll easily admit. He was into his thirties before anyone got his eye again. It was Cibero, who though he wasn't gay, he could play a convincing role. You see, it wasn't Greg he was after, it was his knowledge and military contacts. Greg didn't know he was Family, Sicilian Mafia, and all he was after was getting his hands on some firearms."

"Bloody hell!"

"Greg wasn't exactly heartbroken when he found out, but it was another relationship that hadn't gone anywhere."

"He wasn't heartbroken?" Hunter questioned.

"No, though he'd been hoping he could pass Cibero off as a stand-in, he's only really ever loved Barry."

"Blimey! So how did he get mixed up with Cibero?"

"The Sicilian Mafia was decimated by a couple of zealous magistrates in the eighties, and Cibero fled to the UK. There was some lapsed Family he knew in London. They'd given up crime and were running arcades and nightclubs, and while staying with them, he decided to start a protection racket, but with no contacts, and in need of firearms, he sought out a gay bloke with military contacts in the hope of blackmailing him. So, after being taken for a ride like that, when Greg had to give Cibero a bloody nose on a job that CoT undertook in the nineties, it gave him a great deal of pleasure. He hit him really hard. Nobody's had Greg's eye since Cibero. He's not had so much as a one night stand. Somehow, he manages to get by on his memories of Barry."

"How do you know all that?" Hunter asked.

"There comes a time when everyone needs a shoulder to cry on. One day he drank too much and used mine."

"Just living off his memories of their love as boys must be awful. I mean, Barry must've been dead fifty years now."

"Sandy was right," Kelvin said, sniffing. "The world can be really wicked. If it was like my love for you, he's stuck with it. A love as strong as that would never learn how to die."

Hunter put an arm around Kelvin's shoulders, sniffing too.

The chainlink fence was barely waist high, and easily over by a young person, while an older one might have needed to put a hand on the fencepost and scissor-jump it, but none of them needed to attempt any such manoeuvre. Den made four snips with the wire-cutters, wriggled a vertical length of wire upwards, almost like he was unscrewing it, and bit by bit the fence sprang apart.

"That's the way to do it!" Kelvin joked, in a cartoon voice, though softly as he didn't want the Louts inside hearing.

"It's not so easy with water," Den replied, being equally as quiet and giving him a wink.

"Huh? Water?"

"Moses and the Red Sea?"

"Oh, yeah, I read about that. But he had help, didn't he? I seem to remember he got his staff to do it."

Shaking his head, laughing, Den said, "That's good, that's very good. I must remember that one."

"Yes, it was chuckleworthy, a play on a word," said Teresa, studying Kelvin's face. "But why would you be joking about now? You've just made two wisecracks, and I'd say almost like nervous reactions. Are you worried about something? Is there someone or something you don't want to find in here?"

"Crikey, you *are* good!"

"I've had a lot of practice. So, who or what is it?"

Kelvin explained how it wasn't who he didn't want to find in there, it was who he desperately did want to find, alive and well, and why. If Cracker had been killed because of an idea he'd thought up, he didn't know if he could live with it.

"Oh, you'll live with it, alright. You'll live with it because you have to live with it. It's not only Hunter you've to think about, CoT needs you too. Why don't you stop feeling sorry for yourself and try having a little faith?"

"Faith?"

"It's said it can move mountains."

"But if it was only a mountain needed moving, I could have a go at moving it myself."

Happy Harry tried the door, ready to give it one shoulder if it was locked. If that didn't open it, so important was it to get in quickly in case the Louts had another way out, they had everything ready to blast it off its hinges. The door opened.

Rushing inside, with guns ready in their hands, a rapid head count through a fog of marijuana smoke told them there were seventeen Louts in there, in a group by the far wall. Turning to stare at the intruders, most of the Louts looked as nervous as a canary in a cattery. Apart from one of the youngest, they all immediately put their hands up, or on top of their head, and then he did too, after a kick from the one next to him.

"If you don't want to regret it, throw all the weapons you're carrying over here, and be smart about it," Harry shouted.

"We ain't got none," one replied, shouting it back.

While several crew members kept the Louts covered, others checked to find it was the truth. They had no weapons.

"Are any of you known as Cracker?" Kelvin asked.

They all denied they were him, slowly shaking their heads, and then one of them piped up, "I finks Cracker bought it."

"Bought it?"

"Yeah, got shot. I seed 'im go down. Lotsa blood."

Kelvin's heart plummeted to levels he'd not known existed before. He was stunned, and his stomach gripped, hurting.

"Right, well, here's the good news," Teresa said. "We're not here to harm you or turn you in, but unless you want us to come back and do to you what we've done to the General, your street gang days have ended. You need to get a life, start kicking a ball around or something. Be normal."

"Wodja dun tada Gen man?" asked one of the older ones.

"We shall be leaving now. If you follow us to the common, where our vehicles are, you'll see what. And I promise you, we'll do more, a lot more, if we have to come back."

After standing around talking for a while on the common, Greg, Kelvin, Hunter and Grant's team left the others and headed for the chopper. As it took off for home, Grant's team started laughing about the horrified looks they'd seen on the kids' faces. So bad were they, they were pretty sure nobody would need to return. The General's house being little more than a pile of rubble, with just two walls remaining upright of the extension nearest the road, and them only left there so nothing could fly off to damage any nearby properties, had more than shocked the kids. They'd stared at it, aghast. But it was as like nothing to what followed after one of them had asked about the General, and Happy Harry had pointed to the trees, asking them what they thought of their handiwork. One of the Louts had immediately chucked up, and spiralling to the ground in a dead faint, he'd annoyed two of his mates by giving them the benefit of his last meal. Some of the others had had a wobble too, and what looked to be the youngest four kids there had clung on tightly to one another, trembling uncontrollably as they'd stared up into the trees, white-faced. It was without any doubt, there would be a few nightmares, but if they resulted in the kids changing for the better, did it matter? The general consensus was it didn't.

Still affected by the news of Cracker's demise, Kelvin was sitting silently staring down at the floor, deep in thought, and Hunter didn't know what he could do or say that might make him feel better. Knowing he had to come up with something, he reached out and squeezed his hand. It earned him a smile, albeit a forced one.

"I'm alright," said Kelvin.

"You don't look alright."

"Yeah, I am. I've been thinking about Sandy, and trying to work something out. "

"Work what out?"

"He's only thirteen, and yet he's so cool about everything. I know he'll be heartbroken to hear Cracker's dead, he thought the world of him. He had to wipe his eyes when we talked of what might have happened, but he was quite prepared to accept it, like it was just one of those things. And that's been puzzling me. I think I've worked it out now, though. I know how he can stay so cool."

"Go on."

"He has unshakeable faith that everything will always work out within the boundaries of what's intended. Cracker's death will just be God's way of saying he wasn't intended for him."

"Blimey, that's an awful lot of faith he must have!"

"I know. I wish I could be like that, though."

Greg's phone rang. Sighing, and taking it out of his pocket, he answered it. There were only a few grunts, nothing anyone could glean as intelligible over the noise of the chopper, and then the call ended.

Turning to Kelvin, Greg said, "Run up the front and tell the pilot I said he's to turn round. We need to go back and land just short of where we first landed, before making the hop."

"Okay, but why we going back?"

"Teresa's found a Lout who needs urgent medical attention, he's been shot, but being he's a Lout, the kids have told her he won't get it anywhere local, he'll just be put into a cubicle and left there until he's dead."

"Bloody hell!"

Kelvin raced up the front, and Greg made a call to Bangers, explaining the situation. He was bringing in a life or death case, and he needed them to pull out all the stops.

On the way back to his seat, Kelvin had to grab hold of a rail and hang on tightly, as the helicopter almost turned fully onto its side to perform the turning round manoeuvre.

"Crikey!"

Chapter Eleven

Hunter and Kelvin arrived back home at eleven-thirty that morning. Having grabbed a few hours sleeping on the settees, Mary and Andy appeared to be as fresh as a couple of exotic fan-dancers, and not in any way put out by their lateness.

"Sandy's taken one of the bedrooms, then?" Hunter asked.

"Yes, went up about eight o'clock. I don't think he sleeps normal hours, he wasn't a bit tired," Mary replied.

"Went up so we could get some kip, I think," said Andy.

"Why didn't *you* take one of the bedrooms?"

"By eight o'clock, it didn't seem worth it. Besides, what if he'd woken up and wanted something? The settees were just fine. Actually, they're very comfortable," said Mary.

Mary insisted on making them a snack before she toddled off home with Andy, saying she would have dinner ready for them at seven o'clock that evening, so some time had passed before they went upstairs to check on Sandy. They found him in one of the front bedrooms.

"Crikey! He looks so peaceful lying there, not a care in the world," Kelvin said, softly. "It seems a shame to wake him, shall we leave him a bit longer?"

"I'm not asleep," Sandy said, sitting up in the bed. "Did it go okay? You didn't hear anything about Cracker, did you?"

"Yeah, you didn't tell me he was mixed race," Kelvin said.

"I didn't think it was important."

"No, I suppose it isn't, not normally, but it comes in handy if you're trying to identify someone."

The colour drained from Sandy's face. "I-I-Identify?"

"No, not like that, he's okay! He wasn't, though. He'd been shot, two bullets straight through his right shoulder," Kelvin said, grinning. "My guess is, he'll be wanting you to be his right-hand man until he can use that arm again."

"Oh, wow! He's okay?"

147

"Yes, but he's got a mouth on him, hasn't he?" Hunter said.

"Only if he doesn't know you. Why, what did he say?"

"He was out of it until he'd had the operation to repair the damage, he'd lost a lot of blood and it was touch and go for a while, but when he came round, realising he'd been stripped and put into a hospital gown, he made a big point of letting everyone know guys were either showers or growers, and he was an awfully big grower."

"That sounds like Cracker!" laughed Sandy.

Kelvin laughed too. "Yes, and you have to be the partner he calls Slipper. I think it's another boast."

Sandy cringed. "Oh, no, he didn't do that one, did he?"

"Yes, he did. He said it was because there was nothing he liked slipping his foot into better."

"He has done well, but not *that* well!"

"No, we didn't think he had for a moment. Who has?"

"Not many, thank goodness, but they are around."

"Really?"

"Yes, and they're a pain in more ways than one. They need two cherries on their stalk, and as that leaves you feeling like a last week's lettuce, just wanting to curl up and die, it's not good if you've got another client turning up afterwards."

"Crikey! Did you have clients one after another, then? On the hour, every hour?"

"Sometimes, but they were sliding hours. In-between, there was a fifteen minute break for the maids to change the sheets and tidy around, and for me to shower and pretty-up again."

"Bloody hell!"

"If you want to know a funny, none of the gullible girls got showered or prettied up between clients. It was a quick squirt of deodorant and get your chops around that, gorgeous."

"Oh, yuk! Now I'm *really* grateful I'm gay."

Sandy laughed. "Yeah. me too. Cracker said it must be like getting your breakfast toast on an unwashed plate someone's just had a kipper on."

"He's quite a character, isn't he?" laughed Hunter.

"Can I go and see him?"

"They don't want him having visitors until five o'clock, he needs to rest, so we'll take you then, if that's okay?"

"Oh, is it ever!"

"Can you stand some more good news?" Hunter asked.

"Yes, of course I can. What?"

"Everything's checked out okay for you to live with Teresa and Den, and they can't wait to get you home and spoil you, but it may have to be tomorrow."

"Why tomorrow?"

"They've gone back to Leckington Rye, hoping to check up on a few things they'd been told by some of the Louts who'd survived. They couldn't do it earlier, Teresa's a trained nurse and she was needed on the flight bringing Cracker here."

"What things?"

"Things some of the Louts told them about Cracker's home life. They said a lot of bad things."

"And that might not be everything," Sandy said. "He has it a lot tougher than many know. Why, what will they do?"

"Don't go getting your hopes up yet, but if the stories check out, as he's already agreed to it, they'll try to buy Cracker."

"Buy him?"

"If there really is no father on the scene, only a stepmother he was dumped on who spends all the benefits she gets on heroin instead of feeding and clothing him, and who brings a different bloke home for him to call dad every few days, she probably will sell him. With a bit of luck, she'll spend the money she gets on heroin, overdo it, and that'll be the end of that chapter in Cracker's life."

"Every bit of that's true, and more. He often takes beatings off her, bad ones, I've seen it, and with anything she can find at hand. He won't fight back or even push her off, if he can get away, he runs and doesn't go home for days, he sleeps rough, but if they buy him, where's he going to live?"

"Yes, that was a problem. Teresa and Den don't have space for another one, so providing he checks out okay, we said he could have a room here. It's only a five minute walk from where you'll be living, quicker on a bike, and never mind his room will be his own private space, where he can do what he likes, you'll be able use the pools too, won't you?"

"Oh, wow! I've got to have died and gone to heaven, I must have done, you really are angels!"

"Your turn to be an angel will come, one day."

"I really hope so. I'd love to be able to do what you do."

"You will. Apparently, finding angels has become difficult of late," said Kelvin. "There's a shortage of young people to take over from those who are fast getting too old to be doing the active stuff. It's a big worry for some."

"Why has it become difficult?"

"Society has changed. We're now living in an age of 'Look at me, aren't I wonderful?' They reckon next to nobody is who they really are anymore. On and off their phone, today they're a posed selfie, and as for their emotions, how can you tell what they are? When you see an emotion, is it real or are they still pursuing their selfie act, playing out how they want others to see them? It's become impossible to work out what their true morals are, and the moral fibre of someone is very important to us."

"Morals? But what about me? Look what I've been doing."

"You've only done what you've had to do to get by. You're able to accept your lot in life, you wouldn't do anyone down to improve it, and you're not vain. We know the real you."

Hunter said, "If you want to square it with Teresa's beliefs, according to her, society's morals change with the wind, they are nothing more than the fashion of the day, but the morals of us and angels never change. She says you've done nothing to worry about. Mary Magdalene was one of Jesus' favourite people, and she was a prostitute."

"Blinking heck! She was, wasn't she?"

"Don't ask us, we're a bit shaky on religious things."

"Er, there's something I don't get. Why would Teresa and Den want to go back and buy Cracker? Is it because of me?"

"It's because of both of you, really. We'd told them of your feelings for him, and coming round from the anaesthetic, his ramblings left the world and its partner in no doubt of how he felt about you. Apparently, they could've been straight out of a Mills & Boon book, although I'm not sure they publish gay novels. You'll find out soon enough, when it comes to Teresa and Den, love rules all, okay? They came to an easy decision, you two *have* to be able to see each other."

"Oh, wow, they're really nice people, aren't they? Have they always been . . ? What are you really? You might be like them, but I can't keep saying angels."

"We're cups of tea, we make things better."

"Cups of tea?"

"We work for a secret organisation called Cup of Tea, or CoT, and making things better is what we do, but as that's a secret, you'll keep it under your hat, won't you?"

"I swear it, I will. Oh, wow, a secret organisation!"

"Yes, and to answer your earlier question, Teresa and Den have been CoT agents for roughly twenty-five years. Teresa was raised in a small charitable home run by Roman Catholic nuns, which might be why she doesn't like them, and Den was in foster care when he ran away and joined a circus."

"He joined a circus?"

"Not officially. He was thirteen then, but they took pity on him and he helped out. By the time he was sixteen, and it was legally okay for him to be there because he earned enough to feed himself and had a roof over his head, he'd learned how to be a trapeze artist and a high wire performer, and he was doing public shows. It's why he's called Daredevil Den."

"How did they meet? Did Teresa join the circus?"

"No, Teresa trained to become a theatre nurse, and one day she went to the circus after work with a group of nurses. You could say he fell for her; literally."

"He fell? What, from the trapeze?"

"From the high wire. The story goes, it was at the end of his act, and he'd just got across the wire and back with a tray of drinks on his head while riding on a unicycle, when instead of coming down normally, he deliberately fell into the net."

"Why did he deliberately fall?"

"So say, it doesn't usually happen, there's far too much to concentrate on, but he'd caught sight of Teresa while riding the unicycle, and she'd affected him in such a way that he couldn't slowly sail down the rope afterwards with an arm outstretched seeking applause, not in the tights he had on. By falling, he only had to roll off the net and his assistant was there to wrap him in his cloak. Anyway, after changing into his normal clothes, he went back into the tent, sat down next to Teresa, and chatted her up."

"Oh, wow, that's whacky! It's like a fairy story."

"Well, it's funny you should say that, a fairy did turn up for the next performance," Hunter said, laughing.

"Eh?"

"Needing someone with no fear of heights for a one-off job, Greg had had Den checked out and he'd passed as okay. So, after that next performance, he went to his caravan and made him an offer he thought he couldn't refuse."

"And he didn't refuse it, he took the job?"

"Not straightaway. He said it sounded a bit shady, and he'd only do it if Teresa said it was okay for him to do it, and that stumped Greg. There hadn't been a Teresa when the checks were done. So, everything had to be put on hold while he had Teresa checked out. But for Den to feel he ought to have her permission after only one meeting, he's got to be the king of chat-up lines, hasn't he?"

"He must be good. I guess she checked out alright, said it was okay, and he did it, then?"

"Almost, except after learning about Teresa, Greg changed the offer to one neither of them could refuse; a house, cars, a large bank account, and jobs for both for life. He didn't know it, but so serious was Den about Teresa, he'd already planned to stay behind when the circus moved on at the end of the week, not knowing how he'd support himself."

"Blinking heck!"

"Although Greg could've had that job done cheaper, he still did well out of the deal. Those two are so good at what they do, they've become indispensible. About a month after Den undertook that first job they were married, and nine months later along came Donny."

"I hope I can match up to Donny."

"You'll never do that, so don't try," Kelvin said. "Just keep on being you. There's something about you they like, and it's not going to be him. You can bet on it, in their minds, there couldn't be another Donny."

"What do you think it is they like?"

"Well, I reckon the crucifix you wear is a big clue. It says a lot about you. If you can still be wearing it after having to do some of the things you've had to do, you've got to have faith by the bucketload."

"Oh, of course! It's lucky I stopped to put it back on before I went to see why my punter had run off, isn't it?"

"Yeah, but was it luck or was it something else again? I'm still finding it hard to believe, of all the Louts it could have been, we turned back and picked up Cracker. The weird does seem to happen a lot for you, doesn't it? Er, why do you call him Cracker? Does he like taking crack or something?"

"No, don't laugh, his real name's Crawford Jacobs, and as both Crawfords and Jacobs make cream crackers, everybody calls him Cracker."

"That takes the biscuit," joked Hunter.

"Do you know what he was saying when he was coming round? The Mills & Boon stuff?"

"Not exactly, only medical staff were allowed to be in with him then," Hunter replied. "Nobody can understand how he made it half way across London with his wounds. It was a young Lout called Squirrel, checking out what had happened to the Bobbysocks, who found him slumped unconscious in the hotel's car park, and he ran back and told Teresa. It looks as if Cracker thought you were buried under the rubble."

Sandy's eyes dampened, and he wiped them. "Oh, no! Why would he think that?"

"I don't know, but they found him passed out in a position to suggest he'd been kneeling at the time, and according to Teresa, who was at his bedside, it tallies up with what he was babbling as he came round. We didn't get it verbatim, but it was along the lines of him pleading to die, and how it'd be so easy for God to do because he was already half dead. It was probably what he was saying as he'd passed out. Telling God how much you meant to him, and how he didn't want to live without you, he was trying to come up with a million and one reasons why he should die."

There was nothing that could have stopped it. With a long sniff, Sandy's bottom lip went, and his damp eyes turned into waterfalls, flooding down his face.

Hunter and Kelvin dived onto the bed to comfort him.

***

It hadn't come as a surprise when Teresa and Den had told Curly and Dead-eye Dick they were going back to check out Cracker's home life that they'd said they'd go along for the ride. CoT was like a big family, and that bond never stronger than amongst those who made up the armed crews.

With Teresa driving Berty Bus, they turned into Leckington Rye Road a little after midday, and it was a whole different place. Either some of the Hooray Henries had phoned the police while on their way to work, telling them of the bodies, devastation, and most of the Louts being gone, or the police had worked it out for themselves that it was pretty safe for them to return. The road was blocked off a hundred yards or so before where the Bobbysocks had once stood, and there were police officers, and cars with blue flashing lights, armed response officers, forensic teams dressed in white coveralls, and ambulances and paramedics seemingly everywhere they looked. There were even blokes from United Utilities filling in a hole in the road, where as the flames had gone, they'd no doubt disconnected the gas supply to the hotel.

"For fucksake, love, take the next left," Den said. "I've not seen coppers looking so frightened. That armed response unit is a murder waiting to happen."

"They were probably out in the thick of it last night, love."

"Exactly, and it's obvious they're not up to it. None of that lot should have been allowed anywhere near a gun today."

Turning left into Cross Street, that crossed all the parallel roads, Teresa laughed, "Yes, they do remind you of Noddy is playing soldiers, don't they? Oh, look, isn't that Squirrel with a couple of his mates waving us down on the next corner?"

"That's him alright. Did you find out why the others call him Squirrel?" asked Den.

"Yes, I did, actually. Squirrels are a kind of gopher, and as one of the youngest, he's the dogsbody who has to go for this and go for that."

"Oh, that's good, I like it. I must remember that one, love, he and I have something in common."

Pulling up alongside the group of youngsters and opening her window, Teresa didn't have time to respond to the bait.

"Is Cracker oright?" Squirrel asked, wide-eyed in hope.

"Yes, he's fine, he's making a good recovery. I'm glad we bumped into you, we've come back to see his stepmother, but he's told us there's no hope of her opening the door. Do you think she might open it for you?"

"Wodja wanna go there for?" asked one of the other lads.

"Yeah, yer dowanna go there," said another boy. "Mandem don't go there. She'd a dirty Gerty."

"A dirty Gerty?"

"Er, he means it ain't always clean. If ya steps in it, it won't be dog muck," explained Squirrel. "They ain't gotta dog."

"Good God! She's that bad an addict? It's a shit pit?"

"Yeah, didn't fink you'd know 'bout them," said Squirrel.

"Oh, I've heard of them, but fortunately I've never had to meet one. And Cracker has to live like that?"

"Nah, he goes in the backdoor for da barfroom, but he gotta pad outside in da shed, an' he keeps it clean. Wevver's okay now, but in da winter, it's gotta be bad as sleeping rough."

Teresa shook her head in despair. "So, do you think she'd open the door for you? It's a bottom flat, isn't it? What about if you were to knock on the window?"

"Nah, ya got no hope. She's probably still outa it wiv some pigs in there, an' I don't mean feds. She'll kick 'em out 'bout tea time, when she gotta go out an' get anuvver fix. Be sure ta catch 'er then."

"Well, thanks for your help, boys. We'll still have to give it a try, though. Oh, and don't worry about Cracker. He won't be cold this winter. Stay out of trouble, now, won't you?"

"Sure fing!"

With a wave, Teresa drove around the corner, turning right into Gribble Road and parking outside number seventeen. It was a semidetached property that held every promise of what the boys had told them. The top flat had broken windows and looked as if it was empty, while the torn net curtains up at the windows of the bottom one were filthy and doubtless in too bad a state to take another wash, if they'd ever known one. A disgustingly stained mattress took pride of place, on top of all the other rubbish that littered the small front garden.

"My God! How the other half live, eh?" Teresa gasped.

"I hope our health insurance covers us for this," Den said.

"Do we really need to see any more?" asked Curly. "I had to go into a shit pit once, and I can tell you now, it makes you not want to go into another one."

"If we do go in, I'm not sure wiping our feet on the way out will be enough," Dead-eye Dick stated.

"We need to see what it's like for ourselves," said Teresa, opening her door to climb out. "Come along, and don't forget the magic keys."

The magic keys belonged to Dead-eye Dick. A set of small but sturdy tools used to pick locks, they were a memento of his circus days. Circus performers are expected to know more than their own act and be able to step in and cover another, should the need arise. They aren't just the words of a song, it's the way show business works, the show must go on.

Dead-eye Dick had covered the escapologist's act, having to escape from a straightjacket in a padlocked cage before the blazing rope holding it high up in the big top burnt through and he plunged to his death. It was trickery, of course, the padlocks were special ones that didn't have to be picked for real, there was an easy way of opening them, usually done when it seemed all hope of the performer escaping was lost, but even tricks can go wrong. If that one went wrong, and the padlocks didn't spring open when seemingly picked by the paperclip he'd been allowed to hold in his mouth, in reality a feat impossible to do with the size of padlocks used, it wasn't keys he had hidden on him. In case the wrong padlocks had been used, it was a more reliable lock-picking tool. And if it came to having to use it, it paid to know how to pick a lock for real, and hellishly fast. The escapologist he'd covered had come to liking his gin, and as Dead-eye Dick had frequently had to perform his act, he'd practised picking locks until he'd become like greased lightning.

So, when knocking on all the doors and windows didn't get a response, Dead-eye Dick had the backdoor unlocked within seconds. Then, grinning madly, he took several steps back to join Curly, who knowing what to expect had chosen to stand well away. Bravely, it was Teresa who turned the handle and opened the door.

"My God Almighty!" she screamed, almost retching it, and straightaway closing the door again.

"You ought to leave it open to air," Curly said. "If you can get it down to a level you can stand, you won't smell it after a while."

Teresa reopened the door and quickly stood back. "I wasn't planning on staying a while. For the life of me, I don't know how people can live like that."

"I wouldn't exactly call it living, love," said Den.

They gave it ten minutes to air, and then pulling clothing up to cover their noses, they ventured inside. The kitchen was a tip, where on every worktop, in amongst empty beer bottles and cans, half-eaten trays of microwave meals were piled high on top of each other, some of them gone furry. Gingerly, Teresa pushed the living room door open. With the curtains half-drawn, and the filthy nets not letting much light through, it took them a moment to become accustomed to the gloom.

Slowly, they were able to make out a bald, naked man lying full-stretch on the settee. On his back, with his mouth wide open and his throat gurgling, he was testing the furniture to its limits. He had the most enormous stomach any of them could recall seeing in the flesh. With layers of fat flopping off him in every direction, it was difficult to see he wasn't completely naked. Beneath what headed south, the skimpiest of red underpants must have felt like a permanent wedgie.

And then Den pointed to the armchair beside the fireplace, where looking as if they had fallen asleep during copulation, the stepmother was nakedly lying back in the armchair with her legs thrown over the shoulders of an equally as naked bloke. Showing she hadn't done well by choosing him, he'd popped out of his object of desire on falling asleep to slide down onto his knees and snore into her stomach.

"Don't go any further in, love," Den said. "I can see sharps on the floor, in amongst all the dead cans and rubbish."

"Yeah, and it looks like that dog they haven't got has left a present by the other door," said Curly.

"I've seen enough," Teresa said, shutting the door on the scene, and then bundling them outside.

"Not worth giving her money, is it?" Dead-eye Dick asked, while relocking the backdoor.

"No, I reckon she's made more than enough out of Cracker as it is. You can bet she claims benefits to look after him, and it's obvious she's not doing it. No boy should have to suffer a home like that. We owe her nothing."

Chapter Twelve

One-fifteen saw Greg sitting in the Queen's Legs, enjoying the pub's special lunch of the day, a good old-fashioned liver and bacon casserole, while thinking of returning home later that afternoon. Halfway through his meal, his red phone rang.

Greg's red phone ringing told him it was probably going to be the office calling; his London office. Not an everyday call that he would receive on his other phone, this one would be scrambled. He took it out his jacket inside pocket, and seeing the screen bore the legend, 'Top Bell,' he quickly wiped his mouth on the napkin and answered it.

"Toby!" he said, with a laugh. "Missing me, are you?"

"Yes, it's annoying, there's been no one here to throw my paper planes back, but it's not why I called. We've had alien contact, and they'd like it to become of the fifth kind."

"Really? My, my, my, my, my?"

"Yes, MI5, and the man himself. They're shitting bricks up here. Since not long after that shindig where those two clubs were hit yesterday, there's been suspected terrorists moving around on a scale never seen before and they can't keep up with it, they don't have the manpower. The suspicions are, with so many armed police units going down, it would be a good time to carry out an atrocity, but they don't have a clue what it might be."

"And they think we'd know?"

"After having it cleared by the PM, they were hoping to get Johnny Mo to come to their rescue, but I'm afraid he's past anything like that now, all the old gang are," said Toby. "As Kamal put it so succinctly, there comes a time in life when you just can't get your legs up behind your ears anymore."

"He doesn't mince his words, does he?"

"Kamal has never minced. He does keep a close eye on us, though. They all do. They reckon you should give it a poke."

"Me? What in hell could I do? I can't get my legs anywhere near my ears, I'm not *that* far behind them in age."

"I know, but from some of the reports you've put in lately, and especially the one this morning, they reckon you have an affinity with a couple of young guys who can."

"They've read that report already?"

"Yes, and Johnny and Karl agree, that recent recruit and his other half could have been them when they started out."

"They are rather good, I'll grant you that, but they really think they're that good?"

"They do, and there's a way to prove it. Tell them what the job's about and see if they want to do it. When they say yes, bring them to the office at nine o'clock tonight. They'll be needing bow ties if we take them to anyone from MI5. A lot of those clowns have a target painted on their back."

"I never thought there could be another Johnny Mo. I mean, in today's terms, he made billions because there was nobody who could come close to matching him. After it got out that he'd stopped what would have been World War III, countries were outbidding one another to hire him and his crew."

"Yes, I know, but he didn't follow the money, did he? He'd only go for those with a just cause. I find it strange how the world's biggest heroes are the ones it forgets the easiest."

Greg laughed. "Don't let him hear you calling him a hero. I did that when he stopped what was happening to us boys at a church home for boys on Salisbury Plain. I was knee-high to a grasshopper then, and he didn't thank me, I thought he was going to give me a slap. He didn't, of course, he saw to it I got a good home. With MISIC involved, my adoption was all done and dusted in a month, and I couldn't have wished for better parents. Er, tell me, Toby, why are we so eager to be putting our necks on the line for the establishment?"

"Just in case."

"Eh? In case of what?"

"In case before long there shouldn't be an establishment. It could mean there'd be no us too."

"Jumping Jehoshaphat! You think it could be *that* big?"

"Well, the country has taken quite a number of terrorist hits since Johnny and his crew retired and moved onto the island, and nobody has asked for their help with any of them. Being they never sought publicity or did any interviews, next to no one remembers them today, but for MI5 to have dug so deep that they've found someone who does, they must be wearing brown trousers in Thames House."

"You've such an eloquent way of putting things, Toby. I'll be there, the office at nine o'clock, and I'm pretty sure they'll be with me."

"Oh, I'm certain of it. Johnny might be old now, but some things never change. He doesn't know how to be wrong."

"Right, well, in that case, perhaps you'd better make a few more paper planes. I'll see you tonight."

***

Sandy had been watching the clock all afternoon, willing it to go faster. So, at spot on five o'clock, they walked into the room where Cracker was recovering. He was sitting up in the bed, watching television, and if he hadn't had his arm in a sling and his shoulder bandaged, Sandy would have leapt on top of him.

"Don't you go believing what they told you, Slipper," said Cracker. "I don't do no bawling."

"Yes, you do, and they know we've bawled together, I've told them all about us. Don't worry, when I found out what you'd been saying as you were coming round, I peeled a few onions too."

"I thought you was dead, man."

"Nah, I'm not got rid of that easily. Did you know, with a bit of luck, we'll only be living a few minutes apart? I was told I could visit you anytime, your room would be your own private space, and there were swimming pools we could use."

"Straight up?"

161

Sandy giggled, "That's the way you like it, isn't it?"

"Steady on, man. They'll hear you."

"Don't worry, they're the same as us, and they're angels."

"Really? Er, they're angels?"

"Like angels. Some sinners they save, but some are so bad, they have to send them back to their maker to be judged."

"I guess I got lucky, then?"

"No, you just never got to be bad. I told them your biggest fear was being cut up one night by the gang because you still hadn't proved yourself."

"Oh, man, you don't keep nothing back, do you?"

"Why would I, when all they've done for me is give, give, give? Teresa, the nurse with you when you came round, and her husband, Den, are going to be like my mum and dad, and Hunter and Kelvin, over there, are going to be like your big brothers. You wait till you see your house, it's a mansion."

"And it all depends on a bit of luck?"

"Yeah, well, maybe that's only words. I'm pretty sure the wishes of angels don't often get refused. What happened to you? How did you get shot?"

"Oh, man, it all went tits up on the underground, when we changed to get the tube to Piccadilly Circus. We didn't stand a chance, the local gang was waiting for us."

"And they shot you?"

"No, we got off light there. They stole our weapons, gave us a beating and let us go. They had to be ready for the next train. Anyway, it meant I'd nothing on me at the Man Club. When we had to rush in, firing guns and lashing out with knives and machetes, like a load of others, all I could do was flap my arms about and make a lot of noise. Honestly, man, it only needed the Birdy Song."

"And that's when you got shot?"

"Not long afterwards. They was waiting for us too. They'd cleared the club, so for them it was like shooting fish in a barrel. Those of us with no weapons ran back out, and that's when the feds opened fire. It was the feds who shot me."

"It was the police who shot you?"

"Yeah, there had to be well over a hundred there, and more than half of them armed, just waiting for us to come out. I went down straightaway, and that's when our seniors and the General's men opened fire from the car park. Not one fed got away, they wiped out the whole lot, armed and unarmed, and then they moved on. Knowing it wouldn't do to be caught with all them dead coppers, I managed to get up and make it back as far as the Bobbysocks. You knows the rest."

"Blinking heck! Didn't they shout out, 'Stop or I'll fire,' or something?"

"You been watching too much television? Half them are so scared they shoot anyway. It's why they clear the area. If you ain't got a weapon, they'll soon plant one on you, man."

"Only a few coppers would've been bad, but the good ones have to go along with it if something bad happens," Hunter explained. "Since the days of the Peelers, rule number one's always been to close ranks if one of them does wrong."

"With Leckington Louts turning up dead or injured all over the place, the police must've worked out what was going on and they were waiting too," said Kelvin "I've never really liked coppers, but I didn't know some were that bad."

"It's the unofficial rules that are bad, those like you mustn't dob a rogue colleague in," Hunter said. "They're also why so many innocent people go to jail. Once a case gets into court, if evidence should turn up to prove the accused is innocent, those rules say the police have to bury it rather than admit they got it wrong. I know many do, but you mustn't confuse the law with justice, they are two entirely different things."

"Eh?"

"They may say they're Courts of Justice over the door, but they're not, they're Courts of Law where clever people play a game, and whether the accused is guilty or innocent is of no consequence, the cleverest one wins. It means if you're poor you can easily be wrongfully convicted, but if you're stinking rich, and able to afford a top class barrister, you can get away with just about anything. Does that sound much like justice to you? Probably not, but it is the law.”

“Crikey!”

“Cor, I think I’m going to like my big brothers, man.”

“You will, I can guarantee it,” laughed Sandy. “When they sort someone out, they don’t worry about the law, they go all out for justice.”

Greg walked into the room, and looking around, he said, “I thought I’d find you here. I’ve got two bits of good news, and some other news.”

“What’s the good news?” Kelvin asked.

“Teresa and Den are back and getting Sandy’s room ready for tonight. They’ll pick him up here at eight o’clock. And as Cracker’s stepmother was in no fit state to negotiate, and the flat was like a tip, she’ll be getting nothing. They’d prefer it to be here with you two, it’d save them a lot of travelling, but where he wants to live is entirely up to him.”

“No contest! I wants Sandy and my big brothers, man.”

“Then you’ve got them,” Kelvin said, grinning. “Providing there are still no signs of an infection, they told us they’ll be discharging you tomorrow, so you’ll be recuperating in your new home.”

“Oh, wow!” exclaimed Sandy.

“And the other news?” asked Hunter, looking at Greg.

“I’m returning to London tonight; the office, not home. It seems MI5 want a close encounter of the fifth kind.”

“I’ve heard of the third kind, there was that film, but what’s the fifth kind?” asked Sandy.

“An encounter of the fifth kind pretty much means having an eyeball to eyeball meeting,” Hunter explained.

“Blinking heck!”

“And you want us to be there with you, don’t you?” Kelvin asked, excitedly.

Greg blinked, stupidly. “How would you know that?”

“Why else would you have mentioned it? If it wasn’t that, you’d have just said you were going to the office.”

"Yes, well, Toby wants me to ask you if you'd be interested in helping MI5 with a problem they have."

"What kind of problem?" Hunter asked.

"Terrorist related. MI5 reckon there's an unusual amount of activity, more than they can cope with, and they're expecting something big to happen but they don't have a clue what or where. They were hoping Johnny Mo might have been able to give them a few pointers, but saying he was too old now for things like that, he suggested we ask you two."

"Bloody hell!"

"Why would he suggest us?" asked Hunter.

"He sees you in them when they started out."

"But he doesn't know anything about us."

"He knows everything he needs to know. When there are kids living in mud huts in Africa who follow British football teams, technology has made it a very small world."

"So, they all follow what CoT does?" Kelvin asked.

"Until technology became so good that everyone relied on computers, allowing us to finance ourselves, there were a lot years when they were CoT's biggest benefactor."

"I thought it might have been them."

"Yes, and don't forget, although they're not active officers now, Kamal and Tony have both worked for CoT, and Toby is its head honcho today. You see, it's a case of once a CoT member, always a CoT member. Where do you think I found all those people to process the youngsters? Over many years, they have done what we do now. And providing they're still able to get onto their feet, if the bugle sounds, they'll always stand up to be counted."

"Jesus, just how many people are there in CoT?"

"Oh, it's quite an unimaginable number now," Greg said, tapping the side of his nose, and winking.

"Oh, man, this is doing my head in. A camel's worked on a cot, and if you get in it you'll always be in it, and now there's an unimaginable number in it? How big is this cot? And why would anyone wanna get in it? Is it something kinky?"

It took a while for them to get over that.

Eventually, Greg was able to explain everything to Cracker and swear him to secrecy. Sandy then asking Greg if he and Cracker could *both* be members of CoT one day, and his reply of he couldn't see why not, saw the boys hugging so tightly, Cracker came close to popping his stitches. It became abundantly obvious, neither of the lads would ever do or say anything that might put that goal at risk, making Greg feel a whole lot happier about the situation.

"We didn't see any around when we came in, have all the kids been found somewhere to go now?" Kelvin asked.

"It wasn't easy, but it's pretty much sorted," Greg replied.

"Pretty much?"

"We've still got to contact parents or relatives for a couple of gullible from abroad before we send them back, so they're being looked after in a hotel for now, along with the toddlers who'll be flying out Saturday for a life in the sun."

"What about all the others?"

"Old enough to look after themselves for most of the time, they've found homes with some of our members who stood up to be counted. Apparently, once your children fly the nest and have children of their own, if they aren't living nearby, you don't see much of them and it can get a bit lonely."

"Oh, that's brill! And Angelina? Is she okay?"

"Yes, a tearful reunion. Grace and Favour did the handover earlier. Which reminds me, we made a lot out of that job, not only were her parents very generous, we've taken over the General's millions. You'll both need to go to accounts soon."

"Accounts?"

"It's at the end of the storage tunnel," explained Hunter.

"Why have we got to go there?"

"You've got another two bank accounts," Greg said. "And you'll be needing the details to use them."

"We've got *more* money? Why would we have more?"

"You earned it, and we always pay top dollar. Don't knock it. If everything should go tits up for CoT one day, you'll be needing it. You've gone off the government's radar now. I'm afraid there'll be no benefits, or a government pension in old age, for you, but don't worry about it. With the annuity you'll be able to buy, if you even need one by the time you retire, you'll live out your days in comfort."

"Bloody hell! And I've gone off the government's radar?"

Laughing, Hunter said, "After the number of times you ran away from care, I don't think anyone's going to be surprised if they can't find you, do you? To officialdom, it will appear like you've vanished off the face of the planet. Even should someone go looking for you at the address you put down for your driving licence, car registration and passport, they won't find you living there, fruit drop."

"I don't live at number three Pleasant Lane?"

"No, neither do I. We live at number one. Mary and Andy live at number three. They were active agents for CoT until a few years ago, and you see, so we stay off the radar, agents bail one another out with addresses."

"That's devious!"

"As far as officialdom is concerned, our house belongs to Ravel Homes, a company we jointly own now as George and Alfred Ravel, who not only inherited the company registered in Wallee Wupta, but also live in that obscure backwater of India. Accounts see to it that Ravel Homes pays our council tax, our utility bills, and anything else that needs paying. We don't get a mention."

"Crikey!"

"Oh, as they say, and there's more. Wallee Wupta is in fact so obscure that, although documentation exists in India to say the company was legally registered there and the appropriate fee paid in 1944, if anybody went looking for it, they could spend their lifetime searching. As the place doesn't actually exist, they would have to trawl through a mountain of records from the days of the Raj to see if it was one that changed its name on or after the country gained independence, and even then, with so many records destroyed in the civil disputes of that time, still no one could say for definite the place or the company didn't exist. India is an awful big country if you've got to search through every nook and cranny. I reckon most people would just give up looking, don't you?"

"Yeah, I guess so, angel features. I know I would."

Greg said, "Many probably have given up looking. Adding strength to there once being such a place, there are literally thousands of houses in the UK now owned by a property company registered in Wallee Wupta. It's quite surprising what you can buy for a fistful of rupees these days, when you think about it, isn't it?"

"You can say that again!"

"Er, do you think maybe we should adjourn to the cafe and give the lovebirds a bit of space, Greg?" Hunter asked. "I'm not too sure how you'd cope if Cracker was to get discharged before tomorrow."

"Jumping Jehoshaphat! Yes, right, okay, I think perhaps we should," Greg said, immediately rushing out of the door.

"Eh? We're only holding hands under the covers, we're not doing anything," said Sandy, frowning.

"I know, but if you were wishing you were, now you can."

"Oh, man, you's gotta be the bestest big brothers ever!"

Hunter and Kelvin followed Greg out of the room, laughing as they closed the door behind them.

Chapter Thirteen

Hunter drove them to the office, in the Jaguar, with Kelvin riding shotgun and Greg spread out in the back. On arriving there with time to spare, the office wasn't anything like what Kelvin had been expecting. Situated in a Hammersmith side street, apart from having the space to park several cars, it was a very large house not too dissimilar to many other very large properties along there.

Greg explained that being able to park several cars, and the Ravenscourt Park tube station merely a few steps away, had been its two biggest attractions. It was easier to hop onto a tube to get to most of the places they'd want to go in London, rather than spend hours trying to find somewhere to park, and for Heathrow airport and good links to anywhere else, they had the Great West Road and the M4 with all its connections almost on their doorstep. Kelvin guessed it made sense.

With its own entrance, it turned out Toby had a luxury flat that took up the whole of the top floor, with views over the park, and while with its matching window dressings nobody would suspect it from the outside, the remainder of the house was mainly given over to offices. Having seen them arriving, and not yet ready, Toby ran down and invited them up to the flat, where as soon as the introductions were dispensed with, he returned to what he'd been doing with his hairdryer. And it was something that definitely didn't make sense to Kelvin.

"I know you're not Oscar Wilde. Why are you trying to dry a paper carnation you've sprayed green?" he asked.

"Don't ask!" laughed Toby.

"But I did ask. I'll lose sleep over it, if you don't tell me."

"If I said, 'Boy's Own,' you wouldn't have any idea what I was on about, but Greg would, he'll remember it like I do. It was packed full of adventure stories for boys, many of them about spies, and they'd reveal how spies would have to wear something of a particular colour, like a purple tie, or carry a certain newspaper, while standing on one leg and whistling Dixie into the wind, just so they'd be able to recognise one another. Well, I'm sorry to say, things don't appear to have changed much over the years when it comes to MI5. The idiot we'll be meeting tonight wants one of us to be wearing a green carnation."

"No! Really? Are you sure it wasn't a wind-up?"

"Unfortunately, I am sure. All our security services leave a lot to be desired. Why do you think there are so many police programmes on television now? It's the same with the health service and education. If you're not bringing home the bacon, you'd better be good at pumping out propaganda."

"Bloody hell!"

"It's called maintaining public perception," Greg said.

"They're really that bad?" Kelvin asked.

"They aren't the worst in the world by a long way, but like with many things in which the British once excelled, they've slipped a fair old way down the league table," said Toby. "It wouldn't have happened in my father's time."

Kelvin laughed. "Yeah, I remember that from the book. He couldn't half let rip, and he didn't care who to."

"Oh, if you upset him, he's still like that today. He doesn't take excuses, or tolerate fools."

"A lot like you, I'd say, Toby. The apple didn't fall very far from the tree," said Greg.

"Not anymore, I've mellowed with age, something my old man never learned to do. I reckon it's how he'll go, one day, mid-bluster." Toby laughed. "I pictured him keeping up with the videos going up on social media, the ones showing the police being wiped out. Red-faced, his eyes glaring rage and temple veins throbbing, he would have been jumping up and down, thumping a table with his fist, while clouds of steam wafted off him."

"Crikey, he wasn't *that* bad in the book."

"No, but unlike me, he fermented with age."

"Do Tony and Kamal still have something going . . ?"

"You're a nosy one, aren't you?"

"Inquisitive, there is a difference."

"Well, it's no secret. How could it be after that book came out? Yes, they still have something going on. Not so often now, of course, but Kamal still calls my dad Stony because he likes to get stoned, and Kamal is still his can of Heineken; refreshing the parts others cannot reach. And before you ask, my mum's past anything like that now, so on the occasions it happens for Johnny, it's with Karl and Tel, and then after a shower he goes back to her and they cuddle up for the rest of the night. They really are an amazing lot."

"They sure sound like it."

Toby laughed. "Do you know, growing up, I hardly knew a time that someone wasn't having sex in our house? When I was eleven, and they packed me off to boarding school, my biceps were the envy of the dormitory."

"Bloody hell! Er, and you? What happened to you?"

"I turned out straight, if that's what you mean. I married a girl I'd been seeing at a nearby boarding school to mine and we had three boys. Samantha passed away young, the big C, but though the boys are spread around the world now with families of their own, they still call the island their home, and everyone turns up there for Christmas."

"Cor, I'm sorry to hear about Samantha, but I reckon we're going to have to buy ourselves an island in the sun, one day, Hunter. Can you imagine doing it in a beautiful blue lagoon with the wavelets . . ?"

"Just remember I'm sitting here," spluttered Greg. "We're not all bloody rabbits, you know?"

"Sorry, Greg."

"Well, now that Oscar's pretty flower is dry and won't ruin my jacket," Toby said, laughing, and pinning it on the jacket, before putting it on and checking himself in a mirror. "We'd better be making a move. I hope the tube's running okay, we will still have a bit of walking to do when we get there."

"Where are we supposed to meet this clown?" Greg asked, as they hurried down the road to the tube station.

"Unimaginatively, on Lambeth Bridge. He'll walk up to us at ten o'clock on the centre of the bridge. I mean, really! Isn't that just typically stupid? The nearest tube station is Pimlico, so it would have been a lot easier for us to have knocked on the door of MI5 and saved our feet."

"They do like doing all that cloak and dagger stuff," sighed Greg. "But there must be more to it than that."

"Oh, there is. He will ask me if I know London well, and I have to tell him no, but I do know a pick-up line when I hear it. It's some really crazy stuff, isn't it? Anybody would think we were handing over secret information, not just meeting up for a chat."

"Weird, or what?"

"Yeah, I can see I might have to slap my hand across your mouth, fruit drop," said Hunter, laughing.

"Why would you do that?" Toby asked, frowning.

"So he doesn't blurt out something like, 'And now I know what a prat looks like!' Johnny might think he knows us, but it won't be as well as I know Kelvin. Sometimes things will fly out of his mouth without him thinking about them."

"I'm not that bad, angel features."

"Neither of them will suffer fools gladly," said Greg. "And yet I'd say they were both very wise. I suspect St Paul either got that one wrong, or it went wrong during translation."

"St Paul?" Kevin questioned, screwing up his face.

"It was he who coined the saying in his second letter to the Corinthians. 'For ye suffer fools gladly, seeing ye yourselves are wise.' I think you're the living proof, being wise doesn't mean you will necessarily suffer fools gladly."

"Crikey!"

"In that case, don't cover his mouth, Hunter. He might say something I could only dream of saying," said Toby. "Things used to fall out of Karl's mouth like that, still do at times, so maybe Johnny knows you two a lot more than you realise."

Apart from Hunter and Kelvin being given, and told to look after and definitely not lose, Oyster cards that would always work and never need to be topped up, the journey proved to be uneventful, and after a walk that Greg didn't appreciate, they arrived at the centre of the bridge with time to spare.

It was Kelvin who spotted the MI5 guy first. Coming from the direction they had just walked, he had a map in his hand, and as he sauntered across the bridge towards them, he was looking all around, like a tourist might.

"Oh, what a twat!" Kelvin said, laughing. "Who's he think he's kidding? He looks nothing like a tourist. He might have an 'I love London' hat on, but where's his camera and bag of souvenirs? The Houses of Parliament are over there, lit up like a turkey cock's arse, and he's not even got his phone out to take a picture. If that isn't our guy, I'll eat my hat."

"You haven't got a hat," said Hunter.

"No, and I bet I won't have to buy one either."

"He does look as if he's trying to win an Oscar," Toby said, laughing too. "And apart from not being a convincing tourist, I'd say that suit is a dead giveaway."

The man stopped his sauntering on coming up to them, and for a moment he appeared to be studying where his forefinger was on the map, and then frowning, he leaned towards them, saying, "Excuse me, I'm sorry to disturb you, but do any of you happen to know London well?"

Hunter, Kelvin, and even Greg couldn't help himself, they exploded into a roar, staggering about and having to wipe the mirth from their eyes. Toby almost had to shout his expected reply to be heard over them.

"Oh, sorry, sorry, sorry," spluttered Kelvin. "I'm sorry, but that was just so funny."

"Funny?" questioned the man. "You find me funny?"

"Hilariously funny. Your finger was almost in the Thames estuary on that map, and any idiot could tell they were in the centre of London, which is on the other side of where you've folded it. And, anyway, who uses a map today?"

"We've been watching you, and you've had a good look all around several times now. How could you not have seen the Houses of Parliament?" asked Hunter.

"You noticed that?"

"Oh, nothing gets past those two," Toby said. "That's why they're here. Your boss reckons you might need them."

"You spoke to the boss? What, the big boss?"

"He phoned me."

"I didn't know that. No one thought to tell me. I can't say I'm surprised, though. It's been utter chaos since we've had to work with all the other services. They're forever putting new labels on doors, and none of us have a clue who the hell these people are or what they do."

"What *did* they tell you?"

"Only that I had to meet some people on the bridge who could possibly help us with a terrorist threat. Who are you?"

Toby took a business card out of a silver case in his top pocket and handed it to the man. "Tobias Bellingham-Topps is the name, a professor of history and doctor of theology. I am involved in a setup in Hammersmith where we research and correlate historical facts with the stories of religions. One of your lot apparently unearthed the fact my father was with MISIC when it was disbanded, and it was thought I might know if Johnny Mo was still alive. He is, but I'm afraid he's unable to help, he's far too old now, so he recommended you try these two, they work for me."

"Spluttering cauldrons! You're Jesus freaks?"

"No, we're not Jesus freaks, but it sounds to me like you're a Harry Potter freak. The Harry Potter in the books has never existed, but I can assure you, there's indisputable proof that a man called Jesus existed. It's an historical fact. So is it that at the time many said he could do miraculous things. We don't preach anything, it's not our job, we simply join up the dots."

"I don't understand. How could your father have been with MISIC? It was disbanded after it was discovered every one in it was a poofter."

"Yes, I know. I find it unfortunate the monarch has to stay silent. If that wasn't the case, we'd still have MISIC today, and MI5 and MI6 would still be the envy of the world. It was MISIC that earned them that accolade, a load of poofters, and it was thrown away on a prejudice."

Staring at Toby, with his head shaking haughtily, the man retorted, "I don't have anything against gay people."

"No, nobody does. That's why so many still get done over and live in fear. My father's gay. I'm the result of a finding out what he was experiment at university, but that didn't stop him being the best father in the world. He was also the best officer MISIC had, the one in charge when the establishment turned on it."

"Spluttering . . . Er . . . I mean, really?"

"Yes, it had long been known the secret services had more than their fair share of gay men working in them, and though employing them had been against the rules, a blind eye had always been turned, but finding out a bunch of them were in charge proved to be too much for some people."

"I didn't know that."

"There were some in that bastion of the establishment, the House of Lords, who were horrified to find out about MISIC, and they threatened to expose everybody in it was gay. With gay sex in the early seventies only recently having been made legal, gay people were okay to make fun of, or even to have working for you, but to have a bunch of them in charge, and with so much power that they only answered to the monarch, that put a lot of pompous noses out of joint."

"I didn't know MISIC only answered to the monarch."

"No, it really was *the* secret service. I doubt if you know all its directives were stamped, '*Without Question.*' It never saw the need to interfere with a government once, but had it still been around at the time, I doubt it would've allowed us to be taken into Iraq on a wild goose chase. The world might have been a very different place today."

"It had that much power?"

"Yes, amongst all its many responsibilities, it was there to protect the establishment, and should the need ever arise, the steady hand to grab the tiller. Have you ever wondered what would happen if there was the threat of an imminent nuclear attack and we had a prime minister who'd let it be known he wouldn't press the button? It's not an impossible situation to be in if the present government should fall, is it? In the time it'd take to replace the prime minister, it could easily be too late, we could all be dust. I think we'd better hope we don't come to regret losing that steady hand, don't you?"

"When you put it like that, yes, definitely. But why did they all have to be gay?"

"I doubt if they would all be gay today, we live in different times. Back then, gay guys had to look out for one another a lot more than they do now, it's why they were often referred to as family. And when it came to trusting somebody to have their back, it was safer to trust family."

The next couple of minutes were taken up with the rest of the introductions, and then, after Greg had complained about standing about on the draughty bridge, saying his legs might not work if they stayed there much longer, the man took them to a bar, not far from the south side of the bridge. The subject of humour between Kelvin and Hunter, they swapped several giggly looks, the man told them he was 'RS', explaining how they were the initials of his name, Roger Sole, which as they never used them in his department, was not his real name. It was difficult, but they managed to resist saying, 'Pleased to meet you, Mr. R. Sole,' satisfied they had a good idea what at least one of his superiors thought of him.

Without so much as one sign outside, the basement bar was not only easily missed, the two gorillas in suits, guarding the door, left them in no doubt it was exclusive. It was a strange setup. Though it was nothing special inside, the prices alone would have excluded most people, making the gorillas seem superfluous. They ordered their drinks, RS signed a chitty, and they took them to a circular table in the corner, where the

CoT members quickly grabbed the more comfortable wall seating, leaving RS to perch on one of the low stools. Plainly, he didn't like his back towards the door, forever looking over his shoulder, but he didn't complain or ask to move.

"So," Toby said, "I was told more suspected terrorists were moving around since those clubs were targeted than you had the manpower to watch, and there was a suspicion they might be taking advantage of so many police being knocked out and were about to commit an atrocity. I have noticed it still hasn't been officially confirmed any police were killed."

"No, and it's not likely to be confirmed. The story is, it was the Russians spreading fake news on social media."

"You're frightened a snowball might grow until it becomes too big to handle? Just how many police *were* lost?"

"Three hundred and nineteen at the last count, most of them armed, and with casualties in hospitals all over the place, the death toll is expected to rise. Don't believe the hype, London has never had two thousand armed officers available. It lost a third of what it did have last night. With holidays, sickies and shift work to cover, it's in trouble, and if that became public knowledge, every scrote with a gun would be on the streets with it. Did you know there's probably more than ten times the number of illegal firearms in London alone than the police have for the whole of the UK? You can imagine their morale. Resignations and sickies are off the scale."

"And the troops are on standby, are they?"

"Yes, but the generals aren't happy about it. Soldiers didn't enlist to kill their own. There is a fear that they might go over the government's head."

"An appeal to the Queen?"

"She is the vested head of our armed services, and to whom they pledge their allegiance. The government only controls them under a Royal Prerogative. If push were ever to come to shove, they are the Queen's troops."

"Bloody hell, talk about shit and fan!" Kelvin gasped. "Er, you might not have enough agents to watch all the suspects, but what about those you have been able to watch? Where have they been going?"

"Some have left the country for the usual destinations such as Turkey and Pakistan, but most have gone to towns in the north of England, with quite a few moving to Scotland."

"Moving? So they've not just taken a trip, they've actually moved home, like lock, stock and barrel?"

"Many aren't what you'd call materialistic, they don't go in for possessions, but it would seem so. Annoyingly, it means they can put everything into a couple of bags and a suitcase and just move on. Even when we're watching them, it's not uncommon to discover they've done a moonlight flit over the back fence."

"You don't watch front and back?"

"Not for most, we don't, only the ones we're really worried about. We simply don't have the manpower. There are over twenty thousand people of interest to us, you know?"

"Crikey! There's that many roaming around?"

"Yes, so imagine how many agents we'd need to watch all of them around the clock, front and back. It can't be done."

"I guess you already had agents in the north and in Scotland watching suspects, but have you added to them by sending up all those in the south whose targets have moved up there?"

"Yes, and it wasn't easy to do at such short notice, but MI5 and others have had to make huge commitments to bolster what we had up there. We've sensitive areas up north and in Scotland, including the Faslane nuclear submarine base."

"Oh, well, at least they should be safe."

"Safe? What do you mean, safe?"

"I don't think they've worked it out, fruit drop. Least of all our MI5 friend here," said Hunter.

"No, I don't think they have either, and that's frightening."

"Worked what out?" RS demanded, almost angrily.

"What's frightening?" asked Greg, a puzzled look creeping over his face. "Do you know what's going on?"

"Haven't you worked it out?" Hunter asked.

"It doesn't look like any of them have, angel features. I'm not sure they're going to believe us."

"Let's not turn this into a three act play," Toby said. "What is it we're missing?"

"The atrocity won't be in the north," Kelvin explained. "It will happen in the south, probably in London. And as they've gone that far to get away from it, I reckon it will be a nuclear bomb. Any other type would be survivable much closer, but not one with a nuclear blast and radioactive fallout."

"Jumping Jehoshaphat! Are you sure?"

"It seems the most logical explanation to me. It's got to be something enormous for them to move that far away. A nerve agent would disperse long before it got out of London, and anything like poisoning the water supply wouldn't see them moving, they'd just avoid drinking it and buy bottled water."

"I wish Johnny wasn't always right," Toby sighed, shaking his head. "He said they would work it out."

"You believe them?" RS asked, wide-eyed.

"Yes, that explanation does sound logical, and if you don't believe it, you'll be gambling with millions of lives."

"But most of the suspects don't know each other. How did they get wind of something like that happening? What would make all of them move at the same time? It wasn't anything by phone or email, we do keep a close eye on them."

"If they don't all know each other, there must be something they have in common," Kelvin said. "My guess is a website or a social media page, one you don't know is sympathetic to their cause, where things appear that make sense to them but not to you, like the radio messages broadcast during the war. Something along the lines of: London's climate will soon be too hot for ducks. Sensible ones are flying north to nest."

RS froze for a moment, and then he pulled his phone out, selected the top name in his list of contacts, and as soon as it was answered, he blurted, "Rachel, RS here. There's a group of people I'm bringing in who've convinced me we might have a mango call. You're going to have to hit the button."

"Crikey! Mango is your code for an attack on London?"

"It covers it. Hitting the button will see Communications getting a message to some top brass, telling them to attend an immediate meeting. Come along, they won't hang about, we need to make a move," RS said, standing up and hurrying for the door.

Greg groaned, he wasn't sure his legs would hurry, or even make it to Thames House, but they did and they were met by six men in suits. Not having to be processed and presented with visitors' passes, as the group had expected, at a cracking pace, the suits almost fast-marched them upstairs to the room where the meeting was being held. Looking very much like an old-fashioned boardroom, with a highly-polished wooden table surrounded by chairs, the six men in suits left them with the five men in suits who were sitting around the table at the far end. Kelvin found it funny, and bit his tongue, wondering if there was a tailor somewhere around there doing a job lot price on suits; they all looked pretty much the same.

The one at the head of the table invited them to sit down at the other end, and once the introductions were over, where all the suits made a note of their names on notepads in front of them, RS explained Kelvin and Hunter's theory. It turned out the only name they needed to remember was the one at the head of the table. He was Philip Silvers, a name that had seen both Greg and Toby stifling a chuckle, and he asked all the questions, while it seemed the other four were just there to debate the answers with him when invited, although debate might be too strong a word. Agreeing with him on just about everything, as frequently happens at board meetings, it soon became obvious, they had brown-nosing down to an art.

"And you have nothing as evidence for any of this?" Philip asked. "It's all purely conjecture? Based on what?"

"Sherlock Holmes," replied Kelvin.

"Sherlock Holmes?" blustered Philip, blinking stupidly.

"Yes. If you eliminate the impossible, whatever remains, no matter how improbable, it must be the truth."

"And what impossible have you eliminated?"

"An atrocity happening up north or in Scotland. Terrorists aren't stupid. They'd know a mass migration north would be noticed, and that you'd throw everything you had up there, making that goal pretty much impossible. It's the very last thing they'd do, draw attention to themselves if they were out to commit an atrocity up north. And anyway, if there are so many that you can't keep track of them, there's no atrocity, or even several atrocities at the same time, that would need a number like that to carry them out. It doesn't take many guys to plant a few bombs, or to shoot hundreds of people. So, as it's plainly not that, it seems logical to me, they've moved to get away from something, and though a nuclear bomb might seem improbable, I can't for the life of me think of anything else that would make them go that far. Can you?"

Stunned into silence momentarily, the man proved when it came to blinking stupidly, he could outdo Greg.

"They wouldn't have all have moved north at the same time for no good reason," added Hunter. "I wouldn't rule out the big bang being in the next day or so."

"But a nuclear bomb? You can't just make a nuclear bomb, it's precision stuff. And anyway, if it was of a size that they needed to go that far, I think we'd have known about it. You don't just toddle along to the shops and buy the kind of stuff that's needed to make a nuclear bomb."

"How about a ready-made one bought from a country that doesn't like us?" asked Kelvin. "Russia is good at denials."

"Eh?"

"It wouldn't be beyond terrorists to sneak one in through a container port, and move the container around on the back of a lorry just like any other container. According to a television programme I saw, Gravesend doesn't open or even X-ray most containers, like you, they don't have the manpower. It's why so many drugs come into the country that way. Dealing with loads of perishable stuff, it has a very fast turnaround, meaning there's not much chance of them being detected."

"Holy Mary, mother of God! Have you any idea just how many containers go in and out of that terminal every day?"

"No, but I bet it's a lot."

"Assuming you're correct, how would we find a container with a bomb in it? If they're unable to check them all, I can't see how we could do it."

"But you wouldn't have to check them all, only those that have left there and are parked somewhere sensitive with not a lot happening to them. The terrorists wouldn't have run until the bomb's container was parked up where someone wanted it to be and they were ready to use it."

"I think you might need to wake up whoever scrutinises all those military satellite images," Hunter said. "I know MISIC could, Jenkins had half the British airforce and navy out one night when Johnny Mo and his team shot a traitor, a spy, and the Russian agents who'd come in a submarine to sneak them out of the country, and he had the army out when they found Hitler had survived the war and was addressing a Nazi group near Salisbury, but can MI5 do things like that?"

"No, it can't, but when there are extenuating circumstances, I can bypass the Home Secretary and phone the PM."

"Before you do, you might want to know why the suspects are moving now," said Kelvin. "I reckon it's because that trailer is parked somewhere it became difficult to get to, but it'll be easier now the police will be spread thinner. It's going to be near an armed police presence, like Downing Street, the Houses of Parliament, the government offices in Whitehall, or somewhere like that. It could've been there for some time because after the Westminster Bridge carnage and the copper being killed by the Houses of Parliament, more armed police were deployed and it became difficult to get to. If that's the case, it will have been there for so long now, no one notices it anymore, it's become like a local landmark."

"It does makes sense, I suppose, but if you two are involved in boring stuff like correlating theology with historical facts, how do you manage to fathom out things like that?"

"Protein is said to be good for the brain, and we don't waste any of ours, we recycle it," Kelvin said, grinning devilishly.

Fighting with a giggle, Hunter thumped him, Toby quickly hid his face in his hands, Greg did his best to remain aloof, and not understanding, RS and the five other suits exchanged questioning looks.

Finally, Philip said, "I don't think we got any of that."

"Lucky you. Not that you'd stand a chance with us, I doubt if you'd want any," said Kelvin. "It's family stuff."

Drawing in a long breath, Toby thumped the table with his fist, and then with his eyes streaming, he buried his head in his arms folded in front of him on the table, his shoulders lurching. It was enough to see Greg's aloofness on the brink of taking a tumble. Looking all around the room, he began searching for something to steal his mind away, knowing if he didn't find anything, he'd soon be in a similar state. And Hunter wasn't faring any better. Only a hand clamped tightly over his mouth was holding back a bellow.

Seeing all this strange behaviour promoted another round of questioning looks amongst the suits. And then, perhaps not as stupid as they had suspected, RS suddenly found the word 'family' ringing in his ears. He stood up and walked almost apologetically to the other end of the table, and he whispered the explanation into Philip's ear. The man's eyes opened up wider with every word, and were it not for the return of his stupid blinking, they might well have fallen out.

While RS gave them another performance of a silly stooped walk, returning to his chair, Philip loudly cleared his throat and said, "For the benefit of anyone here as ignorant as I was, I'm told our two young friends are comedians, and possibly good friends of Dorothy. In the context it was said just now, RS has informed me that protein and family stuff are both what we'd call semen."

Thinking maritime — what else in the surroundings? — the other suits looked at each other again, frowning.

It was a gift.

"Oh, do come on, you lot! It really cannot be *that* hard for you to swallow," Kelvin blurted, manically.

The explosion erupting from the CoT team was very loud, immediate, and painful for their stomach muscles. While the suits looked on in amazement, they howled.

"Oh, sorry, sorry," gasped Kelvin, eventually. "I'm sorry, I couldn't resist it. You ask the stupidest of questions. How do we fathom out things like that? How do you think we fathom them out? We use our brains, of course. Maybe some of you ought to try it."

"Yes, perhaps we should," Philip said, staring at each of his team in turn, before looking at Toby. "If there's nothing else we've missed, nothing any of you want to tell us about, RS will see you out. I'm off to ring the Prime Minister. When it comes to kingdom come, I'm not sure all of us would like to be blown there just yet."

"Crikey, you made a joke?"

Chapter Fourteen

To save Greg's legs, they decided to take a black cab back to Hammersmith. It was a funny kind of journey. The driver kept looking in his mirror at them with suspicion. Anytime one of them thought back to Kelvin's hilarious wind-up, they couldn't avoid having a chuckle, and as that would start the others off, it probably came as some relief for the cabbie that Toby paid the fare.

"Are you coming up for a nightcap?" Toby asked, laughing, as the taxi sped off into the night. "I know Greg will, he can smell it in Chestnut Dale if I take the top off the gin."

"You shouldn't buy such good gin," Greg laughed. "I can't get it in my neck of the woods."

"Plymouth Navy Strength?" asked Kelvin.

"How would you know that?" Toby asked, frowning. "You couldn't have seen it earlier, the drinks' cabinet is never open unless I'm using it."

"There's no mystery. It was in the book. It's what Johnny's father drank, only the best, so I guessed it had been passed on from father to son and on down the line, that's all."

"You remember what he drank from that book?"

"Yes, I'm good at remembering things, though not as good as Kamal. I couldn't tell you the page number and the line on which it gets mentioned, but I do remember it was relevant to Johnny's first case, and it was Plymouth Navy Strength."

"How extraordinary."

"We couldn't blame you if you were, but you two are not thinking of hotfooting it to Scotland, are you?" asked Greg.

"Don't be silly," Kelvin laughed. "Now they know what to look for, they'll find that container before morning."

"Do you really think so?"

"Yes, an evacuation of London is out of the question, not only impossible in the time, it would see panic on the streets, tying up thousands who could be doing better things. They'll keep the lid on it and have everybody they can muster out tonight. All the armed forces, the police and secret services, vicars, church wardens, adult choir members, the army, navy and airforce cadets, and even the scouts and boys' brigade, will be searching and phoning in every container they spot."

"With so many looking, it won't take long to find," Hunter said. "There's not likely to be many containers near buildings needing armed police. It would still flatten London and turn it into a no-go area for decades if it was parked in a million other places, but that's where ground zero will be, where it says our ways are wrong, and by whatever they hold dear, they're able to access our very highest places of government to destroy them. They wouldn't use a nuclear bomb unless it was to make the biggest statement ever, one for all who don't believe in their ways to heed."

"You two are like Johnny Mo rides again," said Toby.

"Don't be daft," Kelvin said. "It's only common sense."

"Yes, but not that common today. So, are you all coming up for a drink?"

Hunter and Kelvin conferred, and then Hunter said, "Yes, thanks, but we'd better only have soft drinks. Kelvin suspects you may get another call from MI5 tonight."

"Why would they call us again?" Toby asked, leading them up to the door and unlocking it.

Kelvin explained, "Finding the bomb won't be the end of it, they'll have to make it safe, and I doubt if the bomb disposal guys get a lot of practice defusing nuclear bombs, especially of the type that one will be."

"Type? What type?"

"It won't be like one that's dropped from a plane, or found on the head of a long-range missile. It'll probably be in a big steel box with an electronic countdown that's just waiting to be started, and like as not it will be booby-trapped to go off if it's moved or tampered with. Never mind it'd be too risky to try and defuse it, I doubt they'll have seen any like it."

"And you know how to defuse it?"

"No, of course not. But I've an idea what to do with it."

"What?"

"As it was driven there, moving the bomb must be relevant to inside the container, not to where the container is located, so it needs to be lifted onto a trailer, driven to an airfield and put into a transporter plane that takes big things like tanks, and then dropped into the middle of the Atlantic Ocean, away from the shipping lanes. If it goes off on hitting the water, it won't do much damage there, and if it doesn't, in time the seawater will probably rot it until it's no longer a threat. Er, so the plane can get away if it does go off, they might need to put parachutes on the container and drop it from as high as they can get. I don't think transporter planes go very fast."

"Now I know it for sure. You will have my job one day."

"That's if he doesn't get mine first," said Toby. "His nibs at MI5 might wonder how I managed to get his number, but I'll have to risk it. I'll give him a call and tell him what Kelvin's just said. I'd really hate to see it all go wrong now we've got this far. It was only last week I bought a new box of gin."

"You buy a box of gin at a time?" Hunter asked.

"Yes, why not? It's not going to go off, is it?"

"What he's politely not telling you is that he has to buy it by the boxful with me around. He will drink it, but he doesn't particularly like gin himself," Greg chuckled. "He's more of a whisky and wild, weird women kind of guy."

"Wild, weird women?" Hunter questioned, frowning.

"It's some people's idea of a joke," Toby explained, with a sigh. "I once needed someone to take to a dinner engagement where I was giving a talk, and the demented lot I work with here set me up with somebody they found on an online escort agency, supposedly unaware it was one for transvestites."

"Crikey, you took a bloke in a dress with you?"

"No, I didn't dare. Nothing at all like the photograph, what arrived on the doorstep was a giant of a man in drag, thickly trowelled in layers of makeup, as hairy as a gorilla, and with hands the size of dinner plates. The dinner had been arranged by one of the churches, and it would be full of the clergy, so it wasn't exactly the kind of do where I *could* bowl up with a pantomime dame."

"Bloody hell!"

"It's not I've got anything against transvestites, I haven't and I never will have, just as long as nobody expects me to go to a select dinner party with one that'd make Cinderella's ugly sisters look good. I've never forgiven them."

"What did you do?"

"I told the guy the dinner had been cancelled, paid him his fee, and went on my own. He seemed happy enough."

"That suit of armour sure does get around, doesn't it?" said Hunter, laughing as they went into the lounge and sat down.

"Yeah, it's good fun, though, isn't it?" laughed Kelvin.

Toby sighed again, saying, "I'd better give his nibs at MI5 a ring now. No messing about while I'm on the phone, eh?"

"No, of course not," said Kelvin. "But before you do, I've just thought of something that's likely important."

"What?"

"When the container was dumped wherever it is, it couldn't have been seen to stick out like a sore thumb, it would've had to have fitted in with its surroundings. Looking like it's a tool store for some building work, or renovations, perhaps?"

"Big Ben's had scaffolding up it for yonks," Hunter said.

"Yes, I think it's one of the first places I'd look. It's hardly any distance from where that police officer was killed and they tightened up the armed police patrols. In fact, I'm pretty certain the workmen working on the clock and tower would use that entrance. In which case, it's possible the Houses of Parliament could think the container had been put there by the men doing the renovations, while they could think it had something to do with other work going on in the Houses of Parliament. I know they're forever repairing the roofs. Many of them are said to leak like a sieve, but as sometime in the not too distant future a major renovation is planned for the whole lot, with parliament moving somewhere else for a few years, they only bodge them up for now.”

“And you’ve just thought of all that? What, while you were laughing about my dinner engagement?”

“Yes, why wouldn’t I? I can think of more than one thing at a time, can’t you?”

“Not if the things are poles apart like that, I can’t.”

“Toby had a pretty normal childhood, fruit drop. Following up more than one train of thought at a time doesn’t work for everyone. We can do it because we’ve *had* to do it.”

“Silly me! With so many like us in CoT, I’d forgotten he’d had a pretty good childhood.”

“Take my word for it, Kelvin. No one could ever accuse either you or Hunter of being silly,” said Greg. “And after the performance you’ve given tonight, I’m now inclined to agree with Toby. Johnny Mo does ride again, only this time round there are two of him.”

“Bloody hell, Greg, don’t embarrass us.”

“Yes, steady on there, we’d prefer our heads to stay the size they are now, thank you very much. Besides, have you ever seen a remake of a film that’s been anywhere near as good as the original? As much as I admire Johnny Mo, if one day we should do something memorable, I’d like it to be for us doing it, not for us being like someone else.”

“That’s how I see it too, angel features.”

Shaking his head, Toby said, “I shouldn’t argue with them, Greg. Dragons are strange beasts. I’d say it’s the very same dragon, but now it goes by two other names.”

“Crikey, you don’t actually believe there are such things as dragons, do you?” Kelvin asked, with a look of disbelief.

“Well, you might like to know, the formula we abide by in our historical research prohibits us saying conclusively that there’s never been dragons. It’s the same with many of the miracles attributed to Jesus Christ. The number of reputable people who made a record of seeing them exceeds by more than ten times the number we’d have to see unpassed to write them off. That formula easily writes-off just about everything else of fable, so we have no logical reason to suspect it might be wrong. In fact, tests found if we tweak it to even a quarter of the way to writing-off dragons, it begins to write-off most of what we *know* to be true of today."

"That's weird!"

"It's certainly something we don't understand."

"There are more things in heaven and earth, Horatio, than are dreamt of in your philosophy," laughed Greg.

"Huh?" Hunter frowned.

"It's Shakespeare," Kelvin explained. "It's from Hamlet. I haven't read it, but it's one of the quotes I remember."

"Very good," said Toby. "If you can accept there are things we shall never understand, you will live a happier life. There isn't proof for everything, sometimes you need faith."

"Crikey, Sandy would love you!"

Toby made the phone call. It turned out to be an extremely long one, unbelievably long, where many people at the other end were being called on to rush around excitedly using their phones, and they sat throughout it in silence. Finally, the call ended, and putting his phone away, Toby said, "Officers at the Palace of Westminster have just discovered a container parked where you said, almost under the Elizabeth Tower, or Big Ben to most people."

"Bloody hell! I hope they aren't poking about inside it."

"No, they won't open it, Bomb Disposal is on its way."

"How do you know they won't?"

"Those officers have sophisticated equipment. One bit also now used in many airports, a radiation detector about the size of a mobile phone, is going off the scale if they get anywhere near the container."

"It's leaking radioactive stuff?"

"Probably not enough to harm anyone unless they sat on it for a few weeks, the detectors are ultra-sensitive. Apparently. they can go off if someone with a thyroid condition has taken radioactive medicine in the last week or so."

"Crikey!"

"The PM's called a COBRA meeting for first thing in the morning, if we're all still here, and the RAF at Brize Norton is currently checking the feasibility of your idea of dropping the container into the middle of the Atlantic."

Hunter laughed, "Wouldn't it be funny if it turned out to be a consignment of luminous watches?"

"Bog off! We'd be the laughing stock of the world!"

"I can't see anybody parking a load of watches there, of all places," Toby chuckled. "I think we're safe. It didn't sound like MI5 will be there, but his nibs says they'll be wanting us somewhere handy for the container."

"Why would anyone want us there?" Kelvin asked.

Toby grinned. "I don't know, but being you've been correct about everything so far, maybe someone thought it should be a family affair. Anyway, Counter Terrorism Command has a car on its way for us. It's probably in charge of operations, so it's possible it has people who want to pick your brains too."

"It's sending a car?" Hunter questioned.

"Yes, thankfully. Greg's done enough walking, and there's no way we could go in one of our cars. All the roads will be closed around the Palace of Westminster, so if we were to be waved through because ours came up flagged as DNH, and one of the Counter Terrorism guys noticed, it could quickly turn awkward. They aren't like MI5."

"Yeah, and possibly more than awkward," Kelvin said.

"Why aren't they like MI5?" asked Hunter.

"Contrary to what most people think, MI5 has no powers of arrest, it has to call on the police. Even MI6 isn't what people think. It may only kill someone if a directive to kill them has been issued by a Secretary of State, and as that happens about as often as a flying ostrich, it puts it closer to Basildon Bond than to James Bond."

"Oh, thanks for that, Toby. I liked the Bond movies."

"Nothing has to be real for you to like it. Not something I'd admit in front of RS, I enjoyed all the Harry Potter films."

Considering the traffic would likely be snarled up for miles with a busy part of London blocked off, and probably before any diversion routes could be set up, the car arrived a good deal earlier than they'd expected, with the reason for it soon becoming apparent. Kris, the driver of the plainclothes car, dressed to look nothing like he'd anything to do with the law, told them to hold on tight, he'd be flooring it. And floor it he did. With its normally concealed blue lights flashing, and its siren wailing so mournfully loud that it was putting the fear of God up everybody else on the road, he had the car flying through gaps with barely an inch to spare. It didn't take long for him to get them there, with one of only a few times he'd slowed up when he eased off the accelerator just long enough for two armed police to wave them through the gates. Inside, for the whole length of the circular road, police vehicles were haphazardly parked everywhere, many with their blue lights still flashing, and those who'd arrived in them were standing around in small groups, some in uniform, others not.

"Crikey, if you could turn that into a funfair ride, I'd never get off it," said Kelvin, as they bailed out of the car.

Laughing, Kris said, "You might not have been frightened, but I was terrified. The last people I took for a ride like that, one of them threw up over the back of my neck."

"Oh, gross!"

"Any idea who we're supposed to see here?" Toby asked.

Kris looked all around. "No, not really, it looks like officers from a lot of other divisions got the shout too. That's our big boss in the suit, talking to the Met's Chief Constable by the doors, but it might pay to avoid him. If I were you, I'd have a word with the bloke in the dinner jacket over there with those four armed officers. It looks as if he was at a function when he got the shout. Anyway, he's our Chief Inspector Miles, and he'll probably know more than most."

"More than the big boss?"

"I'd say a million times more. The top brass are always the last to know anything."

Toby chuckled, "If you want to know something about your car, you ask the mechanic, not a director of the garage, eh?"

"That's how it works," laughed Kris.

Miles watched them walking over to him until nearly there, before he took a few steps towards them, holding out a hand and saying, "You must be the Sherlock Holmes lot. I'm glad you could make it."

They all smiled at the man, taking the jibe, but as soon as the introductions were over with, Kelvin asked him why so many police officers were there, seemingly hanging around doing nothing but chatting to each other, and why were there only six officers with serious firearms, with two of them tied up on guarding the gates. He told him he thought it was more than a bit foolish.

"Foolish? Why would it be foolish?" Miles questioned.

"If anything was to kick off, with so many unarmed officers here, they'd be like sitting ducks, falling over one another in a rush to find cover," said Kelvin. "It is only six with serious firearms you've got here, isn't it?"

"Yes, and that's enough to deter anybody coming into the area, let alone kicking off, especially as most the plainclothes officers here carry guns too."

"Apparently, it isn't enough," said Hunter.

"It's not?"

"No," Kelvin said. "Hunter has obviously noticed them too, but it seems your officers have been too busy chatting to see we've got company. They were probably here before any of those officers turned up, so it doesn't look as if they bothered to search and secure the area."

"Good God! How many have you seen?"

"Two with firearms have poked a head around the corner of the building, and it's a job to tell, they're in the shadows and there are too many leaves still on them, but there could be more in those trees on the left of the container. Some of the branches aren't moving like the others in the wind, possibly because there are people standing or sitting on them."

"They got past security coming in, but now it's turned into a vicar's garden party, they can't get out," Hunter said.

"The thing is, though, are they hiding in the hope of starting the countdown, have they already done it, or have they only come to change or check the battery hasn't run down?"

Miles groaned, "Christ knows! You seem to be the experts on everything around here, you tell me."

"I'd say the odds are they haven't started it. If they had, it's likely they'd have tried to shoot their way out of here when only a few officers discovered the container, before any more could turn up. This lot aren't out to become martyrs."

"How do you know they aren't?"

"If they were, they'd have made a big thing about it and detonated it the day they brought it here. As they didn't, I'd say they originally intended to use it as the threat behind a list of demands, and probably still detonating it after they'd got away even if those demands had been met."

"Demands? What demands?"

"Who knows? They could've been anything from releasing prisoners to us stop bombing somewhere. I reckon it went tits up when those on Westminster Bridge were mown down and the policeman was killed on gate duty here. Security was tightened up, and as they couldn't get to the container after that, they shelved their demands rather than risk being seen as a bunch losers who couldn't carry out their threat if their demands weren't met. They'll only be here now because they knew your armed officers would be spread thinner after you lost so many the other night, but unless you've received some demands already, their intentions this time are anybody's guess. Not that it matters. With so many suspected terrorists fleeing north, we can be pretty certain they were intended to end with a bang."

"You two wouldn't want a change of job, would you?"

"Don't be daft! We can do as we please. We wouldn't want to be one of your lot, obeying orders and waiting somewhere, not knowing our heads could be blown off."

"But you're waiting here now."

"Yes, but the difference is, if anything kicks off, we know how look after ourselves, while as tonight and the other night has proved, your lot don't. They didn't bother to search and secure the area, or if they did it wasn't done competently, and now they are just standing around, as Hunter said, like sitting ducks at a vicar's garden party."

"It would only take one of those hiding from us to lose his nerve and half of your officers here could be dead in the first few seconds," Hunter said. "Most of them haven't even got a bulletproof vest on, not that they're likely to do much against some of the high-velocity stuff found on the streets today."

"You ought to listen to them," said Toby.

"What, you think they know more about this kind of thing than our trained officers?"

"Well, I do know they know more about it than you. In case you hadn't noticed, we only need to duck down on hearing the first shot to be shielded by several cars. I've no doubt it's why Hunter and Kelvin walked into our personal space and forced us to stand here. You, on the other hand, will have at least two steps to make before you even reach a car."

"Good God!" Miles gasped, quickly taking those two steps and joining them.

"You might want to consider, still no one here has noticed what these two noticed within seconds of arriving."

"I know whose advice I'll be following if it kicks off, Toby, and it won't be that of a noddy," Greg said, chuckling.

"No, I'm with you on that one," said Toby.

"A noddy?" Miles retorted.

"Yes," Greg said. "It means a foolish, inept person. In my youth, it was a common name used for a policeman. Perhaps it should become fashionable again. If you aren't going to get rid of all the unarmed officers here, you could at least send them into the building where they'll be safer."

"Too late now," said Hunter. "One of the arseholes has just fallen out his tree."

"Take cover! Get down!" Miles screamed, at the top of his voice, his arms madly waving about, while unceremoniously being pulled to the ground by Hunter, where he discovered the Sherlock Holmes team had been way ahead of him.

Not helping many of the nearby officers, they turned to see why the man had been screaming, making them unmissable for the bloke who'd fallen out of the tree. Excitedly shouting, 'Allahu Akbar!' he began spraying them with fully-automatic rifle fire, cutting them down as he repeatedly fanned his rifle left to right and back again. Hidden in the tree to his left, a colleague immediately began to follow suit, and as the police officers dived for cover in a panic, many of them not making it and falling like ninepins, another four seriously armed guys appeared from around the corner of the building.

It soon became obvious it wasn't a Mickey Mouse outfit; they had top-class weapons and knew how to use them. The four at the corner began firing too, but they were employing different tactics. Holding their rifles still, each of them had picked one of the four armed officers as their target. With the speed of the automatic rifles making any slight movement of the rifle almost inconsequential, the bullets were hammering home as near as dammit on the same spot on the bulletproof vests, and that is their weak point, they cannot take being hit repeatedly in the same place. The four armed officers were dead before any of them had managed to get a shot off.

Without getting up, Hunter and Kelvin surveyed as much of the scene as possible. Bodies were strewn all around, some dead, some groaning, and having found his gun, acting like a Jack-in-a-Box, Miles was taking quick looks over the car's bonnet, and then ducking down to blindly fire his gun in the general direction of whatever he'd seen. Several others there were doing the same thing, with it plainly being nothing but a complete waste of time and bullets. And then they saw the two armed officers at the gates, and they groaned. It seemed they'd likely hesitated, perhaps debating if they should leave their post, and now they'd decided they should.

"Jesus fuck! Are they mad? Those two don't stand a bloody chance. We've gotta do something, Hunter."

"I know, but the arsehole in the tree could be a problem."

"No problem," said Kelvin, and after performing a roll to the next car and back so fast it hadn't attracted any gunfire, he handed Hunter a rifle a dead officer wouldn't be needing again. "That's providing you know how to use this thing."

"I don't, but it won't take long to find out." Hunter pointed the rifle into the air, pressed the trigger, and it immediately burst into life. "Easy-peasy. Ready for it, then, fruit drop?"

"You know me, I'm always ready for it," laughed Kelvin, removing his Glock 19 from his inside pocket. "If you can take out Tarzan and his ape with that thing, I'll see what I can do with the others. They're a good bit closer, I should be able to hit them with a handgun."

Hunter sprayed the bloke on the ground first, so he couldn't run and hide behind anything, and then he turned the rifle on the branches of the tree from where the other one had been shooting, and he kept firing up into them until, with a scream, a body tumbled to the ground. Then, wondering why he'd not attracted any gunfire himself, he turned his rifle on the corner where he'd last seen the other blokes, and he discovered all four were rolling on the ground in agony, not knowing what was hurting them the most, their blown away kneecaps or the fingers missing on their shattered and blood-dripping hands.

"Oh, show off, why don't you, fruit drop?" Hunter laughed, playfully punching Kelvin's arm.

"Sorry, angel features, I thought they deserved to suffer."

Finding it gone quiet, Miles peered over the top of the car's bonnet, and then, standing up, he gasped, "Good God! Good God Almighty! I don't believe it! I just don't believe it!"

"Oh, you'd better believe it," Toby said, helping Greg get to his feet. "If they put their minds to it, those two could take out more people than you have here."

"But how? I was told they were only pen-pushers. Don't they work for you researching history and religion?"

"Yes, they do work for me, and research is a part of the job description, but as you've seen, they have other skills too."

"But why would they have skills like that?"

"Because a lot of people get the wrong idea about what we do. Even RS, an MI5 guy, thought we were Jesus freaks, out to tell the world Christianity is the way to go. We're not, we don't preach anything, but that doesn't stop us being targeted by all kinds of religious fanatics. It's why we have these, we need to be able to look after ourselves." Looking like the pre-European Union British passports with the stiff covers, Toby took two booklets out of his inside pocket and handed them to Miles. "You'll find they cover the lads owning and using firearms, and if you need to have them authenticated, every Chief Constable can do that. I think yours is hiding inside the building, somewhere through those doors over there."

Opening one, Miles screwed up his face, frowning. "They have special firearms licences signed by the Queen?"

"Yes, she is defender of all faiths now, and as our research is important to her, only the Monarch or an Act of Parliament can revoke those licences." Toby laughed. "After everything they've done for you here tonight, I can't see that happening on either count, can you?"

"You amaze me," Miles said, shaking his head, and looking around him. "I will need to have the Chief Constable check them out, of course, but, er, where have they gone now?"

"They're on their way back, behind you, with what looks to me as if it could be another two."

"Another two?"

With Hunter also dragging a bloke to dump at Miles' feet, Kelvin dumped his and said, "We found these two round the corner, almost wetting themselves. They didn't have guns, they seem too wimpish for terrorists, so we reckon they're geeks, brought to check the electronics were still okay. They wouldn't speak English for us, so you can take it they can't."

Miles shook his head again in disbelief.

Chapter Fifteen

It was a fraction after six o'clock, and not that it ever really sleeps, London was waking up again, when Kris gave them a far more leisurely ride home. A lot had happened in the hours up until then, with a fleet of ambulances needed for the dead and wounded, but apart from the few minutes it took for a forklift truck to lift the container out of its parking bay and onto the back of a big lorry, when everyone held their breath, nothing that could be called exciting. For them, it had mainly been standing around. Nevertheless, there was to be a funny point. Before driving away after dropping them home, with a pleading look that defied all denial, Kris asked Hunter and Kelvin if he could have their autographs. When they asked him why he would ever want them, he said it was because they'd be a lot harder to get when they became famous. A nice enough guy, they signed his bit of paper, but with the amount of laughter in the air, they were hardly their normal signatures. He was happy with them, though, and that was all that mattered.

"You do know, with some of the things you two have done, you couldn't afford to be famous, don't you?" Toby asked, as they went indoors and up the stairs.

"Yes, of course we do," Kelvin replied. "We don't want to be famous, anyway. But why did you ask?"

"Just checking, that's all."

Kelvin giggled, "Don't worry, if anyone can read it, they'll find I signed that bit of paper as Kalian Wankers."

"Really?"

"Yes, he did, and I was Huntin A Jackoff," laughed Hunter.

Toby shook his head. "I shouldn't have doubted you. Does kalian have a meaning, Kelvin, or did you make it up?"

"A kalian is a hookah, and not a tart, a hubbly-bubbly pipe where you smoke tobacco or drugs through water."

"And he didn't go to Oxford, not even to meet the students coming out," laughed Greg, as they flopped in the lounge.

Frowning, Kelvin said, "Yeah, if you're a history professor and doctor of theology, how couldn't you know a kalian?"

"I earned those qualifications a long time ago. The word rang a bell, that's why I asked about it, and it started to come back to me as soon as you began explaining it. For centuries, hallucinatory drugs of all kinds were smoked through kalians as part of most religious services. It's possible Jesus smoked one, but as it was so commonplace in those times, it wouldn't have warranted a mention. I did do it for a time, a long time, but it's other people in the offices below who carry out all the research today, not me. Now, although valuable research still goes on here, I only use this place as a front."

"Some days, when not a lot is happening for CoT, it can be so boring downstairs, we land up throwing paper planes at one another," Greg added.

"So, you don't do *any* research, Toby?" Kelvin asked.

"Not much these days, except lend it my name, or rather the letters that come after it. I get informed whenever something important is discovered, and then I'm required to pop my head over the parapet, publishing it and maybe doing a few talks, but it's not something I've ever really wanted to do."

"Bloody hell, don't tell me you landed up doing it because of your grandfather on your mother's side? He was a fire and brimstone vicar, wasn't he?"

"Something like that. When I grew up, youngsters did what was expected of them. I can't complain, though. How could I with the life I've had?"

"Good, was it?"

"Extraordinarily good. There are few places in the world I haven't seen, I've got money coming out of my ears, and just look at the family I've got. A lot of it isn't blood-related, and yet you wouldn't find a better one. I was nine when I joined it, and I'm told it was the same before, there's never been one argument in the family."

"Crikey!"

"You just make sure your family is the same."

"Mine? There's only me and Hunter, and we'd never argue over anything."

Toby laughed, "Yes, for now. Johnny and Karl had parents, but it's not through their parents they have the family they've got today, is it? Anyway, haven't you and Hunter just taken on a brother and his partner who lives nearby? According to Johnny, you've already started building your family."

"Bloody hell, we have, haven't we?"

"It looks like it, fruit drop. You wouldn't want to change or get rid of them, would you?"

"No way! I like the idea of picking ourselves a family, and I'd say we chose well there."

"That's good, I do too," Hunter chuckled. "I'm wondering now how long it'll be before we need to extend the house."

"Ages, we've still got three spare bedrooms. which reminds me, we'll have to make a move soon, angel features. Cracker should be moving in today."

"That'll be fun. We didn't get any sleep last night, and we can't just show him his room and leave him to it."

"If Sandy's with him, he might be hoping we do."

"Trust you to think of that!"

"Oh, I know what I wanted to ask, Toby. What were those booklet things Miles gave back to you last night? He looked us over a bit funny when he said the Chief Constable had verified them but he had to keep it under his hat."

"And you'll have to keep it under your hats. I hold licences for everyone we issue with firearms, but it's best they don't know about it. They are more than what they appear to be."

Kelvin frowned. "Why is it best they don't know?"

"If they thought they could just go around shooting people and not have to worry about it, it wouldn't be good."

"Why wouldn't they have to worry about it?"

"They're special licences, they bear the Queen's signature, and the chances are they wouldn't be prosecuted."

"Bloody hell! And Hunter and I have got one?"

"Yes. Not that you'd have been prosecuted for stopping the terrorists last night, Miles might have got a bit funny about it if you weren't licenced to use firearms. So, not wanting his lot turning up here sometime in the future and getting bolshie because he believed you hadn't got licences, I thought it best to show him you had, special ones. In readiness for any such situation arising, I'd taken yours with me."

"What's so special about them, and why would they bear the Queen's signature?"

"It came about after MISIC was disbanded. My father had to go to the palace for a second Dubonnet and gin to formally tell Her Majesty it had been disbanded. Usually, it only used to happen once to introduce the new leader. He thought that was that, but it wasn't that. It turned out some of the faceless people behind the throne, the spokespeople you sometimes hear about from Buckingham Palace, weren't happy."

"They weren't?"

"No. You see, my father wasn't known for his love of the establishment, but he had always been, and still is, known as a royalist. So, shortly after he became involved with CoT, he was summoned to the palace again. To cut a long story short, the faceless people had come up with a way that, as far as the palace and Her Majesty's subjects were concerned, a *likeness* of MISIC was hidden in CoT. It could never be admitted, but it was some of them and MISIC that had launched CoT."

"Crikey, the important people with a bit of clout?"

"Yes, and with MISIC gone, CoT members had no one to help them if they were caught operating outside the law. So, as that wasn't good, they dug around until they found a long forgotten power of the Monarch; named seconds."

"Somebody who can fight in place of someone else?"

"They were the seconds who fought duels. Named seconds were different. They travelled the country in small groups to ensure the interests of the Monarch were being upheld, and in all matters they were the Hand of the Monarch."

"Do you mean they had the power of the Monarch?"

"Not exactly, but to go against anything they said would be like going against the Monarch, and as in those days that was treachery, the penalty was death."

"Bloody hell!"

"Resurrecting this power, my father, and others he deemed as suitable, became Her Majesty's named seconds. And as all those we give guns to today become her named seconds, that authority and their legal right to bear arms gets stamped with the Queen's signature. It means if the police were to charge a named second with an offence, it would be like charging the Monarch with the offence, and on taking up their position, all our Chief Constables are made aware of it. So, although we shouldn't rely on it, it's very unlikely to happen. The same as our armed forces, our police officers swear their allegiance to the Monarch. It is their place to accept neither Her Majesty, nor her named seconds, would *without just reason and right* contravene any of *Her* laws or do anything that would be to the detriment of *Her* subjects or visitors to *Her* realm. But, as I said, it's probably best our armed crews don't know that."

"Crikey, not half! So, did you have to go to the palace for a Dubonnet and gin when you took over?"

"Yes, but don't go getting excited about it. It's etiquette to take one sip, smile approvingly, and then put it down and not touch it again."

"What a waste!"

"Er, being as I told you it was probably best that our armed crews didn't know they were named seconds, I'm finding it strange you haven't asked me why I'd tell you two."

"We're not stupid, we'll both have worked that one out."

"Yes, we have, and you'd better not be thinking about it for a long time yet," Hunter added.

Greg laughed, "Two streets ahead, as usual, Toby."

"I know, I find it remarkable. Don't worry, guys, I'm not planning on anything in the immediate future, but as it would feel wrong to put any difference between you, all being well in a first for CoT, the day will come when you will both need to practise a curtsy."

"Crikey, I don't know about a curtsy, I don't think either of us would be that brave, but if I like the drink I'm given, you can bet etiquette will go out of the window. Anyway, with a bit of luck, it won't be for a long time, we'll have a king by then. Do any of you happen to know what Charles' favourite tipple is?" Kelvin asked, grinning.

"I've heard he's partial to a single malt," Toby replied.

"Oh, that's all we need!" Hunter said, laughing.

"You don't like whisky?"

"No, it isn't that, it's what whisky does to Kelvin."

"It doesn't agree with him?"

"Oh, no, it's much worse, it works like a switch on a certain part of his anatomy. We'll be lucky if we get out of the room before he jumps on me."

"It's not that bad, angel features."

"You wouldn't want to bet on it, would you?"

"Um, no, maybe not. I only bet on certainties."

"Crikey!"

"Hey, bog off, Toby! I do the crikeys around here."

Laughing, Toby raised his hands in surrender.

After talking so much, where time had moved on, Hunter and Kelvin were given some breakfast before leaving at eight o'clock. Nothing special, Toby made everyone tea or coffee, and a round of toast that they covered in marmalade. Not that there was the smell of a kipper, their plates were spotlessly clean, the lads shared a private joke over it, giggling on and off throughout the snack, but not letting on. And then, shortly after that, Toby and Greg watched them through the window as they drove away, heading for home.

"I don't think we've any fears there, Toby," Greg said. "It's like they were made for the job. When the time comes, you'll be leaving the ship in safe hands."

"I know. They really are like what I've been told of Johnny and Karl in their early days, they share the same soul."

"Yes, and from everything I've seen, neither of them is in the slightest bisexual. They won't have that bridge to cross."

"That's true, there'll be no need of a Tel like there was for Karl when Johnny's hormones swung the other way. How Tel turned it into three sharing that soul within only minutes of them first meeting is beyond me. It defies all logic."

"What does logic know? The complications of your family has never stopped it from working, and better than any other I've come across. Do you think the family Hunter and Kelvin are putting together will turn out the same?"

"I don't know, that was puzzling me. I'm sure they'll make it work, but what the setup will be is anybody's guess."

***

As Hunter was driving, it was Kelvin who phoned ahead to check if Cracker could be picked up. The guy who answered said he was clear of any infection and they could pick him up at anytime, but as they'd been unsalvageable, unless he was going to leave in a hospital gown flapping in the wind, they'd need to bring him some clothes. So, laughing at that thought, on arriving in Puffney Bigshot, they parked in Bangers' car park and took a slow walk to the shops in High Street.

They decided to try Hawthorns, the department store where Kelvin had bought most of his clothes. But then, not knowing what Cracker would like, or even sure of the sizes he'd need, it soon turned into a nightmare. They were about to give up and walk back and ask him about his sizes and taste, when someone tapped them on a shoulder, and they spun round.

Sandy asked them, "What are you doing in here? Did your job go alright last night?"

"Crikey! Er, yes, it did, and we're here to get Cracker some clothes to take him home in, but why are you here?"

"Sandy's also buying clothes," said Teresa, laughing, as she walked up to them. "I've had my orders, I stay out of sight and let him get on with it, until it's time to pay, of course."

205

"I'm getting a bike, a phone and a laptop too!" Sandy said, excitedly.

"Yes, we'll have to buy all that for Cracker, but the bike he can pick himself when his shoulder's better, it's hard enough finding him just a set of clothes he might like," Hunter said, sighing. "You wouldn't happen to know what he'd like and what sizes he'd need, would you?"

"Of course, I would. I know everything about him," Sandy said, grinning. "He likes flowery shirts, like the blue one over there, fifteen collar, medium fit; jeans with a thirty waist and twenty-eight leg; quality trainers size ten; and if you've got to get pants, not boxers. He doesn't like it bouncing around."

"Bloody hell, you really do know him!"

"Every inch, intimately," Sandy said, winking cheekily.

Teresa shook her head, fighting off another laugh.

"Did he settle in okay," Hunter asked her. "No problems?"

"No, no problems, he's settling in just fine. It might take a while for him to adjust his sleeping pattern, though. He had us up talking until the early hours." The laugh escaped. "He's very frank about things when he's talking, says it exactly as it is, and with some of the things he's got planned for you two, it's got me and Den hoping you'll be able to cope."

"What things?"

"She's sworn to secrecy," taunted Sandy, grinning. "You'll just have to wait and see, won't you?"

"Crikey!"

"Yeah, they must be good."

"Is it alright if I come over to see Cracker as soon as we've finished shopping?"

"Yes, of course, we told you anytime, but you might want to give it a couple of hours or so. It doesn't pay to rush things when you're shopping, you'll get home and find you've got a load of stuff you don't like."

"Alright, I won't rush. See you later, then."

Feeling happier, Kelvin and Hunter bought the blue flowery shirt and everything else as Sandy had suggested, and when ten minutes later Cracker got to see what they'd bought him, his face lit up like Blackpool promenade.

"Oh, man! They's the biz!" he gasped, sitting up in bed and fighting to get his hospital gown off.

He pulled the gown off over his head, with a struggle, and he managed to get all the fiddly packing bits off the shirt, but he had to ask them for help to put it on. And then, once he'd removed all the other packaging, it came to putting the rest of it on, and with his shoulder bandaged and arm in a sling, that proved to be a problem too. Now sitting on the edge of the bed, he had to ask them for help again.

"Jesus!" Kelvin gasped, turning round to look at him, from by the door where he and Hunter had been talking while they waited. "You really can't get them on by yourself?"

"No, I tried. It's not going to bite you, man."

"Are you sure? If that's a massive grower, the way you told the nurses, then I want a chair and a whip, like a lion tamer."

"Oh, don't embarrass me, man. I was messing with them, I always muck about if I'm nervous. I'm happy with it, but it's nothing special for a guy with some black blood in him. It isn't going to grow until it's out the door and up the road."

"I bloody hope it isn't. It's a hell of a way from our door to up the road."

Hunter chuckled, "Oh, fruit drop, you can't half come out with them at times. Come on, we'll take a side each."

"Okay, but if it wakes up, I'll be quicker than you at giving it a farewell chop. Crikey, if that's what Sandy means by he's done well, I'd hate to meet his done very well."

It didn't require a farewell chop, it behaved, and they soon had him dressed.

"Thanks, guys. Sandy and I like you two a hell of a lot, you know? We got off over you last night, when you left us in here. You two could have it anytime you wanted it."

"You'd cheat on Sandy?" Hunter asked, shocked.

"No, don't be silly, of course I wouldn't, man. I'd never do that. I meant you could have both of us. We agreed on it last night, anything you want, anytime you want it, it wouldn't be cheating with you two."

"Bloody hell, Hunter! He's dead serious about it."

"I know. We'll have to talk to Sandy when he turns up; find out what's going on."

"Is Sandy coming to see me this morning?"

"Sometime later. He'll be coming to the house, after we've got you home. Has there been anything, anytime with anyone before, then?"

"No, of course not. Sandy had his punters, but they didn't count, they didn't mean nothing to him, they were his work."

"And how about you, who have you had?"

"Aw, don't ask me that, man."

"Why not?"

Cracker looked down, as if he was ashamed. "I've told a lot of lies about girls, I couldn't let the Louts know about Sandy, but he's the only one, and all I ever wanted, man."

"Crikey!"

"So, why would you want to change that now?"

"Because of a book Sandy read a long time ago. First there was two gay guys, a couple, then there was three gay guys, a trio because one of the first was really bi, and then there was four, and as they couldn't agree what to call four, they called themselves a unity because it can cover any nu . . ."

"Johnny Mo?" gasped Kelvin. "The book he read was The Life and Times of Johnny Mo – Private Eye?"

"Yeah, that's the one, man. Sandy reckons because things have turned out the way they has, we're supposed to be your three and four, and I believes him. We's a unity."

"Bloody hell!"

"I bet that's what he was frankly talking to Teresa and Den about last night. It'll be the secret thing he's got planned for us that she couldn't tell us about, and why she said she hoped we could cope."

"Never mind her, *I* hope we could cope! If we're supposed to be like that lot, you do remember the sex lives they had, don't you? They were off their heads on drugs half the time, and what with all the orgies they had, they must've been at it more than any rabbit."

"You wouldn't mind us being a foursome?"

"I didn't say that. Never mind they're both underage, what would it do to us? I'm awfully worried now that Sandy thinks we're supposed to be a unity, though. We know weird things do happen a lot for him, and unless there's something I don't know about, like a foursome isn't weird, I've a funny feeling it could happen."

"Would it be so bad, man? We really do have the hots for you two. I haven't read the book, but Sandy reckons they did okay being a foursome, and sometimes more than four."

"We're going to have to have a long talk with Sandy, when he turns up," said Hunter. "Come on, it's time to say goodbye to the room, we have to buy you a phone and a laptop before we go home, and we need to be home soon, we didn't get any sleep last night."

"Really, man? A phone *and* a laptop?"

"Yes, you're living in a different world now, but you'll get used to it. We did."

"Oh, man, you two's something else!"

It didn't take long to buy him a phone and laptop. Cracker was easily pleased and would have settled for lesser models, but they bought him the best in the shop. Although the phone had everything to do it in abundance, he wasn't the 'Look at me, aren't I wonderful?' kind of person, all he wanted was something that would let him keep in touch with Sandy, and they liked that, it was a good sign. Arriving home, they gave him a guided tour of his new home, showing him where all the things he could ever need were stored, and throughout it they suffered countless cries of, 'Oh, man!'

"So, which bedroom do you want?" asked Hunter.

"The one Sandy slept in will do me great."

"But the bedding in there hasn't been changed yet."

"That's why I wants it, man."

"Blimey, you have got it *really* bad for Sandy! But if you love him that much, why would you want us? Is it because he wants a foursome and he talked you into wanting it too?"

"No, course not. Because of what he had to do, we've both been free to have anyone else we wanted, and though neither of us ever has, under those rules, he could have a foursome at anytime he wanted. It's his faith, man. He says it's what God is telling us we should do, that's why we finds you two as hot as we do each other, and I don't ever doubt his faith, man."

"Crikey!"

"Yes, I know, it's weird. But why *don't* you ever doubt his faith, Cracker? People doubt things all the time."

"It's the only secret I's ever had from Sandy, and if I tells it to you, you won't tell him, will you, man? And you definitely won't think I'm mad, will you?"

"No, I swear we won't. Our lips are sealed."

"And me, I swear it too."

"Louts had to prove they were worthy before they became a teenager, they had to at least cut someone bad, else they were a goner. But I couldn't do it, man, I couldn't hurt an innocent person, so they came for me when I was a week past thirteen, six of them with knives one night on Leckington Rye Road. I thought that was it, man."

"Crikey, what happened? Did you run?"

"No point, they'd get you. I just closed my eyes, so I'd see Sandy in my head, not them as I died. I tried to picture being with him, but it wouldn't happen, all I could see was like a knight with a big sword. He brought the sword up in front of his nose, like in a salute, there was a long screech and a lot of bangs, and I opened my eyes to see a car speeding off, and the six Louts scattered about on the ground. Four were dead, two crippled for life, and yet I was okay, there wasn't a mark on me. I couldn't tell Sandy in case he thought I'd gone mad or was trying to steal his thunder, but I often think that knight might have been one of his angels. If he was, he sure did a good job, man. The Louts never came for me again."

"Jesus fuck, Hunter!"

"Yeah, and if he did, he certainly fucked those Louts."

"It don't make no sense to me, man, but since it happened, I've taken Sandy's faith a lot more serious. If he believes us being a foursome is what God wants, you's not going to find me arguing with him."

"Do you ever have arguments?" Hunter asked.

"Only mess about ones, the giggling kind that often ends up in sex, we'd never have a proper argument, man. Why?"

"The four in that book were the same, and they still are."

"They're real people?"

"Yes, very real. I think our lives are getting weirder by the moment, fruit drop. It's like history wants to repeat itself. It's almost as if it's insisting on it."

"Tell me about it! If it does, I know one thing. Any kids we might want one day, we'll have to adopt. There's nothing in the world would make mine work doing it naturally. That's a bit of history I can guarantee couldn't repeat itself."

"I'm with you on that one. I can't understand how they did it. I know us teasing each other wouldn't help me. If there was a female present it just wouldn't work, end of. Have you and Sandy ever thought of kids in the future, Cracker?"

"We talked about it once, but we never thought there was a hope in hell of it happening, man. Like you, we couldn't do it the real way, we'd have to adopt." Cracker laughed. "Sandy's not even stated his case to you for us being a foursome, and yet the way you're talking, it sounds to me you're bending to it already. I reckon we's going to be a unity, man."

"Slow up there, we've not bent to anything. Crikey, when it comes to you, Cracker, bending would take a lot of thinking about. Besides, you're both underage for anything like that."

"But you *is* thinking about it, man, and hard. I know they's not your guns in your pockets, I saw you put them in a safe."

"Bloody hell! You don't miss anything, do you?"

"No, he certainly doesn't. We'll just have to wait for Sandy to turn up, and see what he has to say about it," said Hunter.

"Yeah, he can put things a lot better than me, man."

"That could be highly subjective," sighed Kelvin.

Fighting off a grin, Hunter thumped Kelvin, playfully, and then telling Cracker he was to make himself at home, it was his home too now and he could do whatever he wanted to, he told him they had to get their heads down for a while, they were going to bed, but he was to be sure to wake them when Sandy turned up.

Sandy arrived at twelve-thirty, riding the new bicycle there that had been bought for him that morning. But by the time he and Cracker had finished talking over a few things, it had got to one-fifteen when they crept into Hunter and Kelvin's bedroom to give them a rude awakening. They stripped down to their underpants and climbed into the bed to lie on either side of them, and as if it was nothing new, and it had always been that way, they cuddled up.

At five-thirty, annoyingly, the four had to break off from what they were doing for Hunter to answer his phone. He sat up in the bed, put it into speaker mode, and collapsing back onto his pillow, he laughed, "Your timing is excellent, as usual, Greg."

"Oh, sorry, have I caught you at it again? It's just I thought you'd like to be updated. It was a standard ISO container, went in a C-130 with inches to spare, and the drop proved uneventful, disappointing a few who were hoping to find out the size of bang. We had the news this morning, but Toby insisted I shouldn't disturb you until now as Johnny would be annoyed if there were any seats going spare."

"Any seats going spare?" questioned Hunter.

"Yes, he's had the layout of the aircraft changed so there'll be four seats for you on the flight to Dragons this Christmas. Er, Dragons is his island in the sun, if you didn't know. He is correct, isn't he? You have had enough time to bond? You are a foursome now?"

"Yes, we're definitely four," Hunter laughed. "But unlike when he had threesomes, foursomes and moresomes , , ."

"Spare me the details, please, I'm far too old to be thinking of such things. I'll let you get back to it," Greg said, ending the call.

Kelvin giggled, "Back to it?"

"That's what he said, fruit drop. It looks like we might have inherited a reputation. Whenever anyone thinks of us as four, they'll be thinking of Johnny's orgies."

How it had happened, they couldn't explain, but it had, and as natural as if it was evolution. The two couples had bonded that afternoon and become a unity. However, for now it was purely a unity of souls.

Sandy had lost his argument that if age was just a number for the old then it had to be just a number for the young, and it was left that if they still felt the same way when they were both of legal age, as Kelvin and Hunter couldn't deny they had come to have the hots for them too, they'd talk about it again then. As Kelvin pointed out, it was down to what they had grown up believing, there was a legal age, even though there'd been others who hadn't believed it and had regularly abused them. So, it was left that for now, while hugging and cuddling were both permissible, and even sharing a bed if it was only to talk, like they had so thoroughly that afternoon, anything more than an affectionate peck would be off limits.

Being Sandy had been having all kinds of sex with clients since he was nearly ten, and Cracker had been having it with him at eleven, and they'd both probably experienced more of life than many twenty-one year olds, none of them was under any illusion it would be easy, or even achievable. After all, sex isn't something anyone can put back in the bottle. When that genie escapes, it's out forever.

***

A week later, Kelvin made it to eighteen, and the following week, Sandy hit fourteen. With no thoughts of combining the celebrations, both had a massive party, with dozens of guests turning up and getting hammered around the pool, with a few falling or being pushed into it. And then, indoors this time as it was the first week of December, there was yet another out of this world party to celebrate Cracker making fifteen. They were burning the candle at both ends, but then, they had more candles than most to burn.

Chapter Sixteen

The four of them had a great time on their trip to Dragons that Christmas. Arriving in the afternoon of December 23rd, the aircraft circled once before landing, giving them a view of the whole island, and they stared down at it mesmerised, like young kids visiting Disneyland for the first time. It was a chartered Boeing 737 laid out inside as a long lounge, where for much of the journey, thankfully, the extended family's noisy young had been looked after up at the front, in the area that might have been for first class passengers on a normal flight.

The island was crescent-shaped, much of it left as nature intended, but going from south to north, it appeared to have a small port and three villages along the south coast, and then a third of the way up, going east to west, was the landing strip with what looked to be a load of warehouses alongside it, and then a little further north, not far from the west coast, many acres filled with sportsfields, swimming pools and buildings said that had to be the four children's homes. North of that, in amongst a wilderness of palm trees, it seemed everything else was part of a rambling estate of farms, animals and strange to them agriculture, until up on the most northerly coast stood an enormous one-storey building surrounding a huge patio area that was littered with tables and chairs, where further in, going towards the centre, many sunbeds and recliners, some under thatched sunshades, were spread around an irregular-shaped swimming pool that had to be of Olympic size.

Spotting a beautiful blue lagoon, one complete with lapping wavelets within an easy walk of the complex, Kelvin shook his head, gasping, "Crikey, Hunter, you don't think the plane crashed and this is heaven, do you?"

"I wouldn't like to say," said Hunter, equally gobsmacked.

"Oh, man, you sure knows all the right people."

Lost for words, Sandy just looked at it all, speechless.

While their luggage went on ahead, on the back of a lorry, with no public transport on the island, they travelled to the homestead on the only thing it possessed large enough to accommodate their number, an extra-long horse-drawn cart with rows of seating. Waiting there to welcome them, and easily recognised by the three who'd read the book, even though time had been cruel to their imaginations, were all the old crew, and they looked remarkably healthy.

After dinner that evening, to recover from the journey, the kids were given an early night, and everybody else sprawled around the pool, where just raising an arm into the air saw a golden-skinned young lad wearing a loincloth appear to fetch them anything they required. Johnny explained that none of the staff were slaves or even servants, they were good friends who appreciated being paid to look after them, and a lot of that was to do with the airstrip. Until he'd had it built, their families had lived on various nearby islands, where the only contact with the outside world had been a supply ship calling four times a year. Now that they had use of the airstrip, their supplies came in weekly, taken to the port to be ferried across to the other islands, and as their children grew up to become good friends who worked for them, it helped the families pay for the delivery service.

It was height of summer there, and apart from Kelvin doing it with Hunter in the wavelets of that blue lagoon to satisfy a dream, they spent many hours enjoying all the other things you can do to have fun on sandy beaches or in the sea. In the evenings and through into the night, in between swimming and diving into the pool, they sipped drinks on that patio, spending many hours lapping up untold stories of Johnny and his crew.

They were the very best of the best of times, but the thing they would all remember the most happened on their second full day there; Christmas Day. It was traditional for Johnny and the whole family to visit the homes, bearing gifts for the six hundred and forty children in them. Given the names of four famous dragons, the houses were Pendragon, Jedwyrm, Sampandraco, and Righteous, and accompanying the family on this Santa trip, they were amazed at just how well the kids were living. Everything a child could ever want or need was there, and it seemed the children knew it too. In every house they were met by deafening cheers and rapturous applause, with happy kids ecstatically jumping up and down, shouting, 'Happy Chriiiiiistmas!'

The really memorable moment, the one that was destined to live forever, came in Righteous. Johnny had asked Sandy and Cracker to each carry a present, without telling them why. As all the other presents were in huge sacks being carried by the family, where as they were pulled out in each house the boy or girl's name would be called and they'd come up to fetch it, the request had seemed strange, but they hadn't bothered to question it.

They discovered the reason for carrying the presents when they went into the dining room of Righteous, where later they would be having Christmas Dinner with the youngest. Sitting at one of the tables, and surprised to see them, Bill and Ben leapt out of their chairs to run up and almost flatten them.

Gulping, Cracker cried, "Oh, little man! It says William on this pressie, I bet you anything it's for you, Bill."

"Of course it is," said Johnny. "It's a special present from you and Sandy. You two must mean a lot to them, they never stop talking about how you used to take them out and play games with them on the common."

"Oh, wow, then Benjamin has got to be for you, Ben, hasn't it?" Sandy said, his eyes filling up and having to be wiped as soon as he'd handed over the present.

"Cor, thankoo, but what you doing here, Sandy? You going to live here too? It ever so good."

"We does lessons, but we has lotsa, lotsa fun," said Bill.

"We can tell," Sandy said. "You're talking almost as good as we do now, and it's only been a few months."

"How now brown cow," Bill giggled, his mouth teasingly accentuating every word.

"We can tell the time now," said Ben, proudly.

"That's brilliant! Have you made a lot of friends too?"

"We got lotsa, lotsa friends. Everyone friends here, there no bad peoples," said Ben, happily grinning.

Kelvin and Hunter sniffed and had to wipe their eyes, doing it almost in unison. Why weren't their lives like that as kids? Every childhood should be that good. You only get one.

From behind, Johnny walked up between them, hanging an arm over a shoulder of each, and asking, "You have worked it out why you were invited to Dragons, haven't you?"

Turning his head towards him, Kelvin replied, "It's to make sure Johnny Mo rides forever?"

"The name isn't important, it's the horses that matter, they need to keep galloping, and from the reports I've seen lately, you've got your work cut out. When it comes to London and all counties south, bar you two, and hopefully your upcoming family, unless you and Hunter do something, very soon there won't be a lot of life left in the stables."

Turning his head, Hunter questioned, "You're talking about CoT's armed crews growing old and there's no crews coming up to replace them, aren't you?"

"I am, and it won't be long before the unarmed crews are the same. You'll need to get your fingers out. Everybody has an age when they lose their speed and focus, and you've got a hell of a lot of people fast approaching it."

"I knew I was right!" Kelvin said, punching the air. "When you lost your speed and focus, you didn't stop riding, though, did you? You just swapped your dragon for a horse called Toby and rode that. For CoT, read Johnny Mo."

"You two really do have the bee's knees. It was Tony first, and after him Toby. You couldn't ask for a better person than Toby, but as a horse, he'd never win the Grand National. He doesn't gallop. It's hard enough to get a canter out of him."

"What about us, then? Would we win the Grand National?"

"I've no doubts about you winning it at all."

"So, if you had no doubts about us, why did you invite us here? It wasn't because you wanted to ask us to search for replacements for the crews, Toby or Greg could have asked us to do that at anytime. There's got to be more to it, and I'd say a hell of a lot more."

"Yeah, I hope we're not losing brownie points, but I've not been able to work that one out either," said Hunter.

"I didn't expect you to, but it's quite simple, really. I rode Tony and CoT went places. I rode Toby and I could only get him to hold the fort. All being well you two will be next, and if I'm still around, I know you'd never let me or anyone ride you, so in the hope of being able to influence the direction you'll be heading off in, I wanted you to see what we do here for unfortunate kids."

"Crikey, you really do care about kids, don't you?"

"Yes, a long time ago, I was one for a while."

"Yeah, but according to that book we read, you were born with a silver spoon sticking out of your backside. Your dad owned companies all around the world. He was a millionaire many times over, and you were given just about everything you wanted."

"I had too much and other kids too little. It's why I used to sneak out of our gated community and play in the slums, and why I eventually became a Mong Kok Warrior. I knew I had to try and help them."

"*That's* the reason why you went on what could only be a crusade for justice and what was right when you moved to England with your mother? Kids getting a raw deal?"

"They were a major part of it, but there are a lot of people who get a raw deal. It was my father who set me up with my first business as a private investigator, don't forget, and after becoming embroiled with MISIC on one of its cases, it was an easy way to go. MISIC used me, and I used MISIC."

"But everyone must know what *can* be done for unfortunate kids, they just don't do it. What you do here is exceptional, they wouldn't need to do the half of what you do, but I still can't understand why you'd want us to see it."

"Reports told me you'd rescued a bunch of kids. Reports told me you had taken one on as a brother, with his partner coming as part of the deal. And reports told me the four of you had bonded to become a unity, just like we did, making our family, but reports couldn't show me your eyes."

"Our eyes?"

"Look into a person's eyes and they'll tell you everything you need to know about them. They are the windows to their soul. We won't be around to look after all this forever, and as it will need looking after, and Toby says he's already too old to think about taking it on, your eyes tell me that when that time comes, there couldn't be anyone more deserving for us to leave the island to than you and your family. You'd fight anyone to the death for your kids. Don't worry, you'll get all the investments that keep it going, and more."

"Bloody hell! But what about Toby's sons?"

"You came over on the plane with them, you'll have seen what they're like. Unless you count a dodgy curry, they've never known a bad time. They couldn't do it, and should it be needed, they certainly couldn't fight for the kids. If someone were to do them down, they wouldn't know how to fight for justice, they've never had to fight for anything. Justice for them is having just ice in a drink. As for their kids, there'd be no hope of them if they were old enough, they're being raised to be snowflakes. They'll be nothing more than pawns, being put upon, with no idea how the real world works."

"Crikey!"

"Yeah, it's more of that weird, fruit drop. It looks like one day we'll be getting that island you wanted."

"Whacky, eh?" laughed Sandy, winking at them.

"Oh, man! He sure do like working in funny ways."

The story you have just read is a work of fiction, of course, but one that's been based on many terrible truths. There is no secret organisation called CoT, but maybe there should be. It is true, we do only get one childhood, and to an extent, what that is like determines the kind of people we become.

Statistics show that in the UK more than 140,000 children go missing every year, with some of them never to be heard of again. Sadly, a few are found deceased, but most have run away from something. Some will have run from their family, others from being in care, with a sizeable number repeatedly running away, where more than a hundred times is now not unusual. But when that many children find running away to live on the streets preferable to where they should be living, hasn't somebody got to be doing something wrong?

Although literary licence has been used to, hopefully, make it an entertaining read, this story has revealed a few of the things that can go wrong. Kids in care should not forever find themselves being pushed from pillar to post, to be used and abused in more foster homes and children's hostels than they care to remember. It is safe, long-term accommodation that they need, somewhere they can feel they belong and call their home. The checks done on foster parents, before and after they're taken on, do appear as if they might be getting better, it does seem as if things are improving, but nowhere near fast enough. What isn't, though, is many children being placed a long way from where they know and went to school and had friends, some tens of miles away. Starting at a new school is a harrowing experience when they're doing it on their own in the middle of a term, and having to do it every few weeks has got to be an enticement to run.

As for the other children who run away, those not in care, what can be said about them? Well, we could say the way the country is going, with the rich becoming richer and the poor becoming poorer at an alarming rate, it won't be long before a large number of them are in care too. Life is getting tough for a lot of people, and if for any number of reasons a child has a disagreement — something that happens all too easily if their parents have turned to drink or drugs, like many have in an attempt to alleviate some of their suffering — they will run away in search of a better life. And running away is not without its risks. There's the genie no one can put back in the bottle to consider. On how, when, and where that escapes can depend a child's whole future.

It seems everywhere you look these days, there's an official wailing about the lack of resources because of government cuts and telling us they're the cause of all our troubles, and you can bet that somewhere nearby they're being matched by a politician with a painted on smile, crowing over how much more the government is spending on everything. It is another terrible truth in the story. Politics is an evil business.

Government statistics show 4.1 million children in the UK are now living in poverty. Up by a staggering 100,000 on last year, it's getting worse. Politicians might need reminding, it is the children of today who grow up to become the society of tomorrow, and if they don't do something to give them a better deal soon, we could all be in for a hell of a ride.